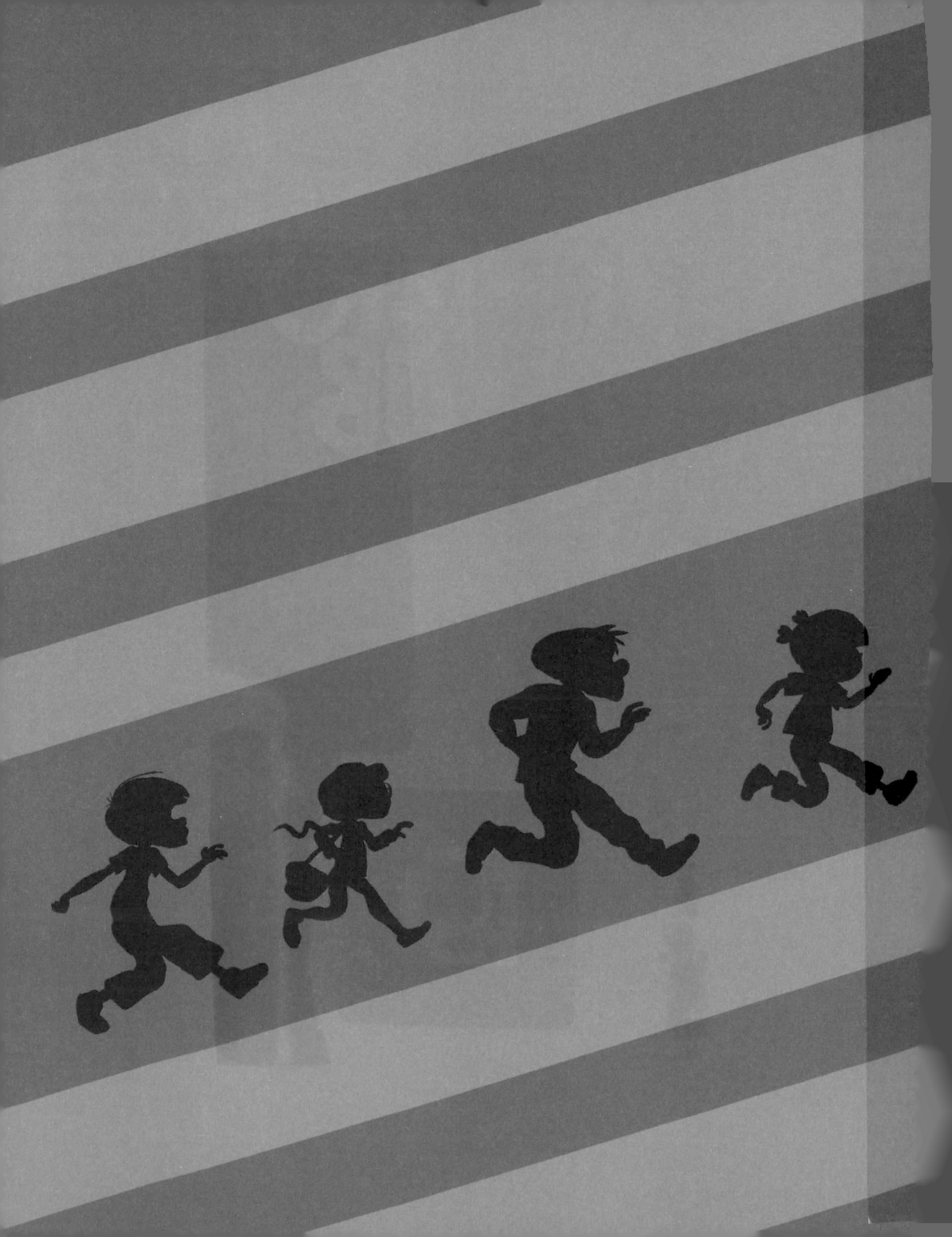

hmhbooks.com

The text was set in Fennario.

ISBN: 978-1-328-52848-3 paper over board
ISBN: 978-1-328-55043-9 paperback

Manufactured in Malaysia
TWP 10 9 8 7 6 5 4 3 2 1
4500756055

MYSTERY CLUB

WILD WEREWOLVES

by Davide Cali

Illustrated by Yannick Robert

Houghton Mifflin Harcourt

Boston   New York

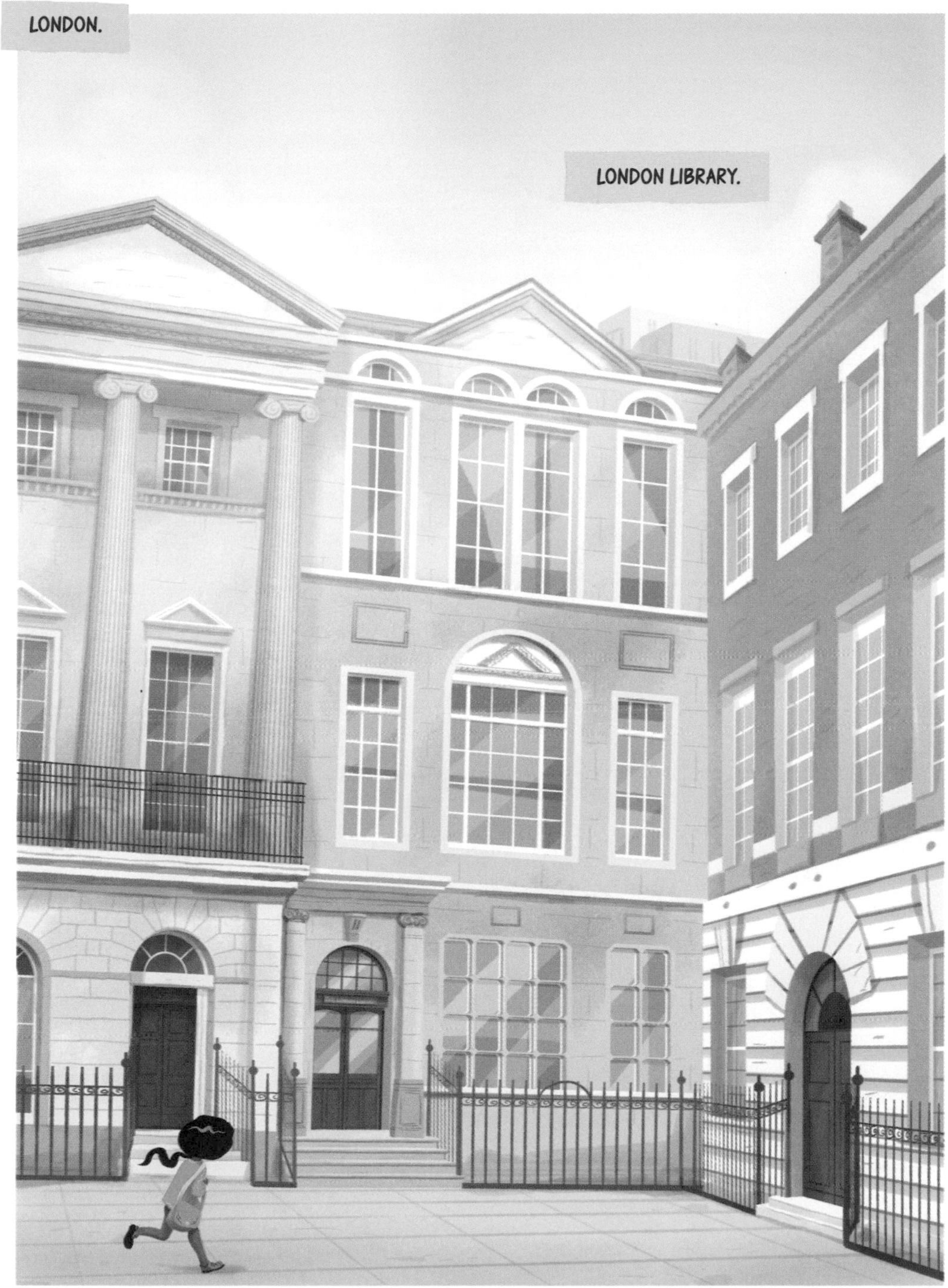
LONDON.
LONDON LIBRARY.

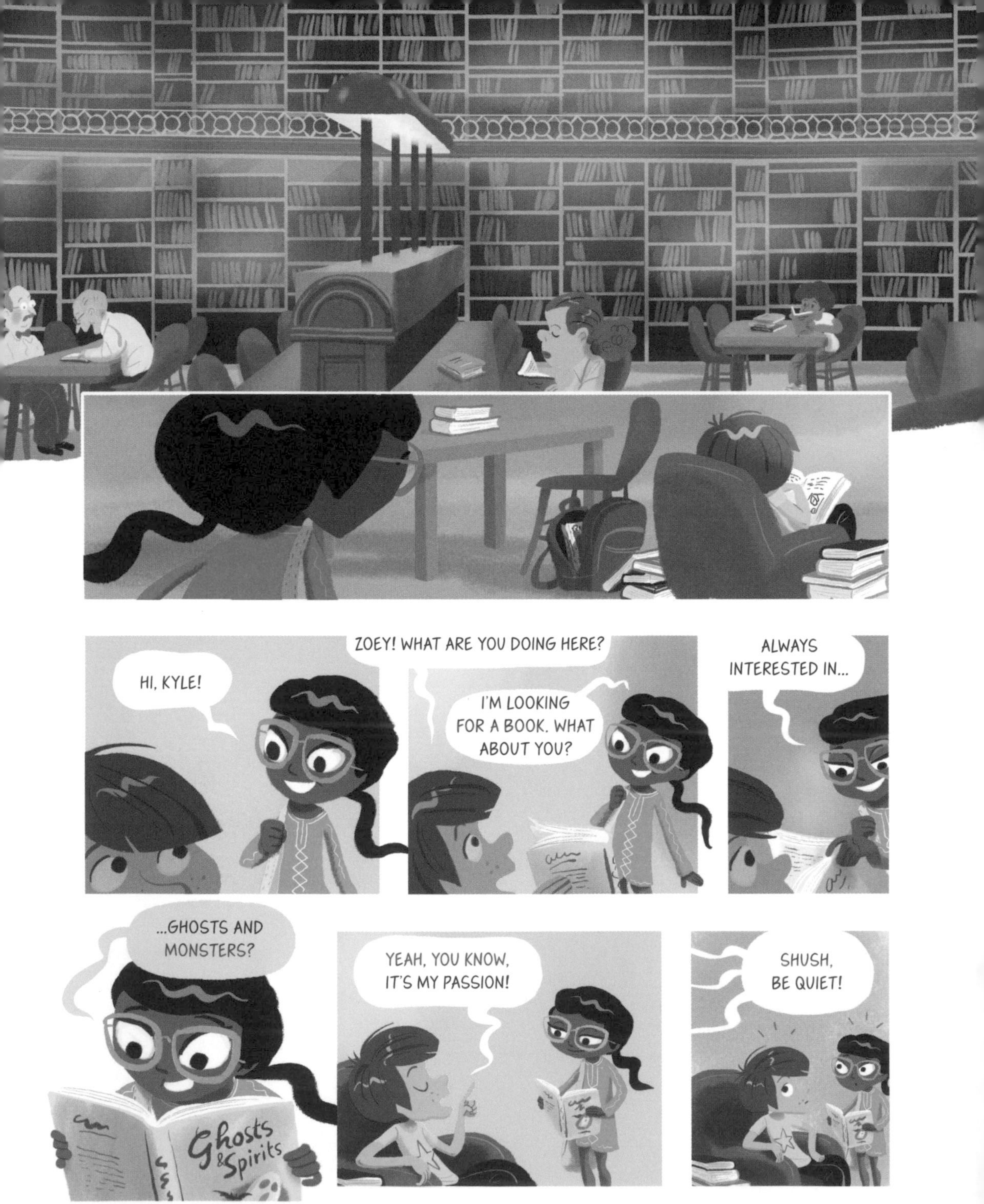
HI, KYLE!
ZOEY! WHAT ARE YOU DOING HERE?
I'M LOOKING FOR A BOOK. WHAT ABOUT YOU?
ALWAYS INTERESTED IN...
...GHOSTS AND MONSTERS?
Ghosts & Spirits
YEAH, YOU KNOW, IT'S MY PASSION!
SHUSH, BE QUIET!

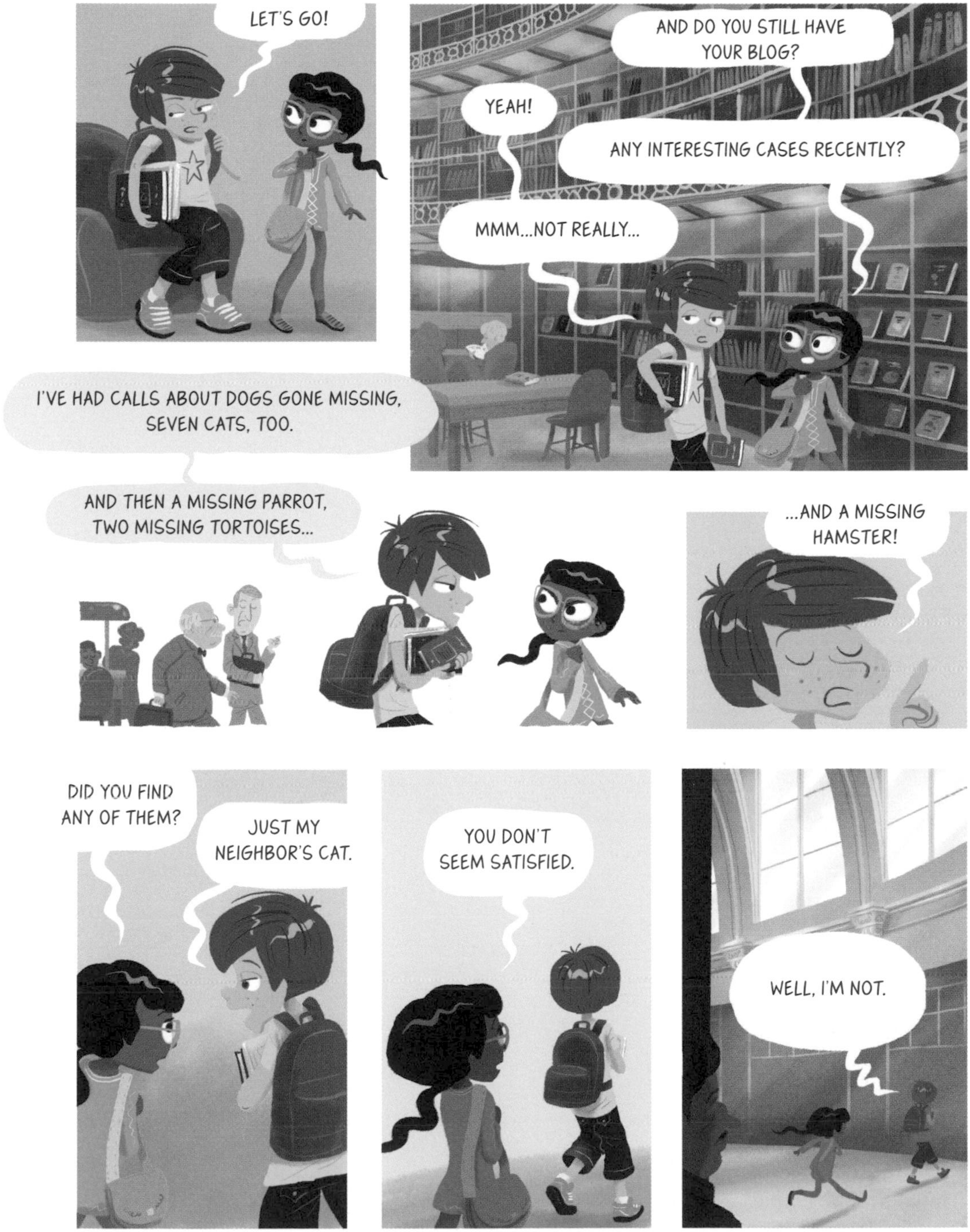
LET'S GO!
AND DO YOU STILL HAVE YOUR BLOG?
YEAH!
ANY INTERESTING CASES RECENTLY?
MMM...NOT REALLY...
I'VE HAD CALLS ABOUT DOGS GONE MISSING, SEVEN CATS, TOO.
AND THEN A MISSING PARROT, TWO MISSING TORTOISES...
...AND A MISSING HAMSTER!
DID YOU FIND ANY OF THEM?
JUST MY NEIGHBOR'S CAT.
YOU DON'T SEEM SATISFIED.
WELL, I'M NOT.

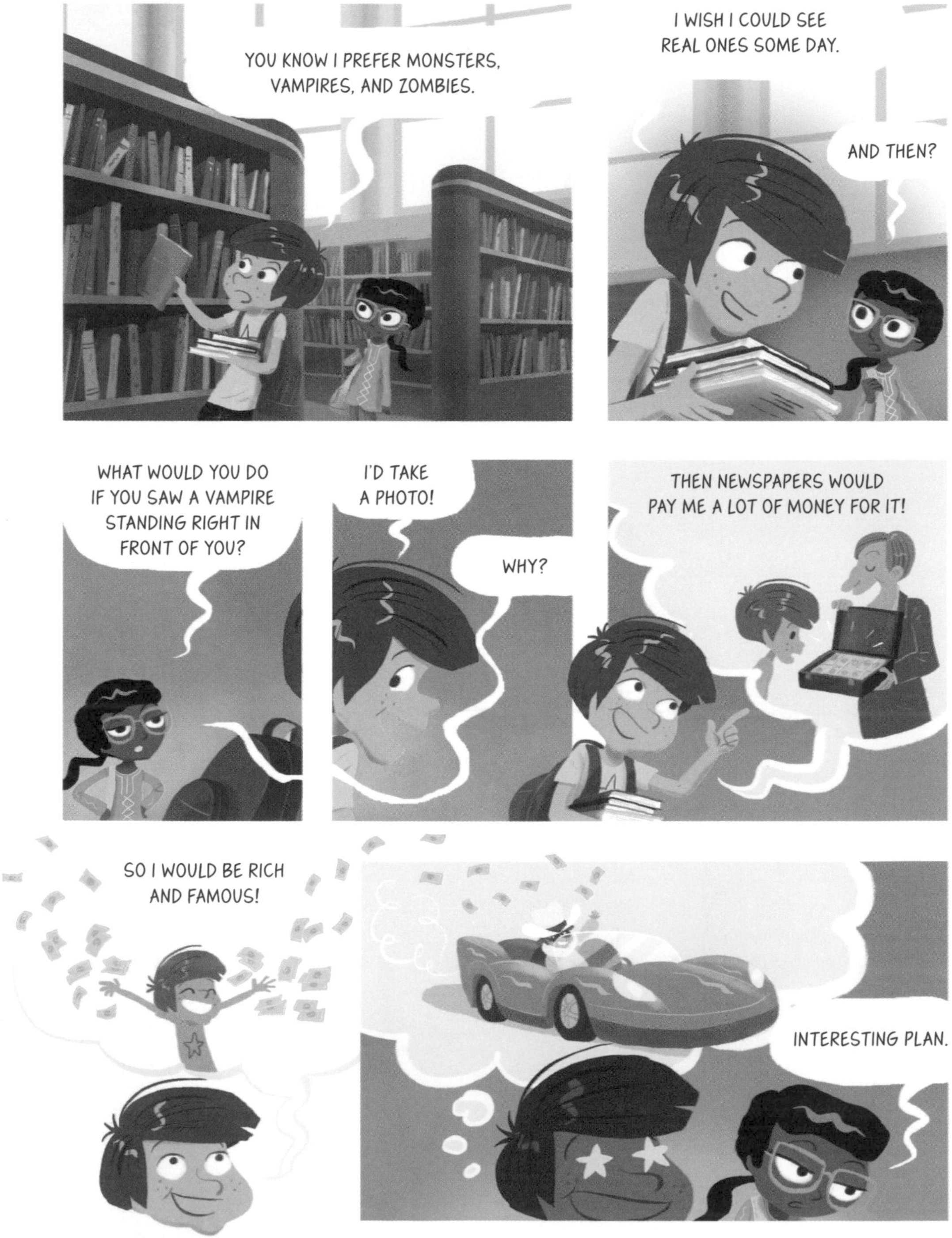
YOU KNOW I PREFER MONSTERS, VAMPIRES, AND ZOMBIES.
I WISH I COULD SEE REAL ONES SOME DAY.
AND THEN?
WHAT WOULD YOU DO IF YOU SAW A VAMPIRE STANDING RIGHT IN FRONT OF YOU?
I'D TAKE A PHOTO!
WHY?
THEN NEWSPAPERS WOULD PAY ME A LOT OF MONEY FOR IT!
SO I WOULD BE RICH AND FAMOUS!
INTERESTING PLAN.

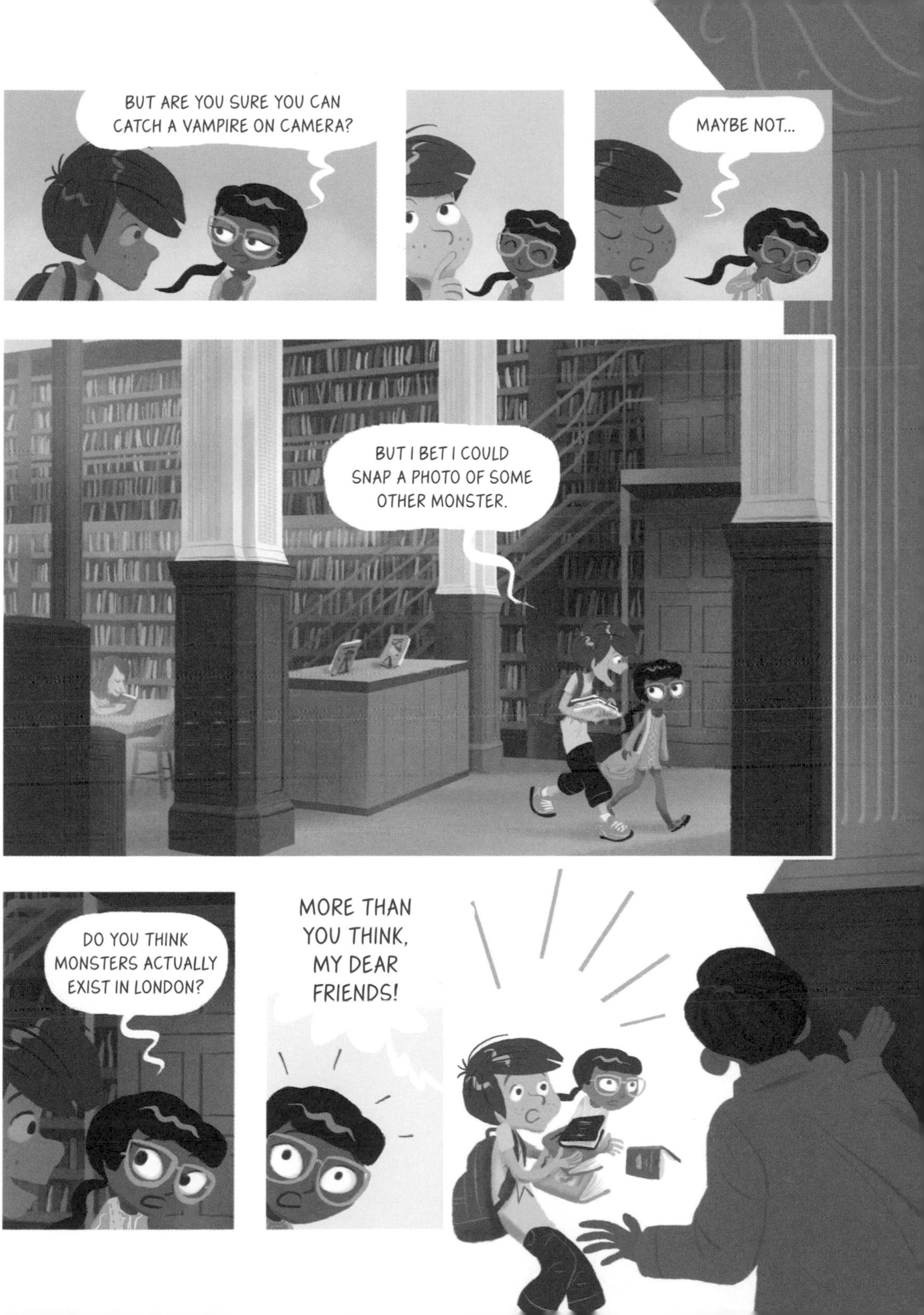
BUT ARE YOU SURE YOU CAN CATCH A VAMPIRE ON CAMERA?
MAYBE NOT...
BUT I BET I COULD SNAP A PHOTO OF SOME OTHER MONSTER.
DO YOU THINK MONSTERS ACTUALLY EXIST IN LONDON?
MORE THAN YOU THINK, MY DEAR FRIENDS!

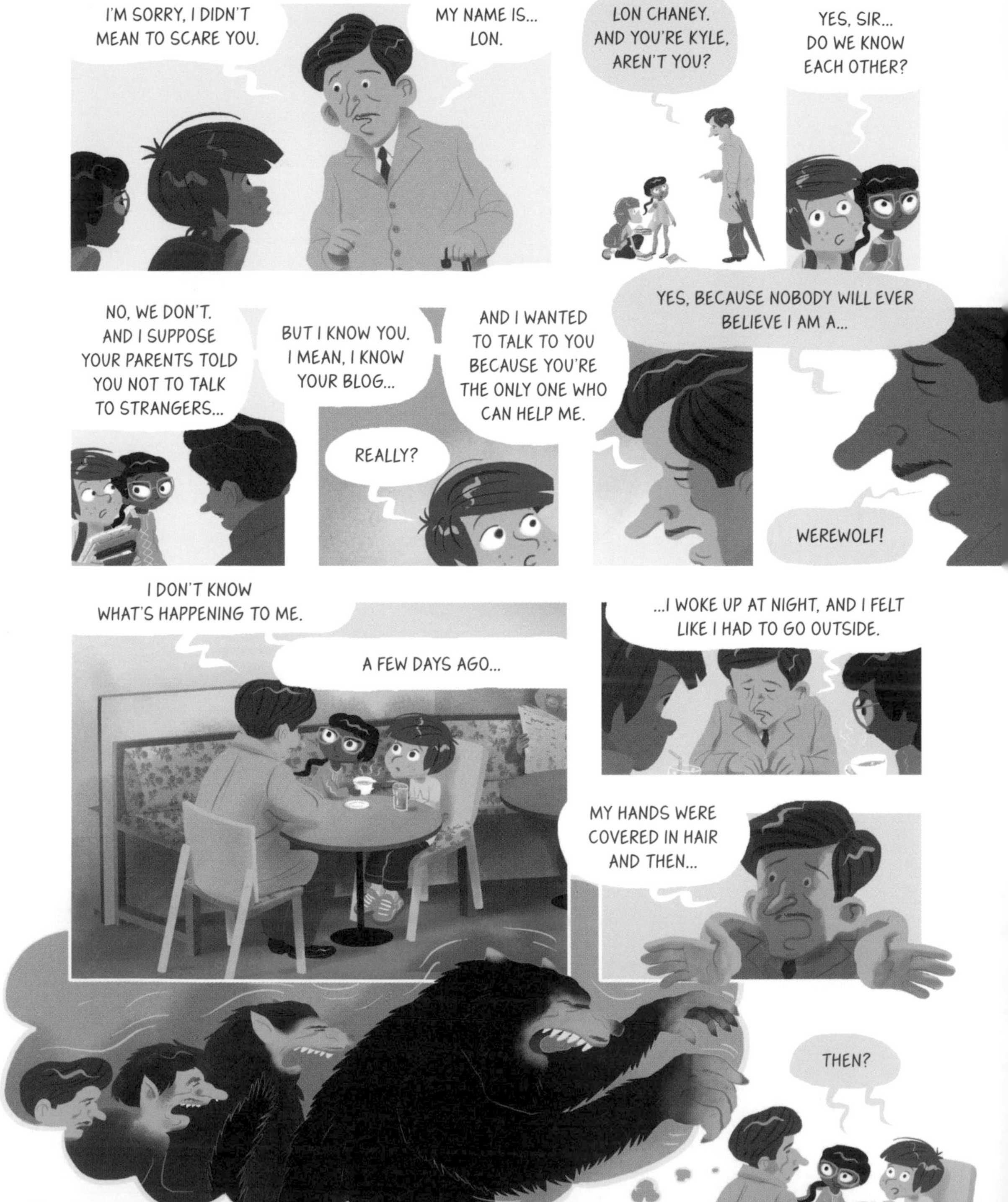
I'M SORRY, I DIDN'T MEAN TO SCARE YOU.
MY NAME IS... LON.
LON CHANEY. AND YOU'RE KYLE, AREN'T YOU?
YES, SIR... DO WE KNOW EACH OTHER?
NO, WE DON'T. AND I SUPPOSE YOUR PARENTS TOLD YOU NOT TO TALK TO STRANGERS...
BUT I KNOW YOU. I MEAN, I KNOW YOUR BLOG...
AND I WANTED TO TALK TO YOU BECAUSE YOU'RE THE ONLY ONE WHO CAN HELP ME.
REALLY?
YES, BECAUSE NOBODY WILL EVER BELIEVE I AM A...
WEREWOLF!
I DON'T KNOW WHAT'S HAPPENING TO ME.
A FEW DAYS AGO...
...I WOKE UP AT NIGHT, AND I FELT LIKE I HAD TO GO OUTSIDE.
MY HANDS WERE COVERED IN HAIR AND THEN...
THEN?

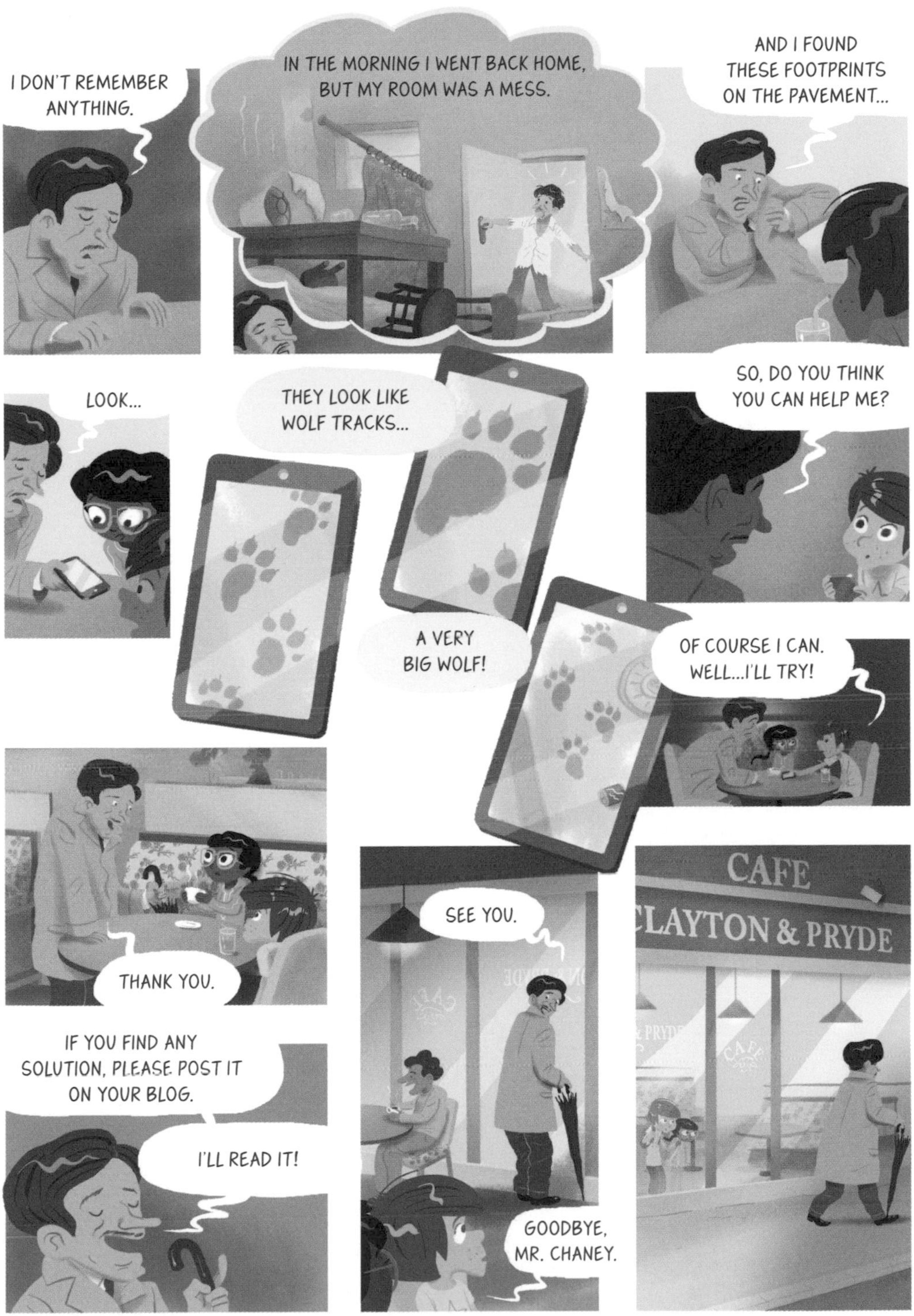
I DON'T REMEMBER ANYTHING.
IN THE MORNING I WENT BACK HOME, BUT MY ROOM WAS A MESS.
AND I FOUND THESE FOOTPRINTS ON THE PAVEMENT...
LOOK...
THEY LOOK LIKE WOLF TRACKS...
A VERY BIG WOLF!
SO, DO YOU THINK YOU CAN HELP ME?
OF COURSE I CAN. WELL...I'LL TRY!
THANK YOU.
IF YOU FIND ANY SOLUTION, PLEASE POST IT ON YOUR BLOG.
I'LL READ IT!
SEE YOU.
GOODBYE, MR. CHANEY.
CAFE
CLAYTON & PRYDE

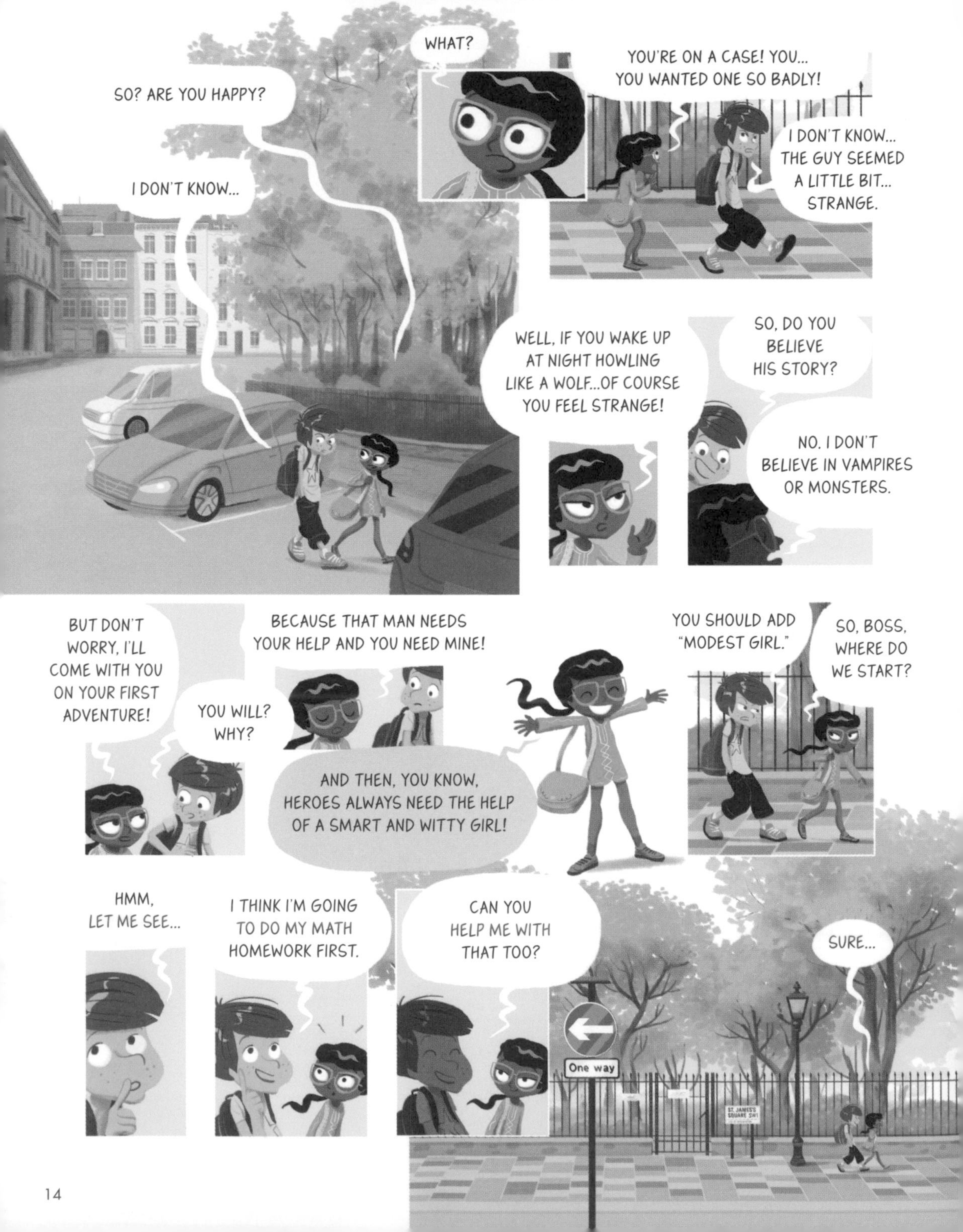
SO? ARE YOU HAPPY?
I DON'T KNOW...
WHAT?
YOU'RE ON A CASE! YOU... YOU WANTED ONE SO BADLY!
I DON'T KNOW... THE GUY SEEMED A LITTLE BIT... STRANGE.
WELL, IF YOU WAKE UP AT NIGHT HOWLING LIKE A WOLF...OF COURSE YOU FEEL STRANGE!
SO, DO YOU BELIEVE HIS STORY?
NO. I DON'T BELIEVE IN VAMPIRES OR MONSTERS.
BUT DON'T WORRY, I'LL COME WITH YOU ON YOUR FIRST ADVENTURE!
YOU WILL? WHY?
BECAUSE THAT MAN NEEDS YOUR HELP AND YOU NEED MINE!
AND THEN, YOU KNOW, HEROES ALWAYS NEED THE HELP OF A SMART AND WITTY GIRL!
YOU SHOULD ADD "MODEST GIRL."
SO, BOSS, WHERE DO WE START?
HMM, LET ME SEE...
I THINK I'M GOING TO DO MY MATH HOMEWORK FIRST.
CAN YOU HELP ME WITH THAT TOO?
SURE...
One way

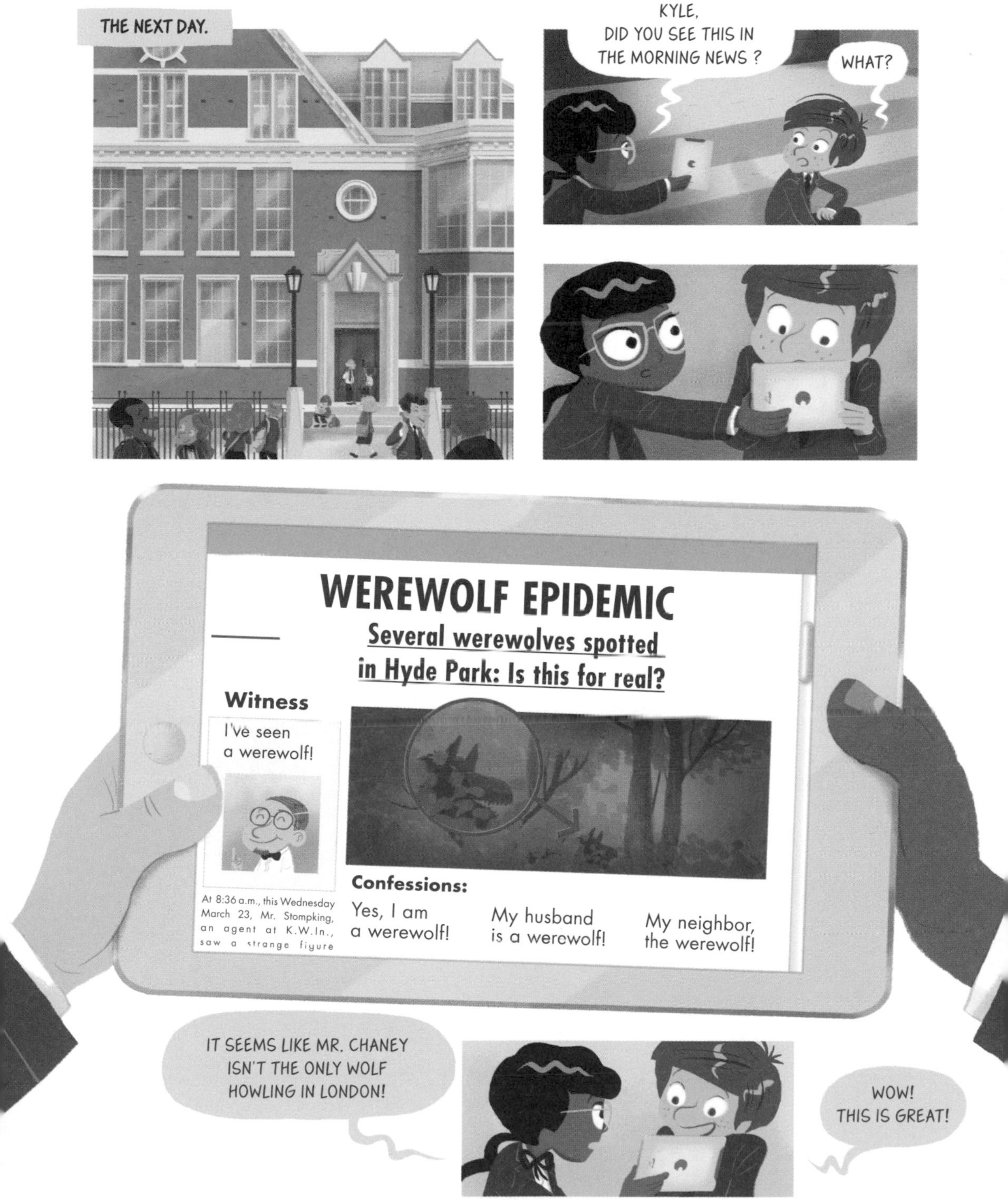
THE NEXT DAY.
KYLE, DID YOU SEE THIS IN THE MORNING NEWS ?
WHAT?
WEREWOLF EPIDEMIC
Several werewolves spotted in Hyde Park: Is this for real?
Witness
I've seen a werewolf!
At 8:36 a.m., this Wednesday March 23, Mr. Stompking, an agent at K.W.In., saw a strange figure
Confessions:
Yes, I am a werewolf!
My husband is a werewolf!
My neighbor, the werewolf!
IT SEEMS LIKE MR. CHANEY ISN'T THE ONLY WOLF HOWLING IN LONDON!
WOW! THIS IS GREAT!

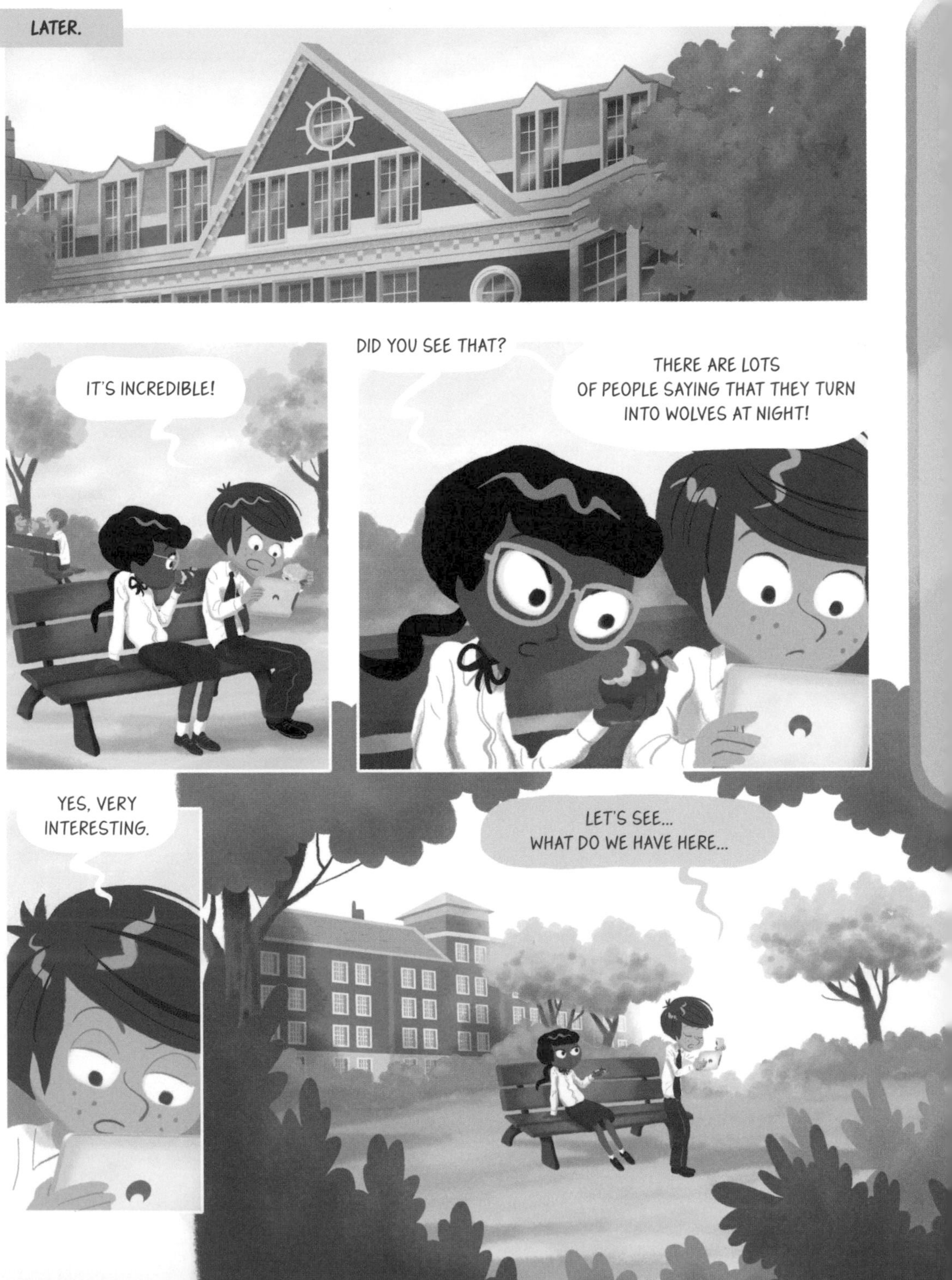
LATER.
IT'S INCREDIBLE!
DID YOU SEE THAT?
THERE ARE LOTS OF PEOPLE SAYING THAT THEY TURN INTO WOLVES AT NIGHT!
YES, VERY INTERESTING.
LET'S SEE... WHAT DO WE HAVE HERE...

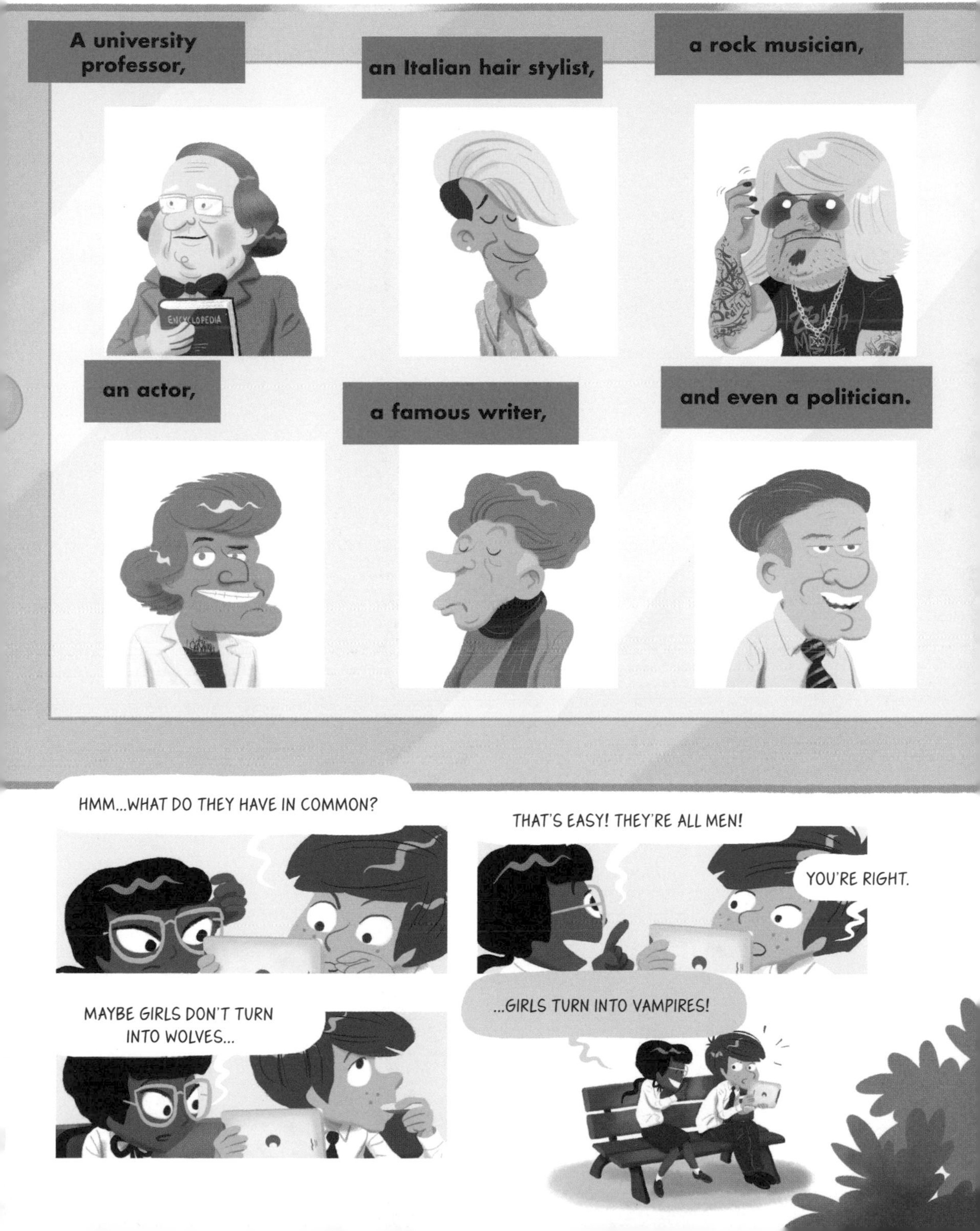
A university professor,
ENCYCLOPEDIA
an Italian hair stylist,
a rock musician,
an actor,
a famous writer,
and even a politician.
HMM...WHAT DO THEY HAVE IN COMMON?
THAT'S EASY! THEY'RE ALL MEN!
YOU'RE RIGHT.
MAYBE GIRLS DON'T TURN INTO WOLVES...
...GIRLS TURN INTO VAMPIRES!

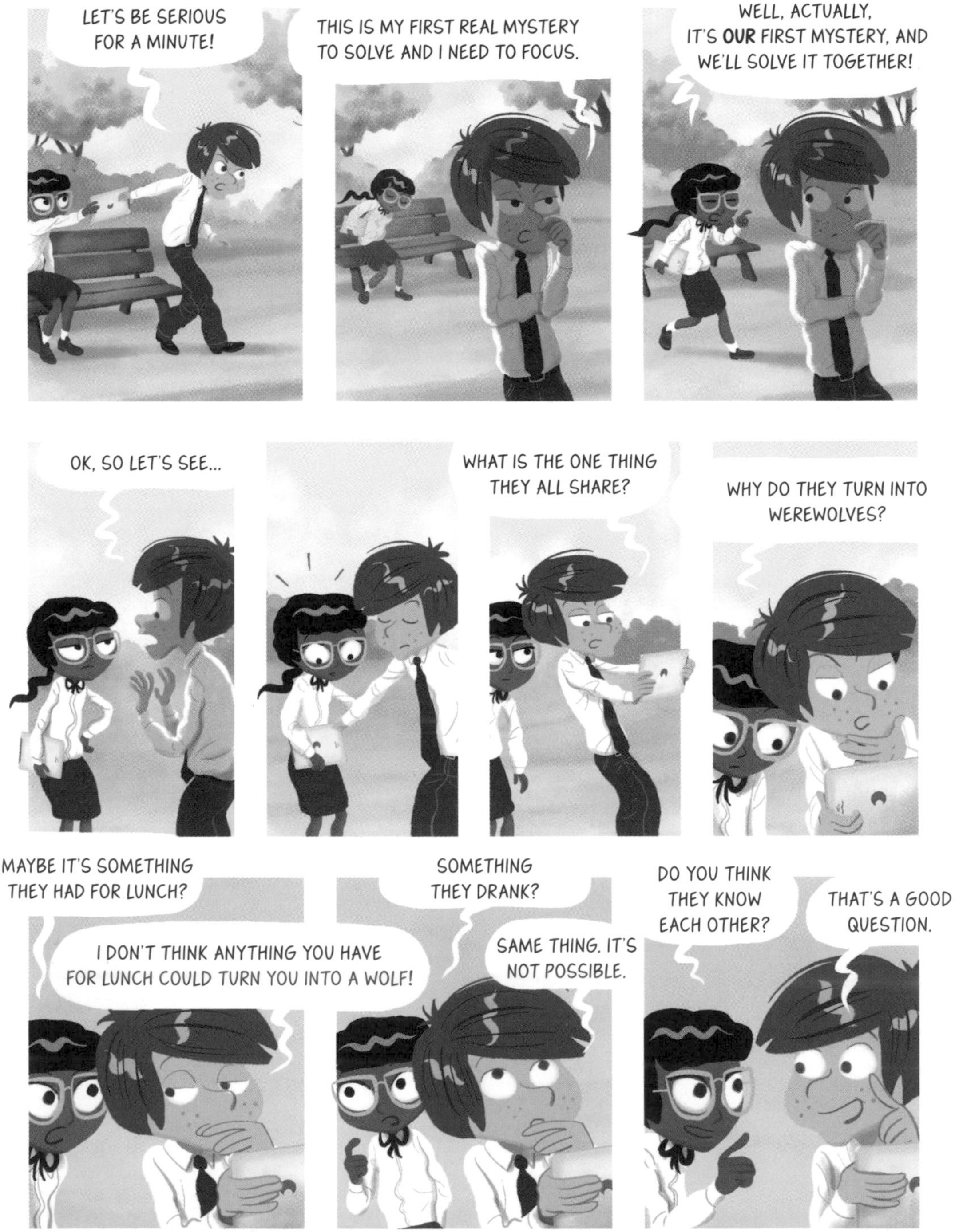
LET'S BE SERIOUS FOR A MINUTE!
THIS IS MY FIRST REAL MYSTERY TO SOLVE AND I NEED TO FOCUS.
WELL, ACTUALLY, IT'S **OUR** FIRST MYSTERY, AND WE'LL SOLVE IT TOGETHER!
OK, SO LET'S SEE...
WHAT IS THE ONE THING THEY ALL SHARE?
WHY DO THEY TURN INTO WEREWOLVES?
MAYBE IT'S SOMETHING THEY HAD FOR LUNCH?
I DON'T THINK ANYTHING YOU HAVE FOR LUNCH COULD TURN YOU INTO A WOLF!
SOMETHING THEY DRANK?
SAME THING. IT'S NOT POSSIBLE.
DO YOU THINK THEY KNOW EACH OTHER?
THAT'S A GOOD QUESTION.

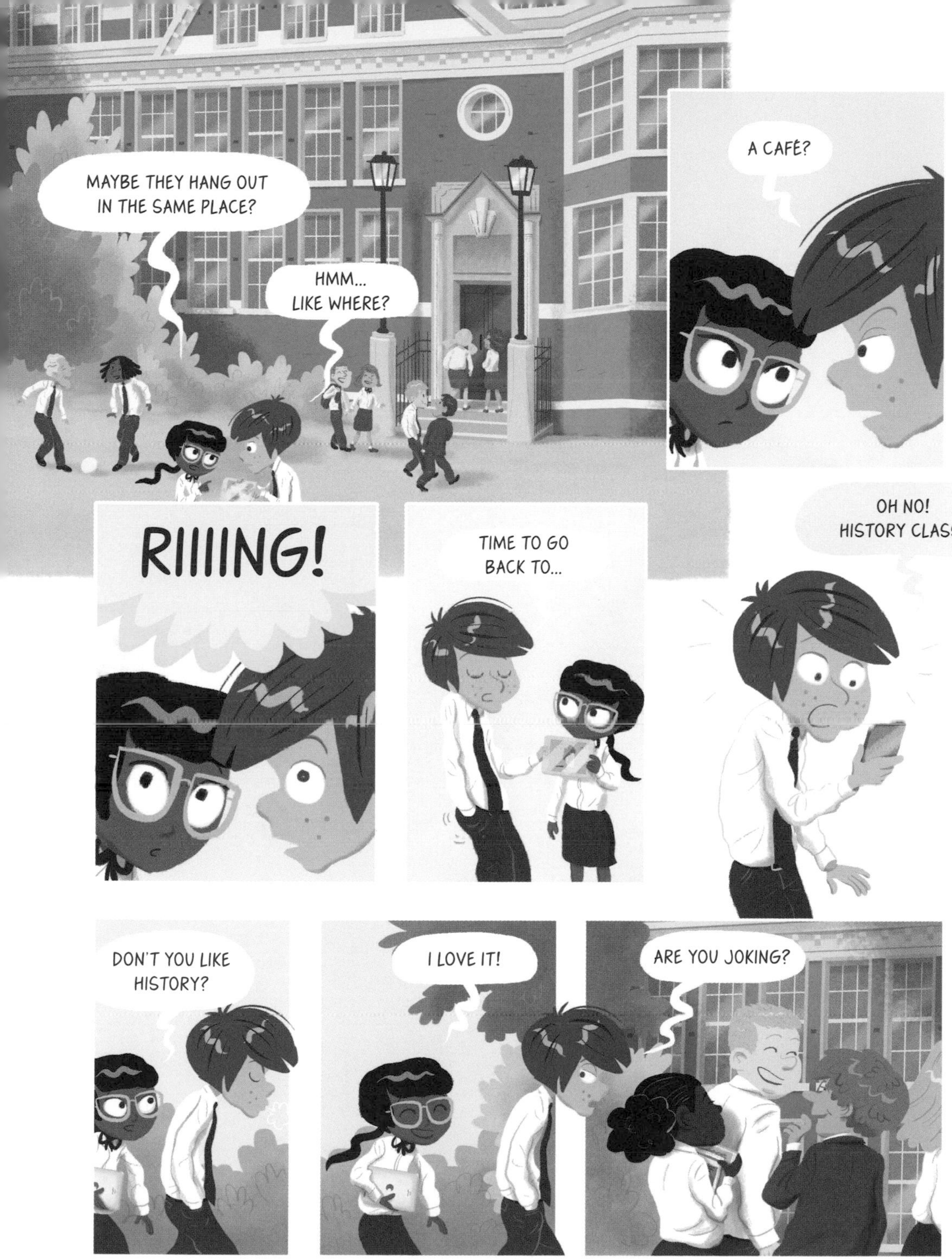
MAYBE THEY HANG OUT IN THE SAME PLACE?
HMM... LIKE WHERE?
A CAFÉ?
RIIIING!
TIME TO GO BACK TO...
OH NO! HISTORY CLASS!
DON'T YOU LIKE HISTORY?
I LOVE IT!
ARE YOU JOKING?

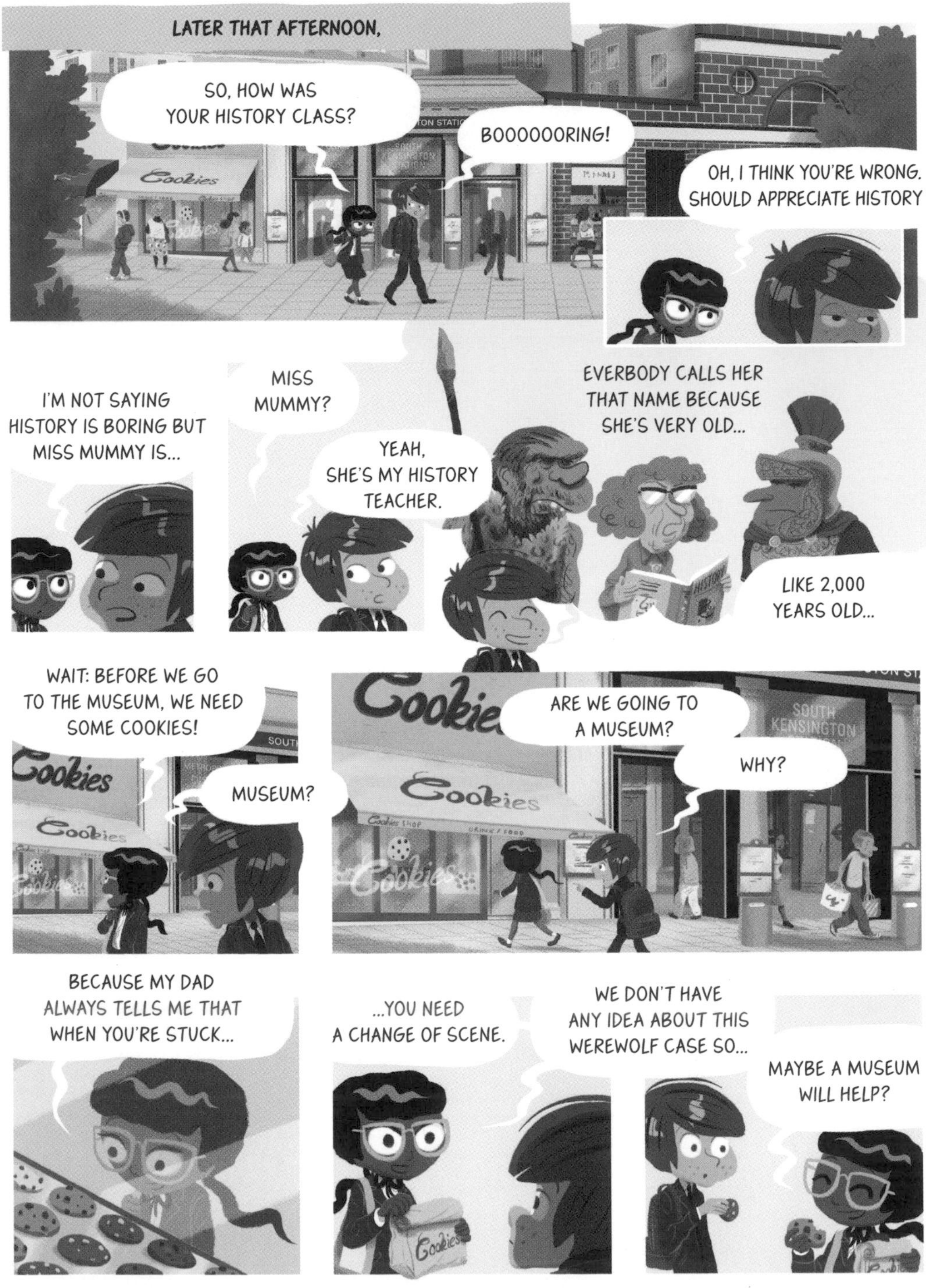
LATER THAT AFTERNOON,
SO, HOW WAS YOUR HISTORY CLASS?
BOOOOOORING!
OH, I THINK YOU'RE WRONG. YOU SHOULD APPRECIATE HISTORY MORE.
I'M NOT SAYING HISTORY IS BORING BUT MISS MUMMY IS...
MISS MUMMY?
YEAH, SHE'S MY HISTORY TEACHER.
EVERBODY CALLS HER THAT NAME BECAUSE SHE'S VERY OLD...
LIKE 2,000 YEARS OLD...
WAIT: BEFORE WE GO TO THE MUSEUM, WE NEED SOME COOKIES!
MUSEUM?
ARE WE GOING TO A MUSEUM?
WHY?
BECAUSE MY DAD ALWAYS TELLS ME THAT WHEN YOU'RE STUCK...
...YOU NEED A CHANGE OF SCENE.
WE DON'T HAVE ANY IDEA ABOUT THIS WEREWOLF CASE SO...
MAYBE A MUSEUM WILL HELP?

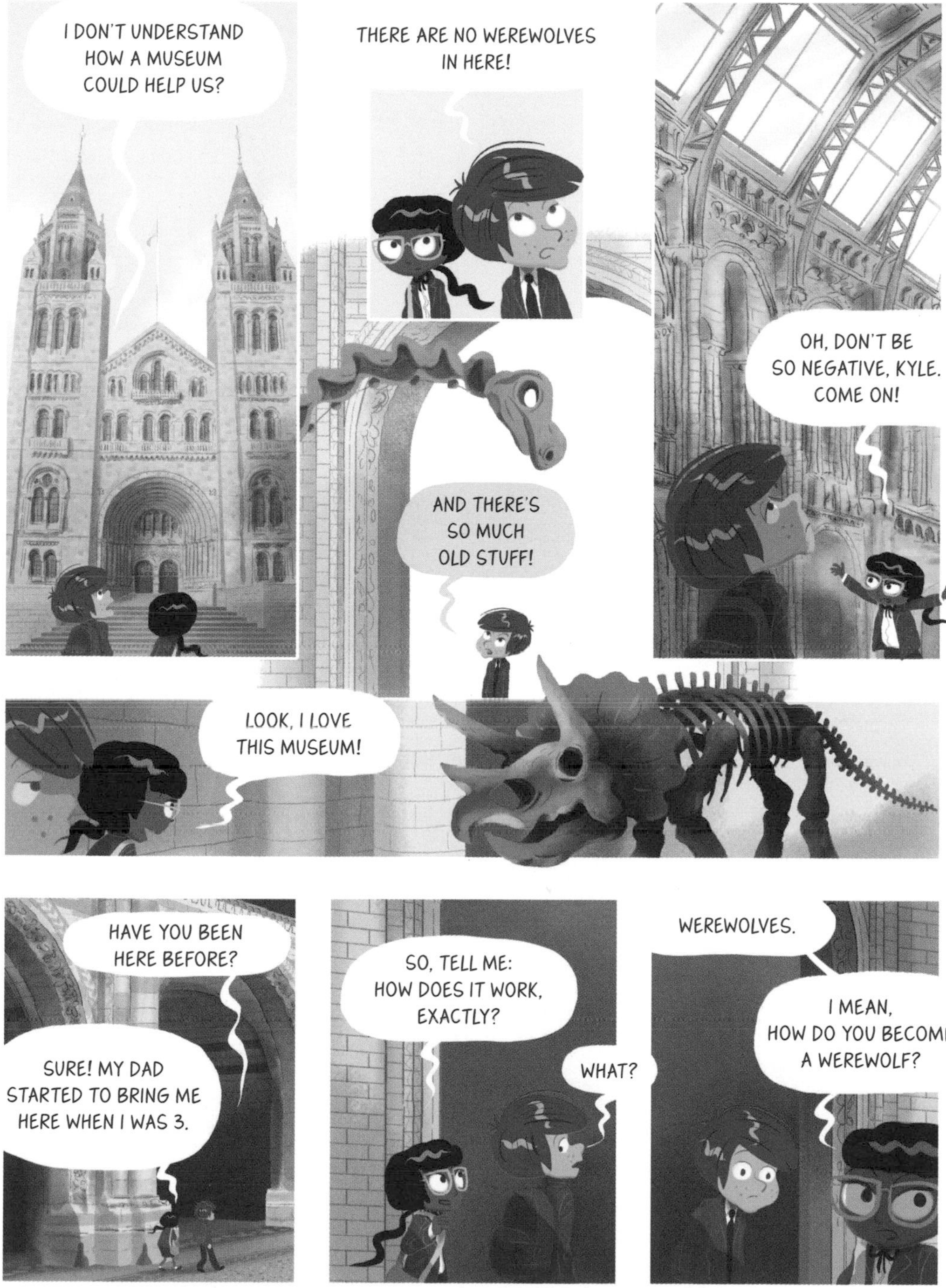
I DON'T UNDERSTAND HOW A MUSEUM COULD HELP US?
THERE ARE NO WEREWOLVES IN HERE!
AND THERE'S SO MUCH OLD STUFF!
OH, DON'T BE SO NEGATIVE, KYLE. COME ON!
LOOK, I LOVE THIS MUSEUM!
HAVE YOU BEEN HERE BEFORE?
SURE! MY DAD STARTED TO BRING ME HERE WHEN I WAS 3.
SO, TELL ME: HOW DOES IT WORK, EXACTLY?
WHAT?
WEREWOLVES.
I MEAN, HOW DO YOU BECOME A WEREWOLF?

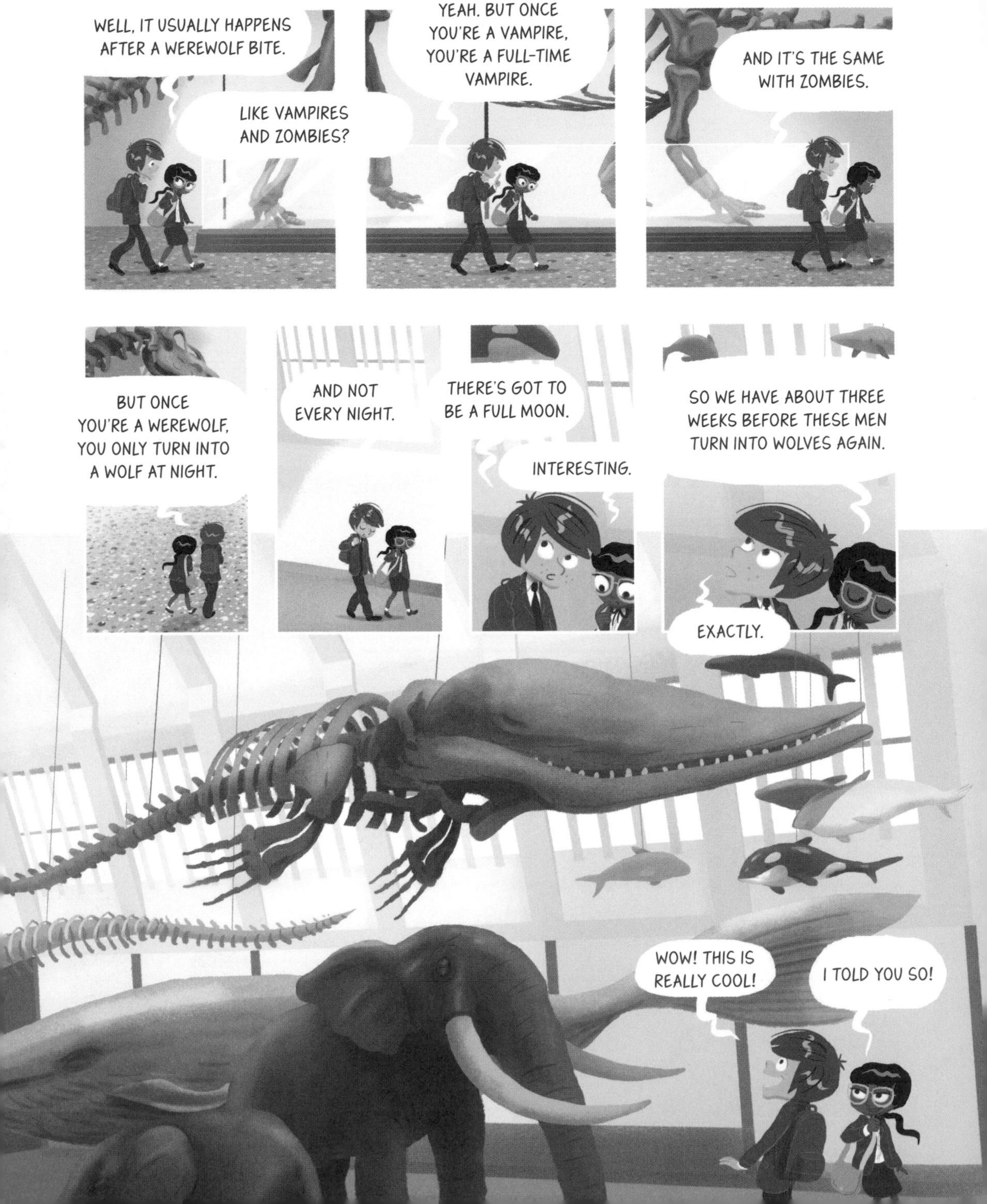
WELL, IT USUALLY HAPPENS AFTER A WEREWOLF BITE.
LIKE VAMPIRES AND ZOMBIES?
YEAH. BUT ONCE YOU'RE A VAMPIRE, YOU'RE A FULL-TIME VAMPIRE.
AND IT'S THE SAME WITH ZOMBIES.
BUT ONCE YOU'RE A WEREWOLF, YOU ONLY TURN INTO A WOLF AT NIGHT.
AND NOT EVERY NIGHT.
THERE'S GOT TO BE A FULL MOON.
INTERESTING.
SO WE HAVE ABOUT THREE WEEKS BEFORE THESE MEN TURN INTO WOLVES AGAIN.
EXACTLY.
WOW! THIS IS REALLY COOL!
I TOLD YOU SO!

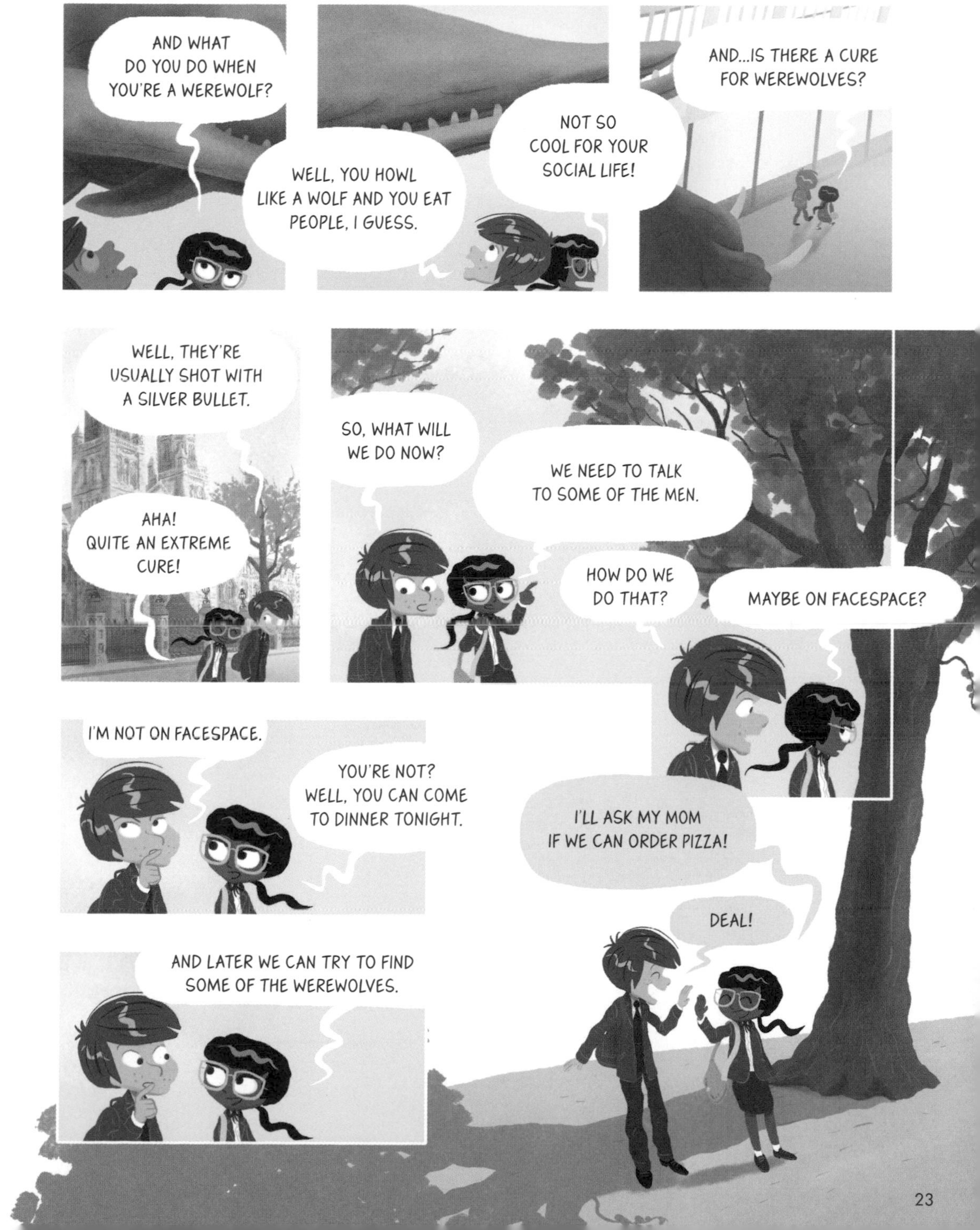
AND WHAT DO YOU DO WHEN YOU'RE A WEREWOLF?
WELL, YOU HOWL LIKE A WOLF AND YOU EAT PEOPLE, I GUESS.
NOT SO COOL FOR YOUR SOCIAL LIFE!
AND...IS THERE A CURE FOR WEREWOLVES?
WELL, THEY'RE USUALLY SHOT WITH A SILVER BULLET.
AHA! QUITE AN EXTREME CURE!
SO, WHAT WILL WE DO NOW?
WE NEED TO TALK TO SOME OF THE MEN.
HOW DO WE DO THAT?
MAYBE ON FACESPACE?
I'M NOT ON FACESPACE.
YOU'RE NOT? WELL, YOU CAN COME TO DINNER TONIGHT.
AND LATER WE CAN TRY TO FIND SOME OF THE WEREWOLVES.
I'LL ASK MY MOM IF WE CAN ORDER PIZZA!
DEAL!

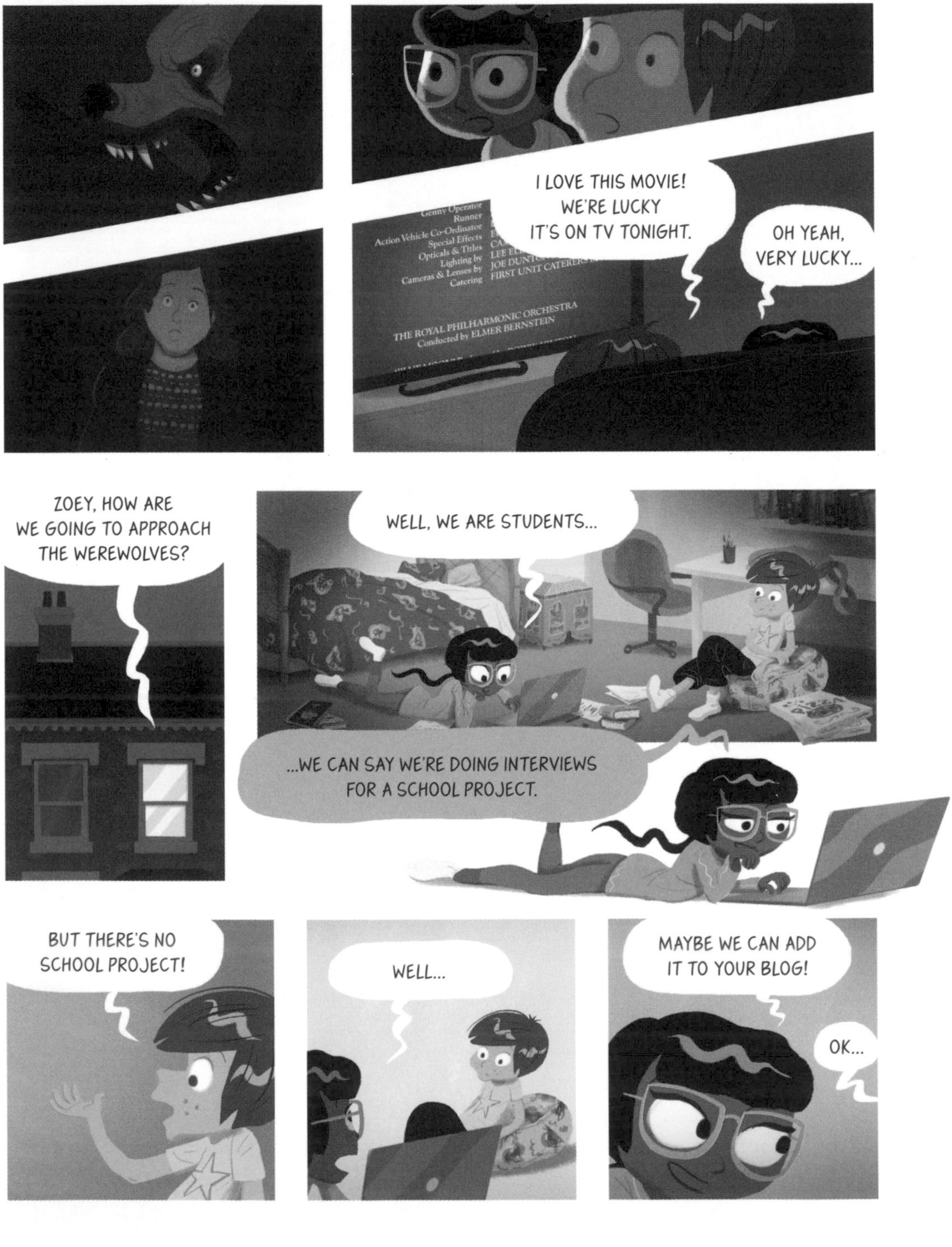
Genny Operator
Runner
Action Vehicle Co-Ordinator
Special Effects
Opticals & Titles
Lighting by
Cameras & Lenses by
Catering
FIRST UNIT CATERERS
THE ROYAL PHILHARMONIC ORCHESTRA
Conducted by ELMER BERNSTEIN
I LOVE THIS MOVIE! WE'RE LUCKY IT'S ON TV TONIGHT.
OH YEAH, VERY LUCKY...
ZOEY, HOW ARE WE GOING TO APPROACH THE WEREWOLVES?
WELL, WE ARE STUDENTS...
...WE CAN SAY WE'RE DOING INTERVIEWS FOR A SCHOOL PROJECT.
BUT THERE'S NO SCHOOL PROJECT!
WELL...
MAYBE WE CAN ADD IT TO YOUR BLOG!
OK...

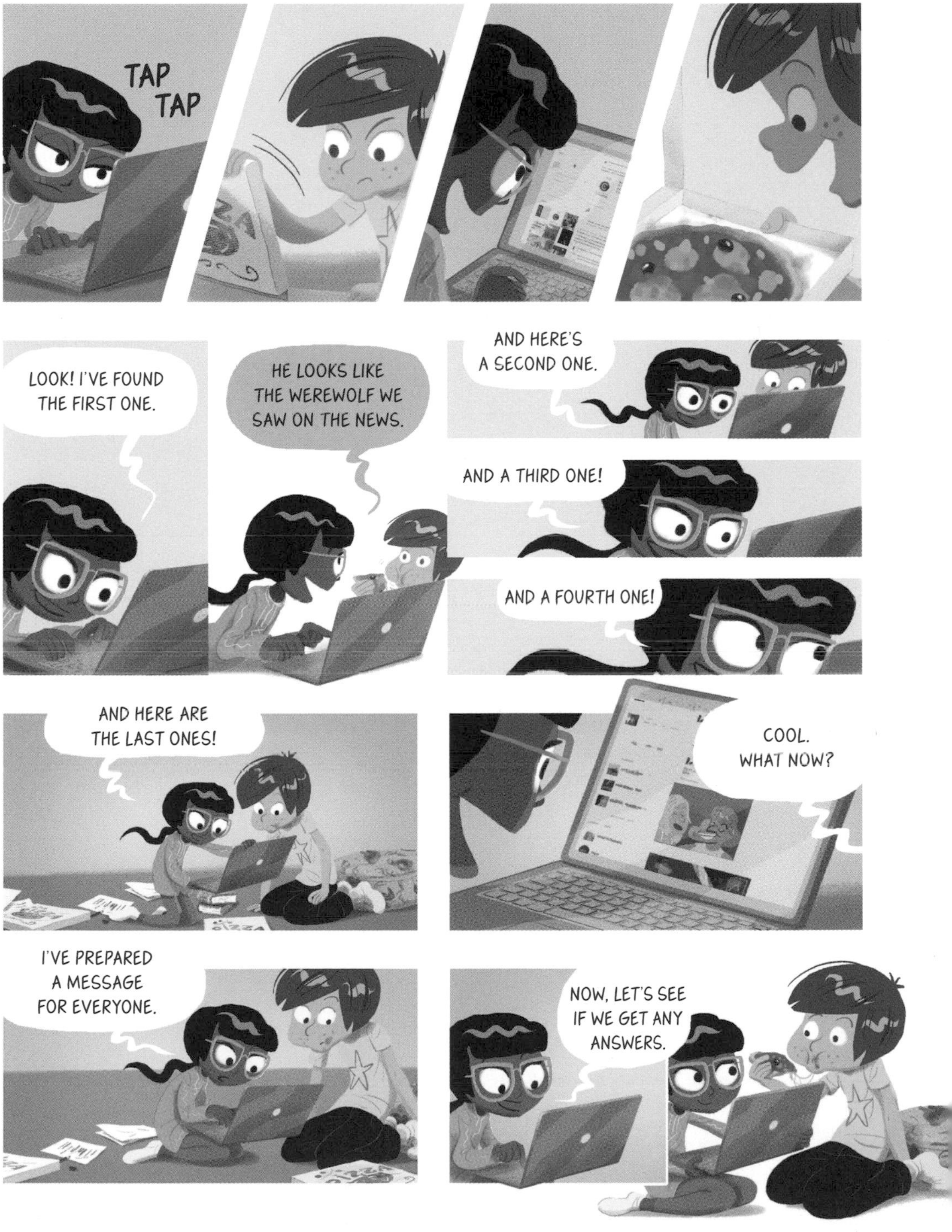
TAP
TAP
LOOK! I'VE FOUND THE FIRST ONE.
HE LOOKS LIKE THE WEREWOLF WE SAW ON THE NEWS.
AND HERE'S A SECOND ONE.
AND A THIRD ONE!
AND A FOURTH ONE!
AND HERE ARE THE LAST ONES!
COOL. WHAT NOW?
I'VE PREPARED A MESSAGE FOR EVERYONE.
NOW, LET'S SEE IF WE GET ANY ANSWERS.

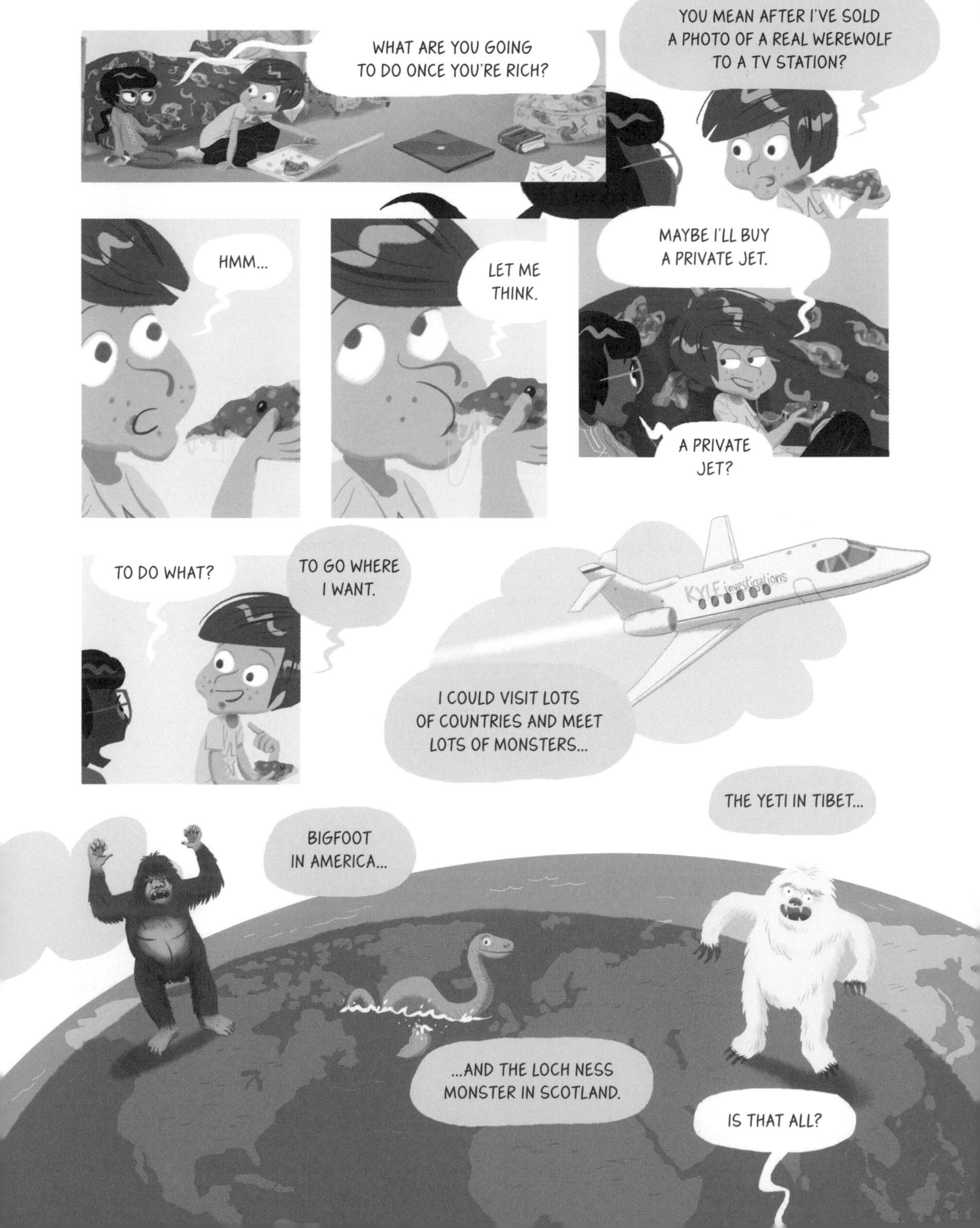
WHAT ARE YOU GOING TO DO ONCE YOU'RE RICH?
YOU MEAN AFTER I'VE SOLD A PHOTO OF A REAL WEREWOLF TO A TV STATION?
HMM...
LET ME THINK.
MAYBE I'LL BUY A PRIVATE JET.
A PRIVATE JET?
TO DO WHAT?
TO GO WHERE I WANT.
KYLE investigations
I COULD VISIT LOTS OF COUNTRIES AND MEET LOTS OF MONSTERS...
BIGFOOT IN AMERICA...
THE YETI IN TIBET...
...AND THE LOCH NESS MONSTER IN SCOTLAND.
IS THAT ALL?

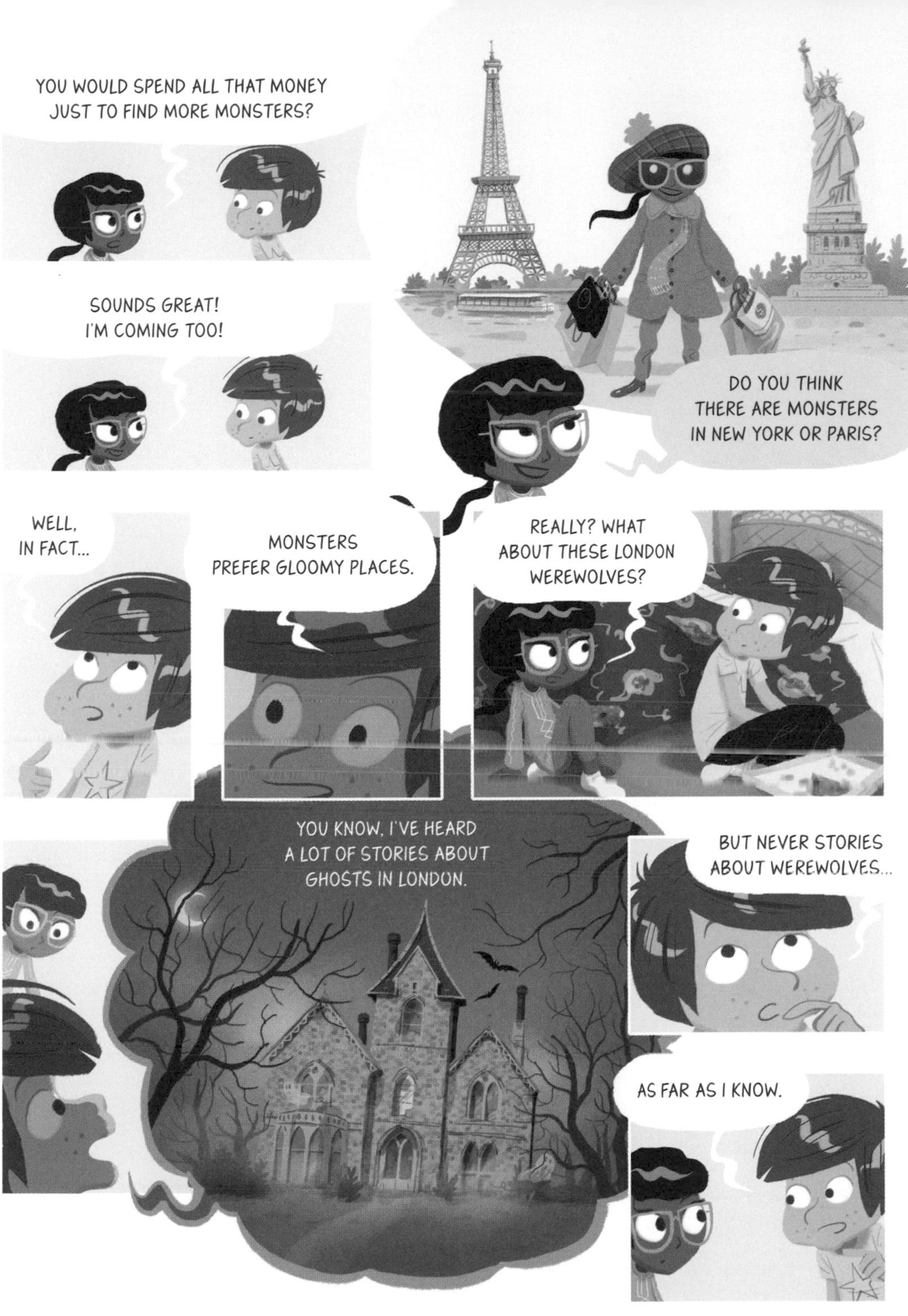
YOU WOULD SPEND ALL THAT MONEY JUST TO FIND MORE MONSTERS?
SOUNDS GREAT! I'M COMING TOO!
DO YOU THINK THERE ARE MONSTERS IN NEW YORK OR PARIS?
WELL, IN FACT...
MONSTERS PREFER GLOOMY PLACES.
REALLY? WHAT ABOUT THESE LONDON WEREWOLVES?
YOU KNOW, I'VE HEARD A LOT OF STORIES ABOUT GHOSTS IN LONDON.
BUT NEVER STORIES ABOUT WEREWOLVES...
AS FAR AS I KNOW.

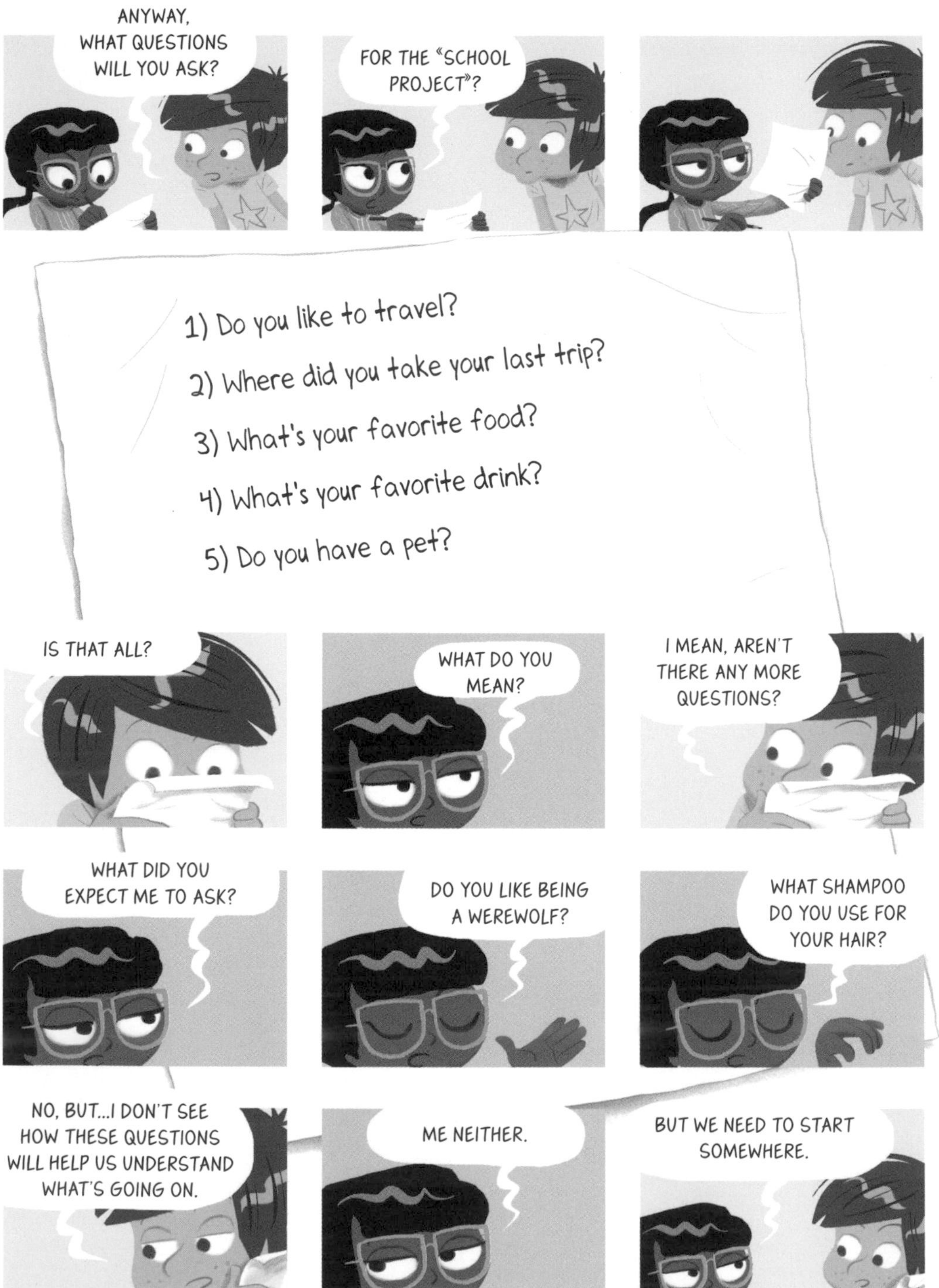
ANYWAY, WHAT QUESTIONS WILL YOU ASK?
FOR THE «SCHOOL PROJECT»?
1) Do you like to travel?
2) Where did you take your last trip?
3) What's your favorite food?
4) What's your favorite drink?
5) Do you have a pet?
IS THAT ALL?
WHAT DO YOU MEAN?
I MEAN, AREN'T THERE ANY MORE QUESTIONS?
WHAT DID YOU EXPECT ME TO ASK?
DO YOU LIKE BEING A WEREWOLF?
WHAT SHAMPOO DO YOU USE FOR YOUR HAIR?
NO, BUT...I DON'T SEE HOW THESE QUESTIONS WILL HELP US UNDERSTAND WHAT'S GOING ON.
ME NEITHER.
BUT WE NEED TO START SOMEWHERE.

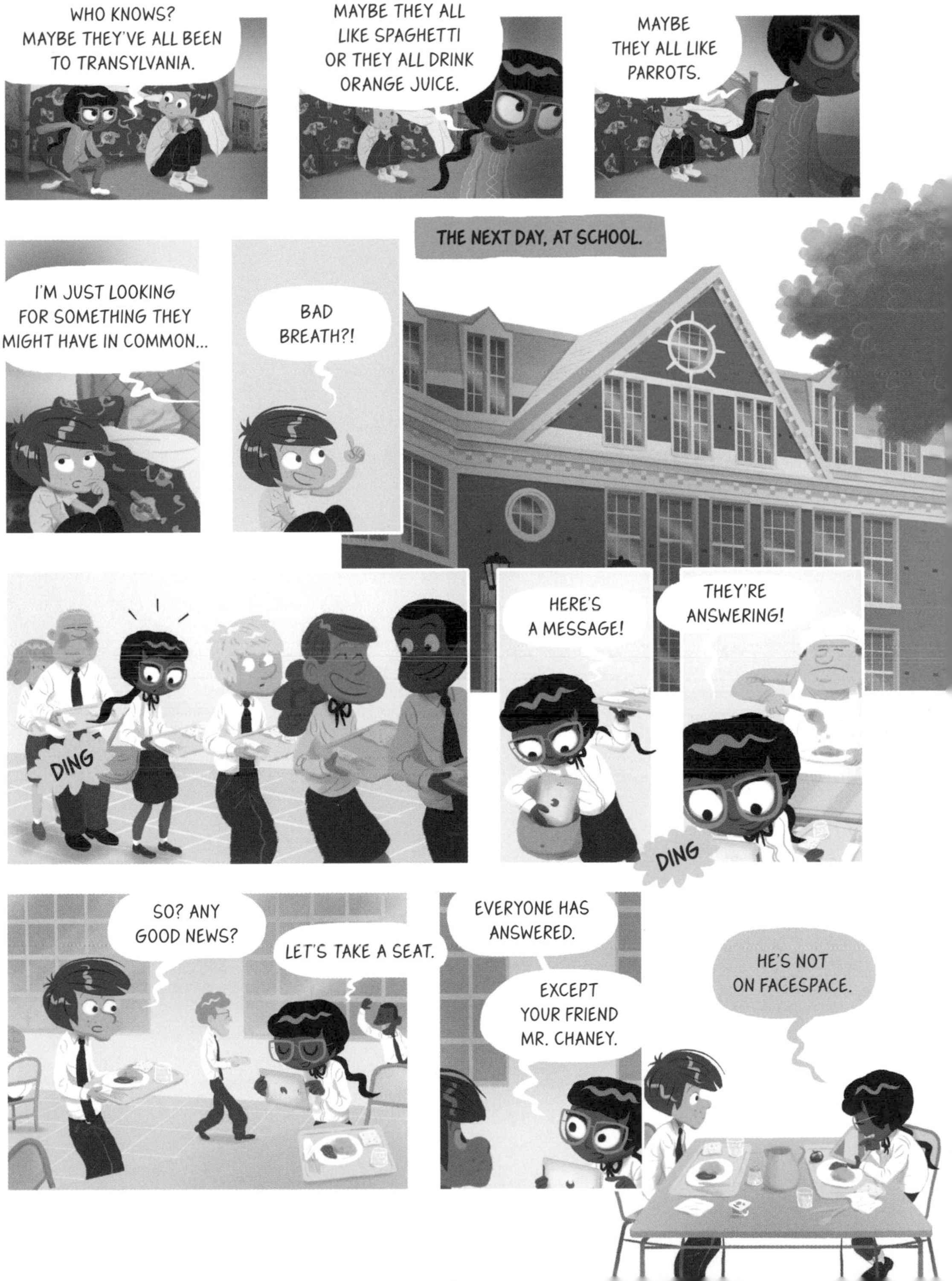
WHO KNOWS? MAYBE THEY'VE ALL BEEN TO TRANSYLVANIA.
MAYBE THEY ALL LIKE SPAGHETTI OR THEY ALL DRINK ORANGE JUICE.
MAYBE THEY ALL LIKE PARROTS.
I'M JUST LOOKING FOR SOMETHING THEY MIGHT HAVE IN COMMON...
BAD BREATH?!
THE NEXT DAY, AT SCHOOL.
DING
HERE'S A MESSAGE!
THEY'RE ANSWERING!
DING
SO? ANY GOOD NEWS?
LET'S TAKE A SEAT.
EVERYONE HAS ANSWERED.
EXCEPT YOUR FRIEND MR. CHANEY.
HE'S NOT ON FACESPACE.

University professor

Do you like to travel? No

Last trip taken: Nowhere

Favorite food: Pork chops

Favorite drink: Cider

Do you have a pet? Two dogs

Italian hair stylist

Do you like to travel? Yes

Last trip taken: Cambodia

Favorite food: Asian food

Favorite drink: Sake

Do you have a pet? Three cats

Rock musician

Do you like to travel? Yeah!

Last trip taken: Greenland

Favorite food: Hamburger
   and French fries

Favorite drink: Beer

Do you have a pet? I like animals
   but don't have any.

Actor

Do you like to travel? Sometimes

Last trip taken: Italy

Favorite food: Every kind of
   Italian pasta

Favorite drink: Red wine

Do you have a pet? Yes, I have
   a couple of turtles.

Famous writer

Do you like to travel? I hate traveling.

Last trip taken: Nowhere

Favorite food: Vegetable soup

Favorite drink: Water

Do you have a pet? I don't like animals.

Politician

Do you like to travel? Yes

Last trip taken: Turkey

Favorite food: Couscous

Favorite drink: Tea

Do you have a pet? Some tropical fish

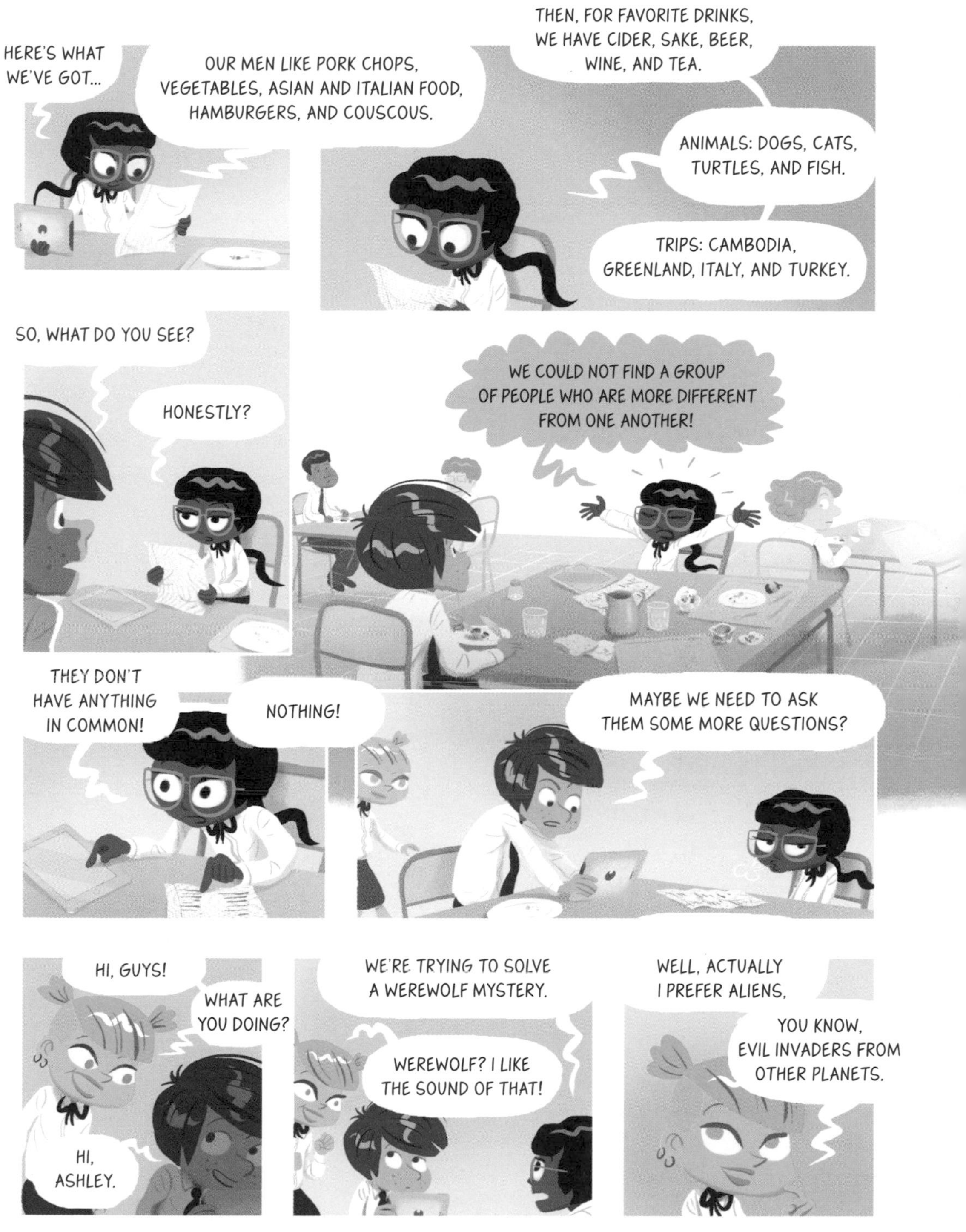
HERE'S WHAT WE'VE GOT...
OUR MEN LIKE PORK CHOPS, VEGETABLES, ASIAN AND ITALIAN FOOD, HAMBURGERS, AND COUSCOUS.
THEN, FOR FAVORITE DRINKS, WE HAVE CIDER, SAKE, BEER, WINE, AND TEA.
ANIMALS: DOGS, CATS, TURTLES, AND FISH.
TRIPS: CAMBODIA, GREENLAND, ITALY, AND TURKEY.
SO, WHAT DO YOU SEE?
HONESTLY?
WE COULD NOT FIND A GROUP OF PEOPLE WHO ARE MORE DIFFERENT FROM ONE ANOTHER!
THEY DON'T HAVE ANYTHING IN COMMON!
NOTHING!
MAYBE WE NEED TO ASK THEM SOME MORE QUESTIONS?
HI, GUYS!
WHAT ARE YOU DOING?
HI, ASHLEY.
WE'RE TRYING TO SOLVE A WEREWOLF MYSTERY.
WEREWOLF? I LIKE THE SOUND OF THAT!
WELL, ACTUALLY I PREFER ALIENS,
YOU KNOW, EVIL INVADERS FROM OTHER PLANETS.

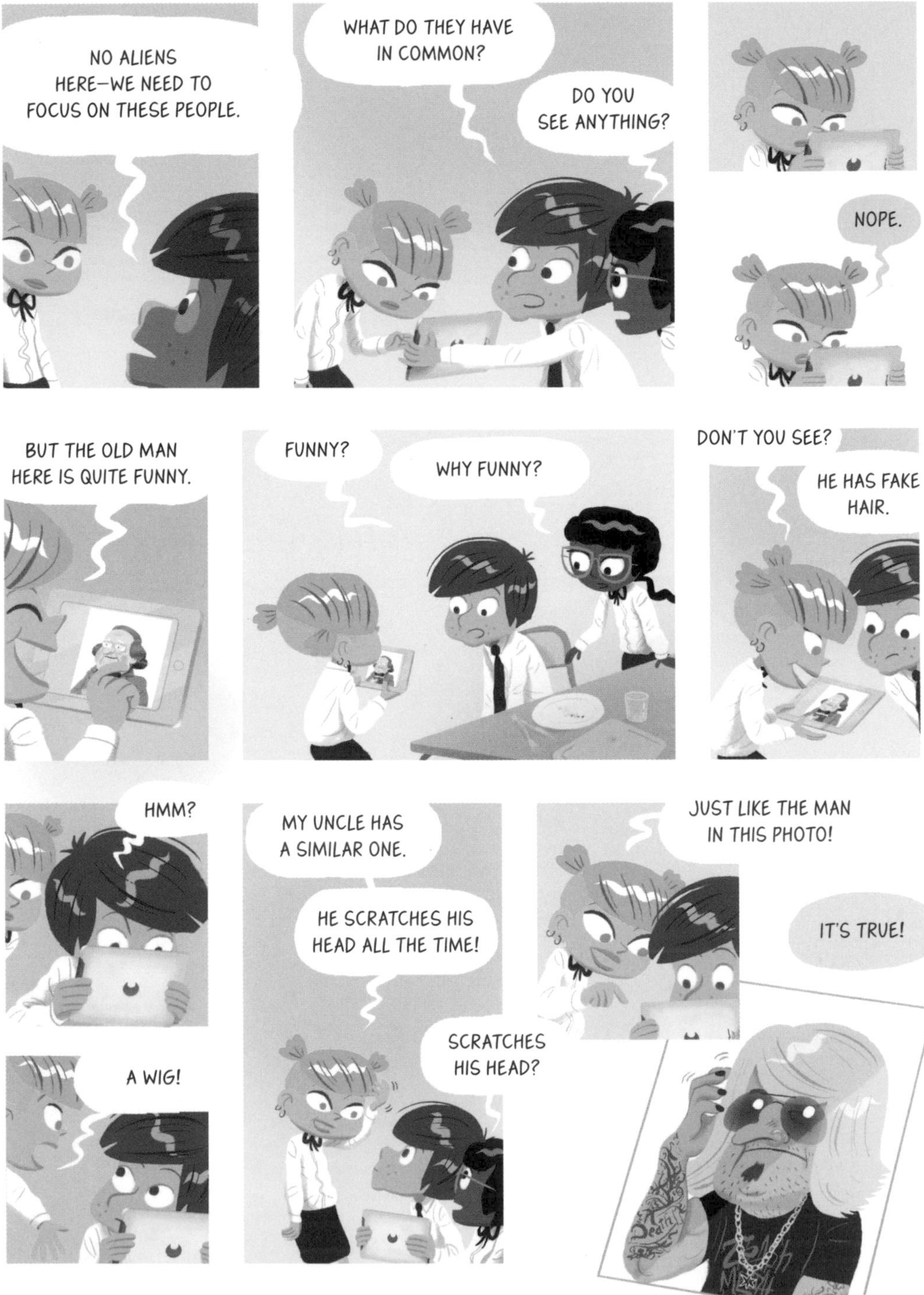
NO ALIENS HERE—WE NEED TO FOCUS ON THESE PEOPLE.
WHAT DO THEY HAVE IN COMMON?
DO YOU SEE ANYTHING?
NOPE.
BUT THE OLD MAN HERE IS QUITE FUNNY.
FUNNY?
WHY FUNNY?
DON'T YOU SEE?
HE HAS FAKE HAIR.
HMM?
A WIG!
MY UNCLE HAS A SIMILAR ONE.
HE SCRATCHES HIS HEAD ALL THE TIME!
SCRATCHES HIS HEAD?
JUST LIKE THE MAN IN THIS PHOTO!
IT'S TRUE!

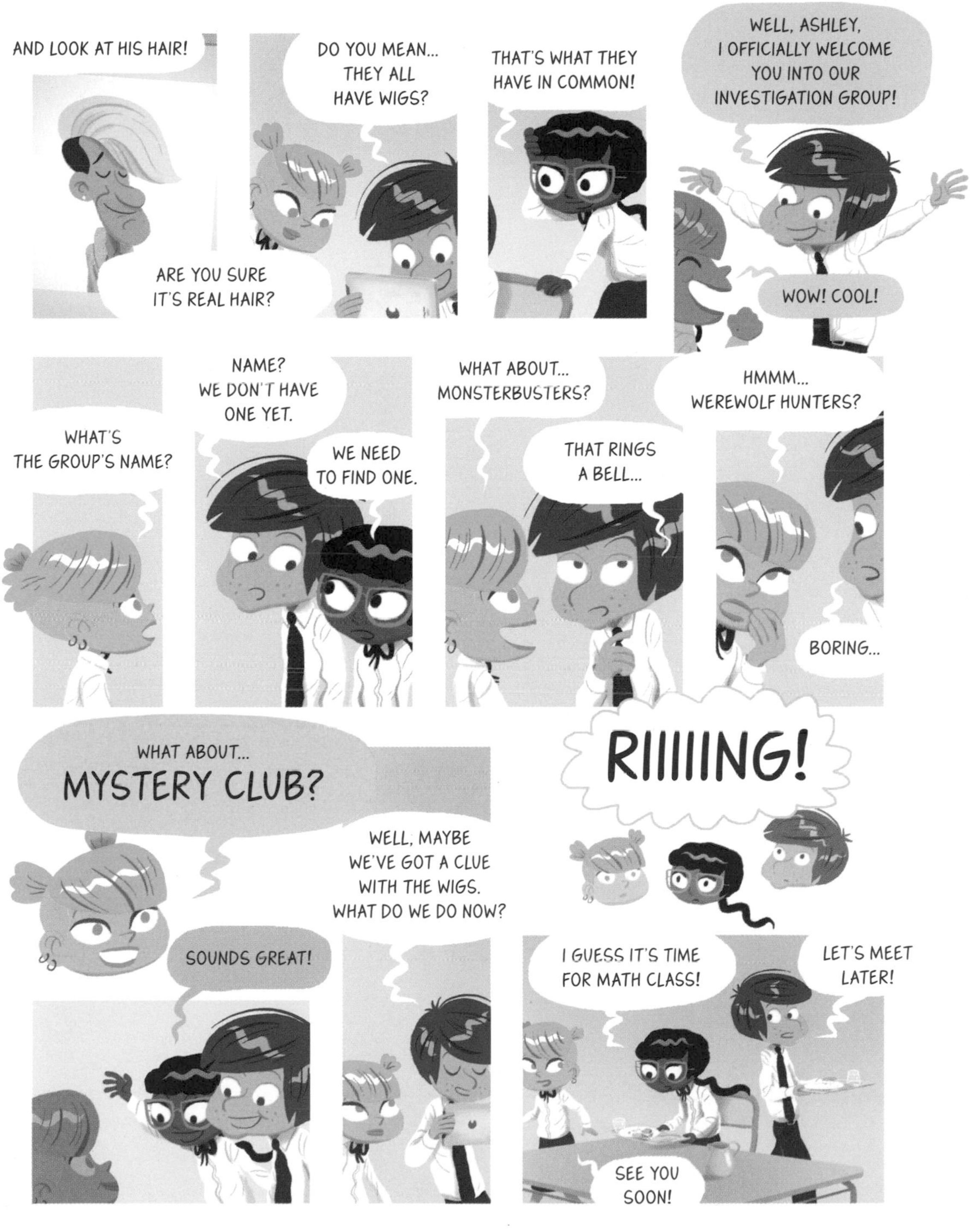
AND LOOK AT HIS HAIR!
ARE YOU SURE IT'S REAL HAIR?
DO YOU MEAN... THEY ALL HAVE WIGS?
THAT'S WHAT THEY HAVE IN COMMON!
WELL, ASHLEY, I OFFICIALLY WELCOME YOU INTO OUR INVESTIGATION GROUP!
WOW! COOL!
WHAT'S THE GROUP'S NAME?
NAME? WE DON'T HAVE ONE YET.
WE NEED TO FIND ONE.
WHAT ABOUT... MONSTERBUSTERS?
THAT RINGS A BELL...
HMMM... WEREWOLF HUNTERS?
BORING...
WHAT ABOUT... MYSTERY CLUB?
SOUNDS GREAT!
WELL, MAYBE WE'VE GOT A CLUE WITH THE WIGS. WHAT DO WE DO NOW?
RIIIIING!
I GUESS IT'S TIME FOR MATH CLASS!
LET'S MEET LATER!
SEE YOU SOON!

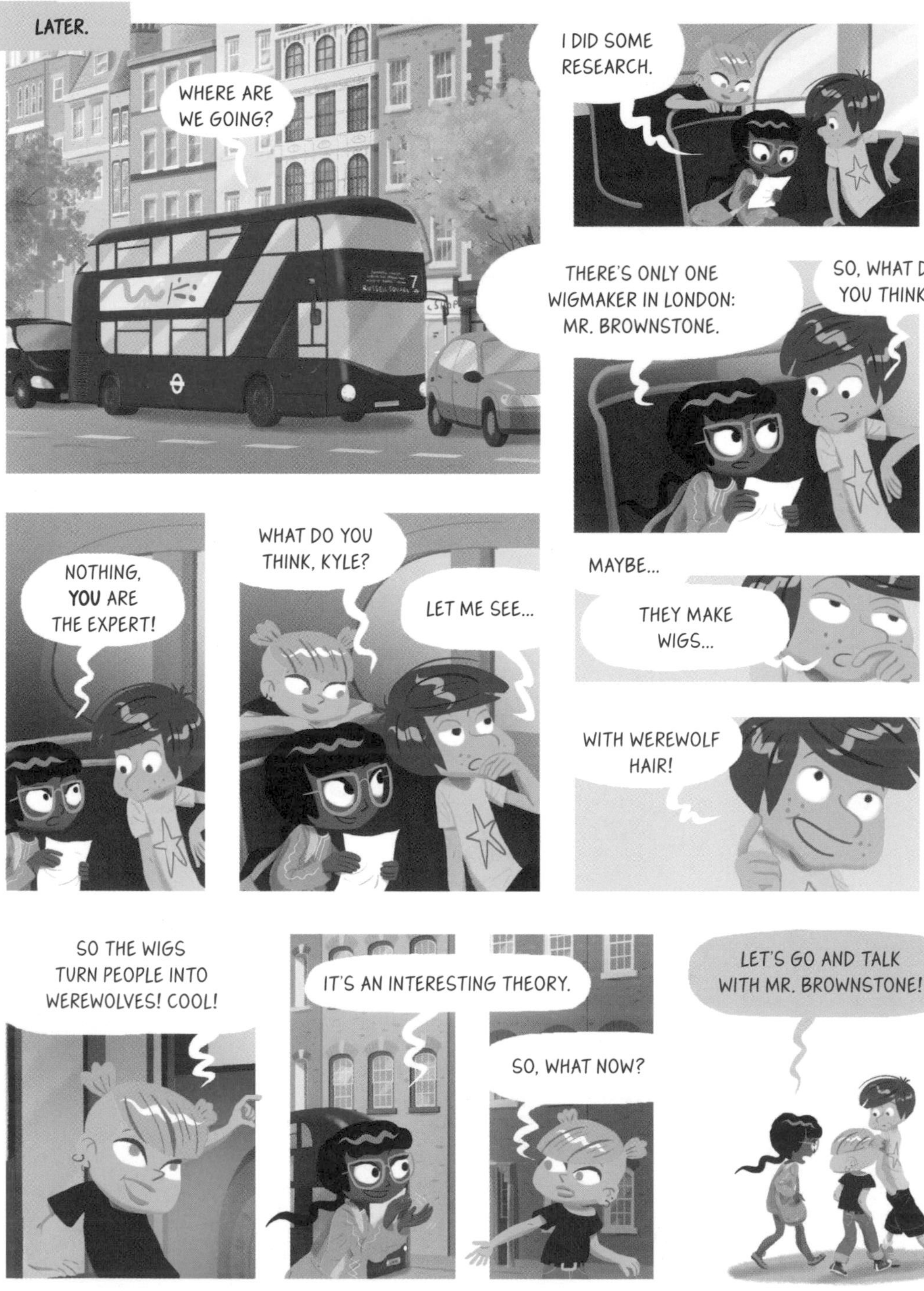
LATER.
WHERE ARE WE GOING?
I DID SOME RESEARCH.
THERE'S ONLY ONE WIGMAKER IN LONDON: MR. BROWNSTONE.
SO, WHAT DO YOU THINK?
NOTHING, YOU ARE THE EXPERT!
WHAT DO YOU THINK, KYLE?
LET ME SEE...
MAYBE...
THEY MAKE WIGS...
WITH WEREWOLF HAIR!
SO THE WIGS TURN PEOPLE INTO WEREWOLVES! COOL!
IT'S AN INTERESTING THEORY.
SO, WHAT NOW?
LET'S GO AND TALK WITH MR. BROWNSTONE!

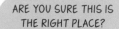

ARE YOU SURE THIS IS THE RIGHT PLACE?

LATER THAT AFTERNOON.

IT MUST BE.

HERE IT IS.

A. BROWNSTONE
WIGMAKER
SINCE 1983

WHAT DID YOU SAY WHEN YOU MADE THE APPOINTMENT?

I SAID WE'RE WRITING AN ARTICLE FOR A SCHOOL PROJECT...

BZZZZZ

WHAT DID YOU DO, KYLE?

NOTHING!

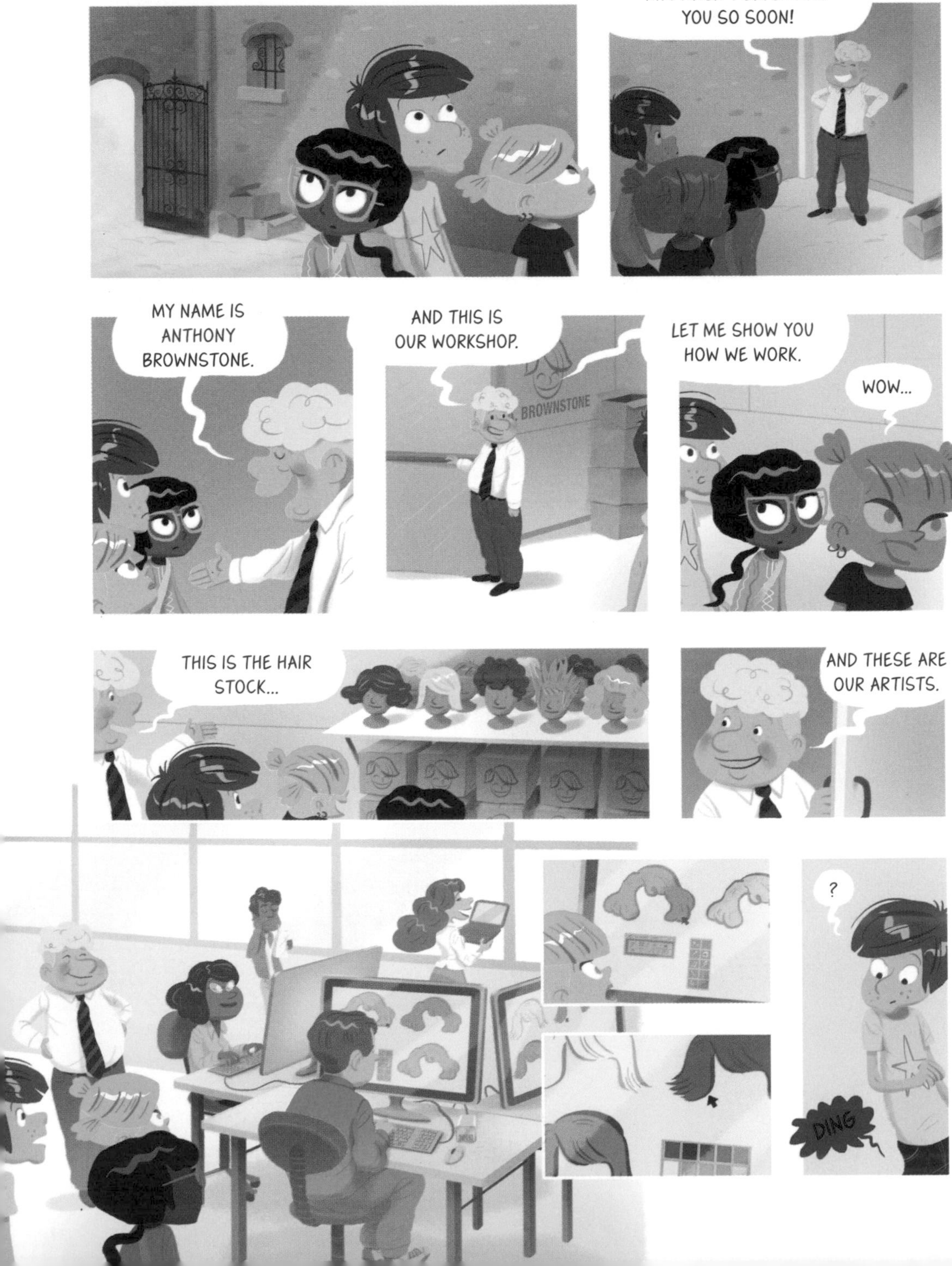
HI! I WASN'T EXPECTING YOU SO SOON!
MY NAME IS ANTHONY BROWNSTONE.
AND THIS IS OUR WORKSHOP.
BROWNSTONE
LET ME SHOW YOU HOW WE WORK.
WOW...
THIS IS THE HAIR STOCK...
AND THESE ARE OUR ARTISTS.
?
DING

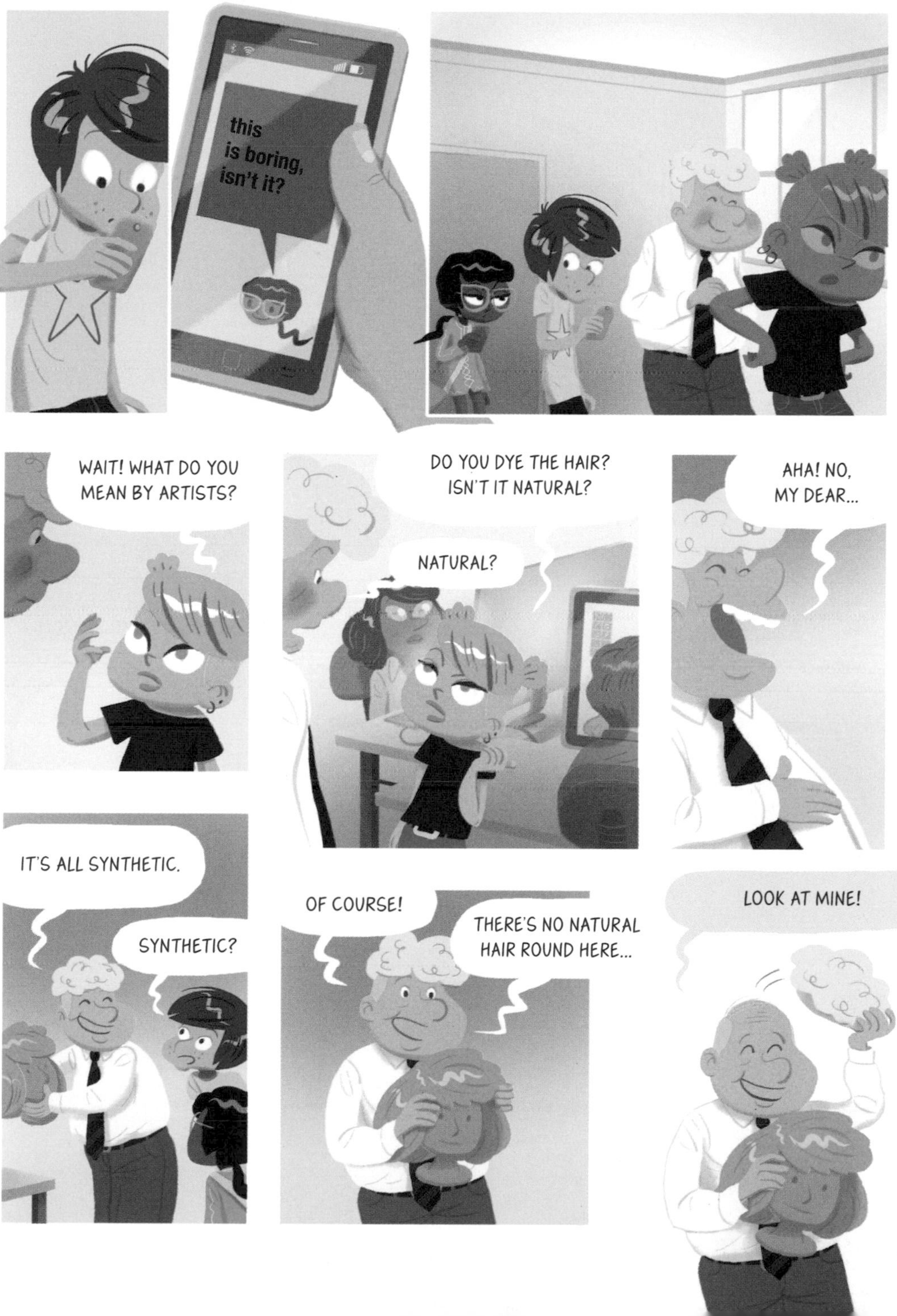
this is boring, isn't it?
WAIT! WHAT DO YOU MEAN BY ARTISTS?
DO YOU DYE THE HAIR? ISN'T IT NATURAL?
NATURAL?
AHA! NO, MY DEAR...
IT'S ALL SYNTHETIC.
SYNTHETIC?
OF COURSE!
THERE'S NO NATURAL HAIR ROUND HERE...
LOOK AT MINE!

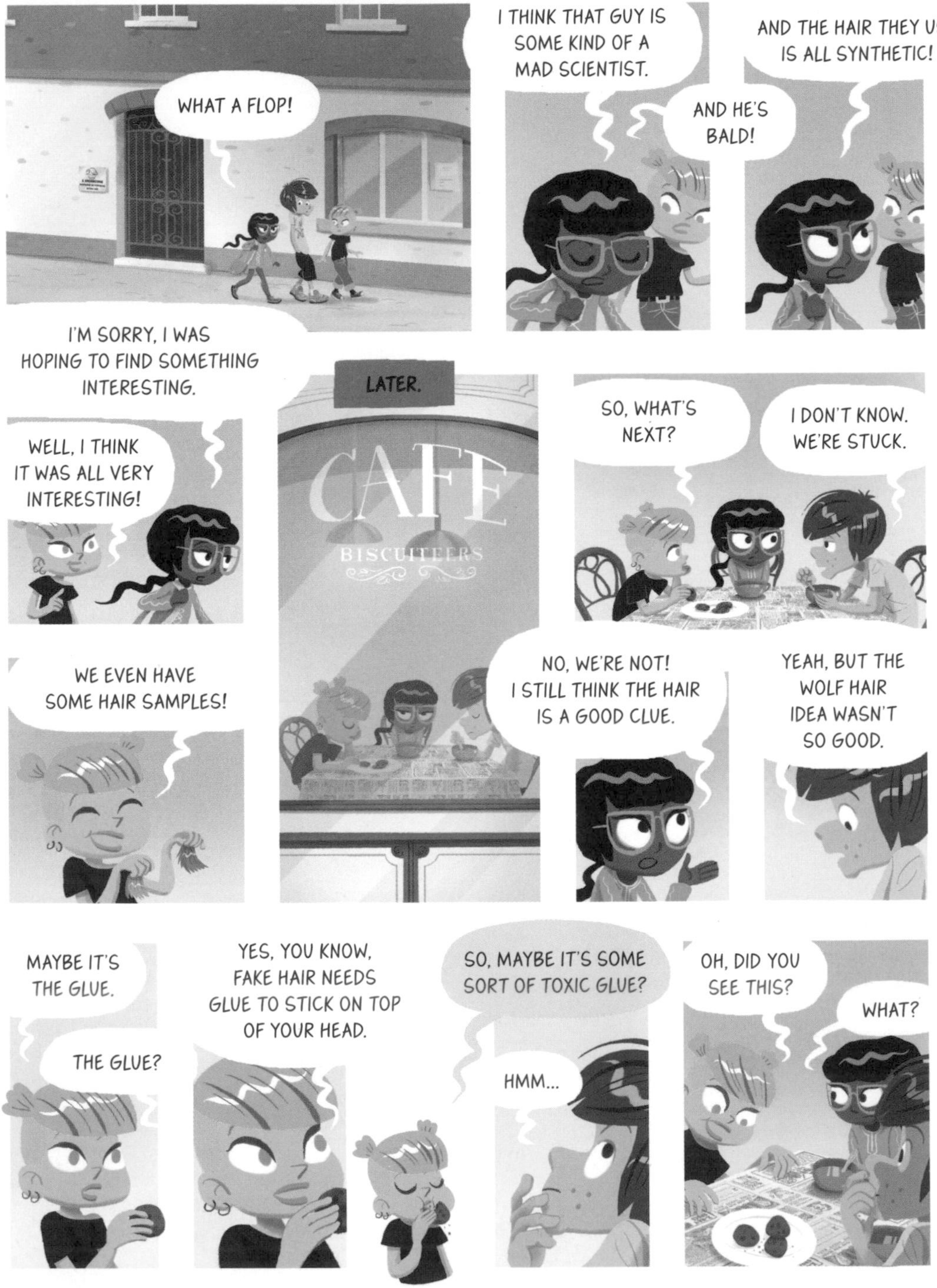

WHAT A FLOP!
I THINK THAT GUY IS SOME KIND OF A MAD SCIENTIST.
AND HE'S BALD!
AND THE HAIR THEY USE IS ALL SYNTHETIC!
I'M SORRY, I WAS HOPING TO FIND SOMETHING INTERESTING.
WELL, I THINK IT WAS ALL VERY INTERESTING!
WE EVEN HAVE SOME HAIR SAMPLES!
LATER.
CAFE
BISCUITEERS
SO, WHAT'S NEXT?
I DON'T KNOW. WE'RE STUCK.
NO, WE'RE NOT! I STILL THINK THE HAIR IS A GOOD CLUE.
YEAH, BUT THE WOLF HAIR IDEA WASN'T SO GOOD.
MAYBE IT'S THE GLUE.
THE GLUE?
YES, YOU KNOW, FAKE HAIR NEEDS GLUE TO STICK ON TOP OF YOUR HEAD.
SO, MAYBE IT'S SOME SORT OF TOXIC GLUE?
HMM...
OH, DID YOU SEE THIS?
WHAT?

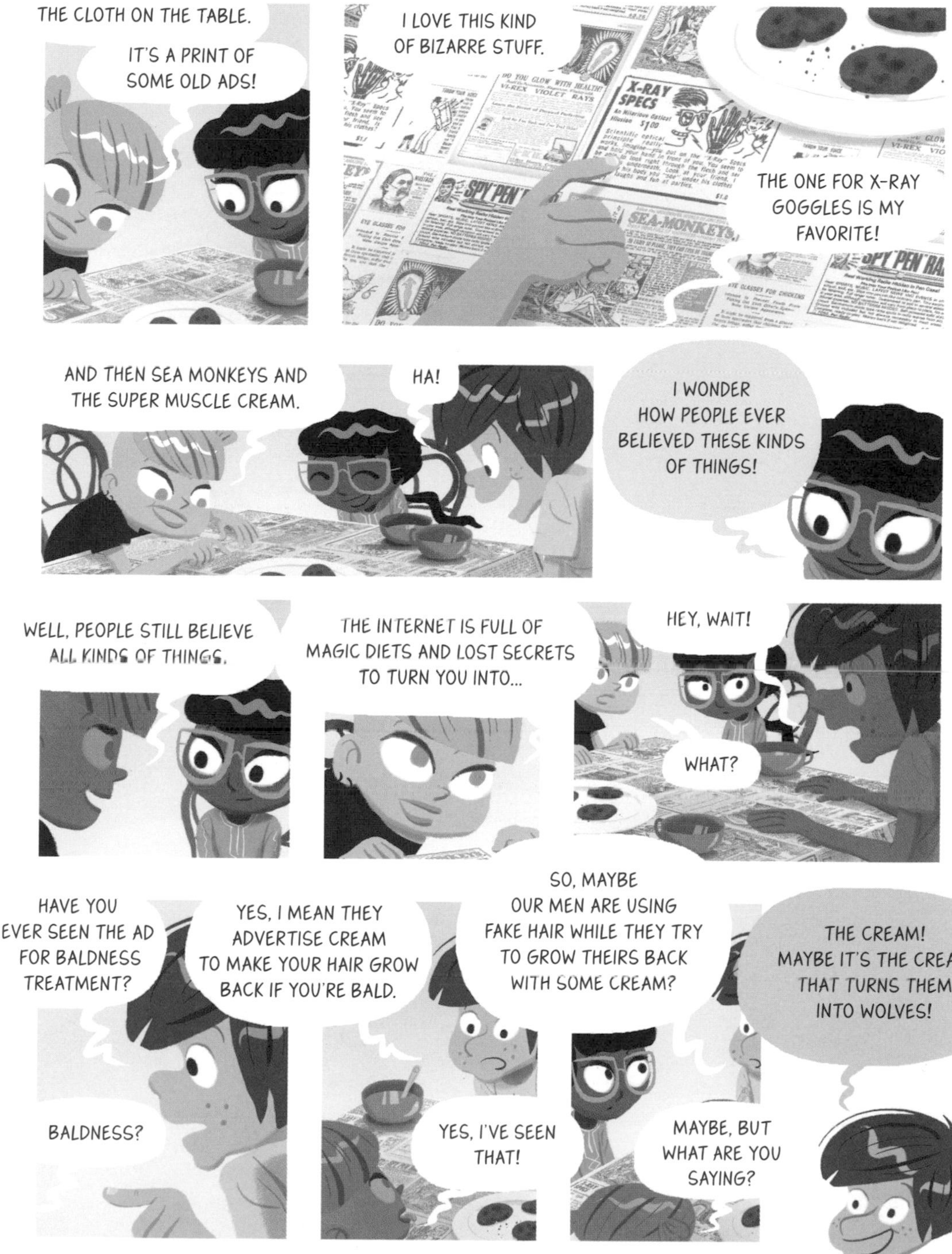
THE CLOTH ON THE TABLE.
IT'S A PRINT OF SOME OLD ADS!
I LOVE THIS KIND OF BIZARRE STUFF.
X-RAY SPECS
SPY PEN
SEA-MONKEYS
THE ONE FOR X-RAY GOGGLES IS MY FAVORITE!
AND THEN SEA MONKEYS AND THE SUPER MUSCLE CREAM.
HA!
I WONDER HOW PEOPLE EVER BELIEVED THESE KINDS OF THINGS!
WELL, PEOPLE STILL BELIEVE ALL KINDS OF THINGS.
THE INTERNET IS FULL OF MAGIC DIETS AND LOST SECRETS TO TURN YOU INTO...
HEY, WAIT!
WHAT?
HAVE YOU EVER SEEN THE AD FOR BALDNESS TREATMENT?
BALDNESS?
YES, I MEAN THEY ADVERTISE CREAM TO MAKE YOUR HAIR GROW BACK IF YOU'RE BALD.
YES, I'VE SEEN THAT!
SO, MAYBE OUR MEN ARE USING FAKE HAIR WHILE THEY TRY TO GROW THEIRS BACK WITH SOME CREAM?
MAYBE, BUT WHAT ARE YOU SAYING?
THE CREAM! MAYBE IT'S THE CREAM THAT TURNS THEM INTO WOLVES!

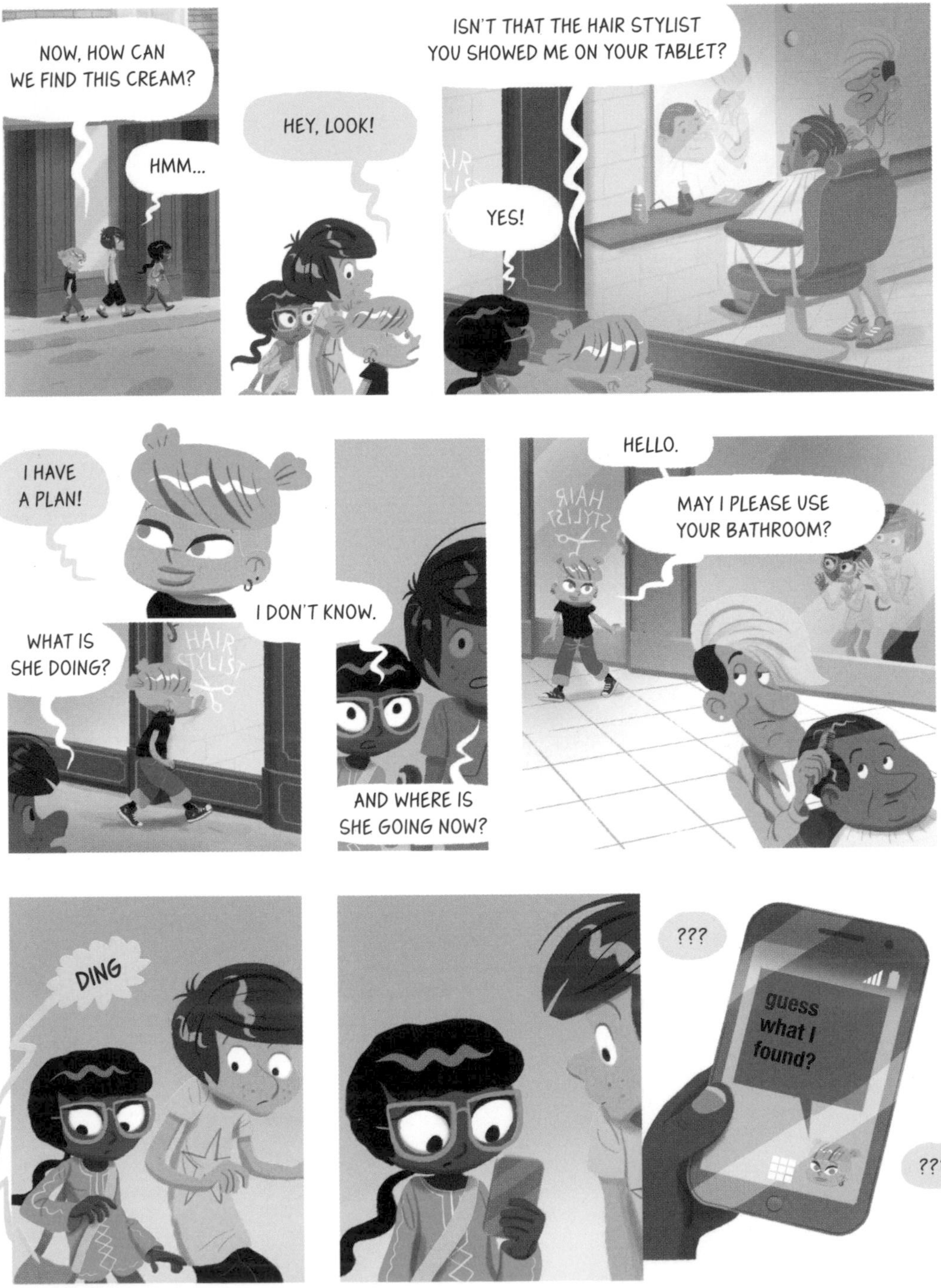
NOW, HOW CAN WE FIND THIS CREAM?
HMM...
HEY, LOOK!
ISN'T THAT THE HAIR STYLIST YOU SHOWED ME ON YOUR TABLET?
YES!
I HAVE A PLAN!
WHAT IS SHE DOING?
HAIR STYLIST
I DON'T KNOW.
AND WHERE IS SHE GOING NOW?
HELLO.
MAY I PLEASE USE YOUR BATHROOM?
DING
???
guess what I found?
???

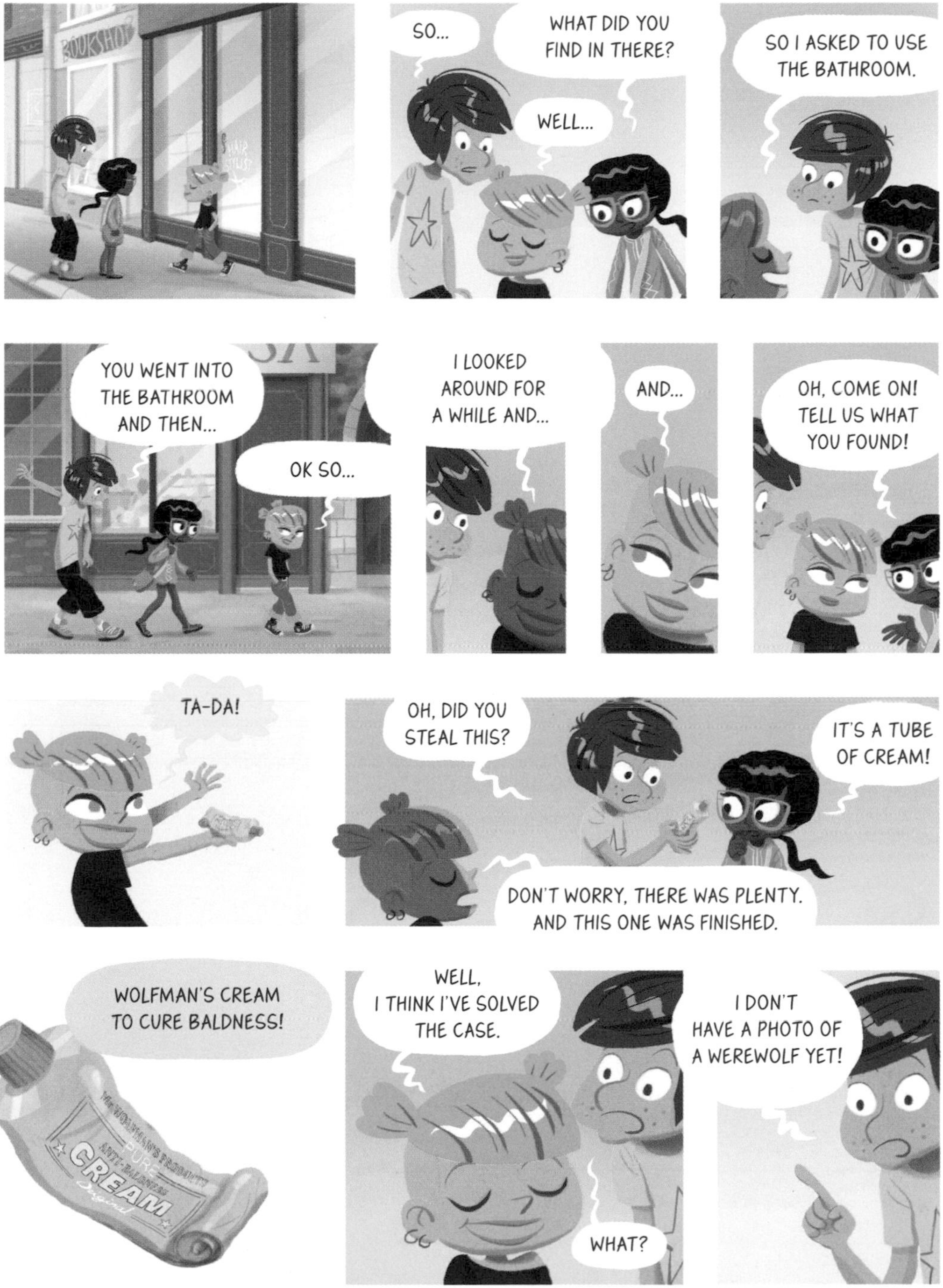
SO...
WHAT DID YOU FIND IN THERE?
WELL...
SO I ASKED TO USE THE BATHROOM.
YOU WENT INTO THE BATHROOM AND THEN...
OK SO...
I LOOKED AROUND FOR A WHILE AND...
AND...
OH, COME ON! TELL US WHAT YOU FOUND!
TA-DA!
OH, DID YOU STEAL THIS?
IT'S A TUBE OF CREAM!
DON'T WORRY, THERE WAS PLENTY. AND THIS ONE WAS FINISHED.
WOLFMAN'S CREAM TO CURE BALDNESS!
CREAM
WELL, I THINK I'VE SOLVED THE CASE.
WHAT?
I DON'T HAVE A PHOTO OF A WEREWOLF YET!

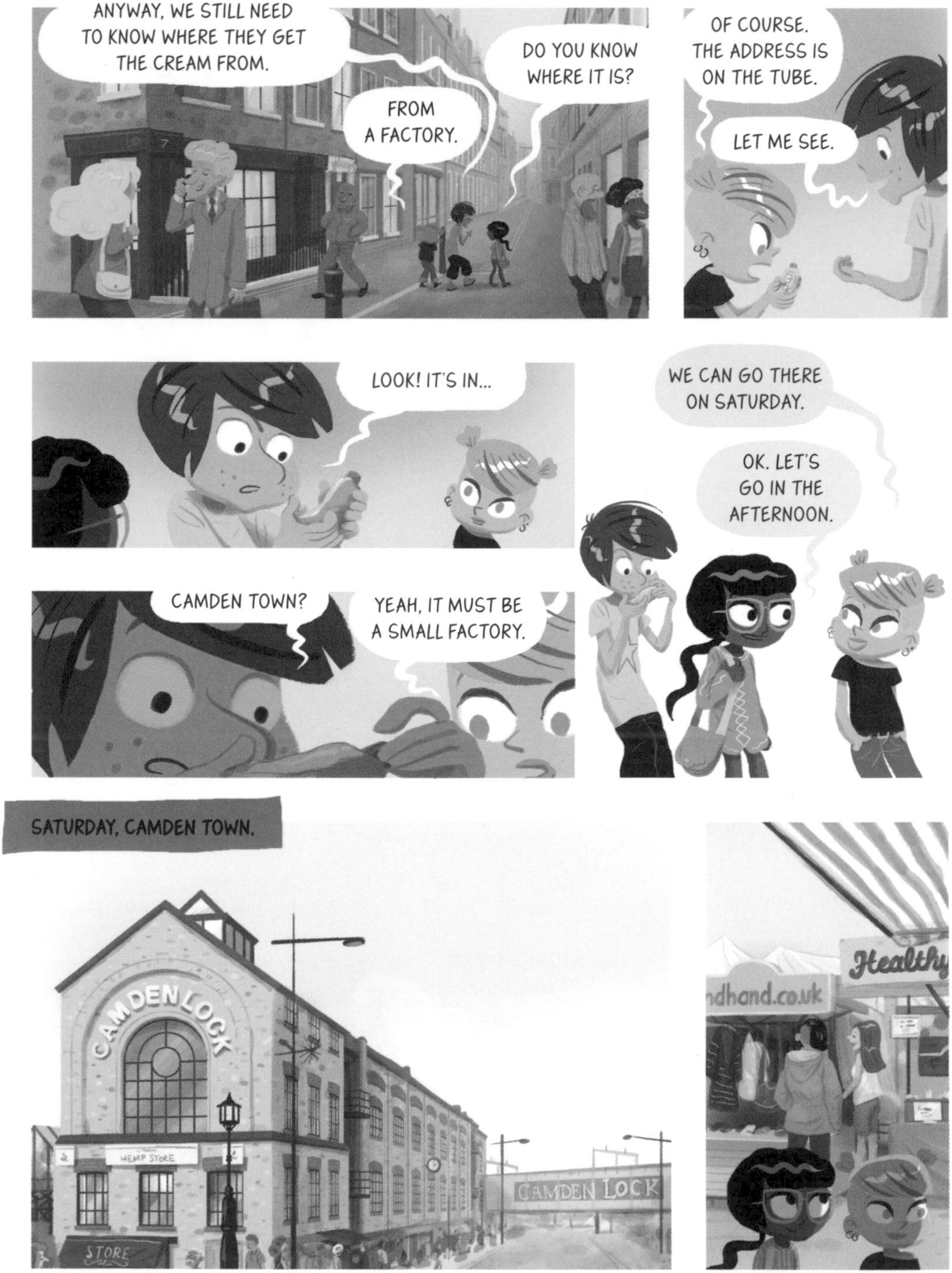
ANYWAY, WE STILL NEED TO KNOW WHERE THEY GET THE CREAM FROM.
FROM A FACTORY.
DO YOU KNOW WHERE IT IS?
OF COURSE. THE ADDRESS IS ON THE TUBE.
LET ME SEE.
LOOK! IT'S IN...
CAMDEN TOWN?
YEAH, IT MUST BE A SMALL FACTORY.
WE CAN GO THERE ON SATURDAY.
OK. LET'S GO IN THE AFTERNOON.
SATURDAY, CAMDEN TOWN.
CAMDEN LOCK
HEMP STORE
STORE
CAMDEN LOCK

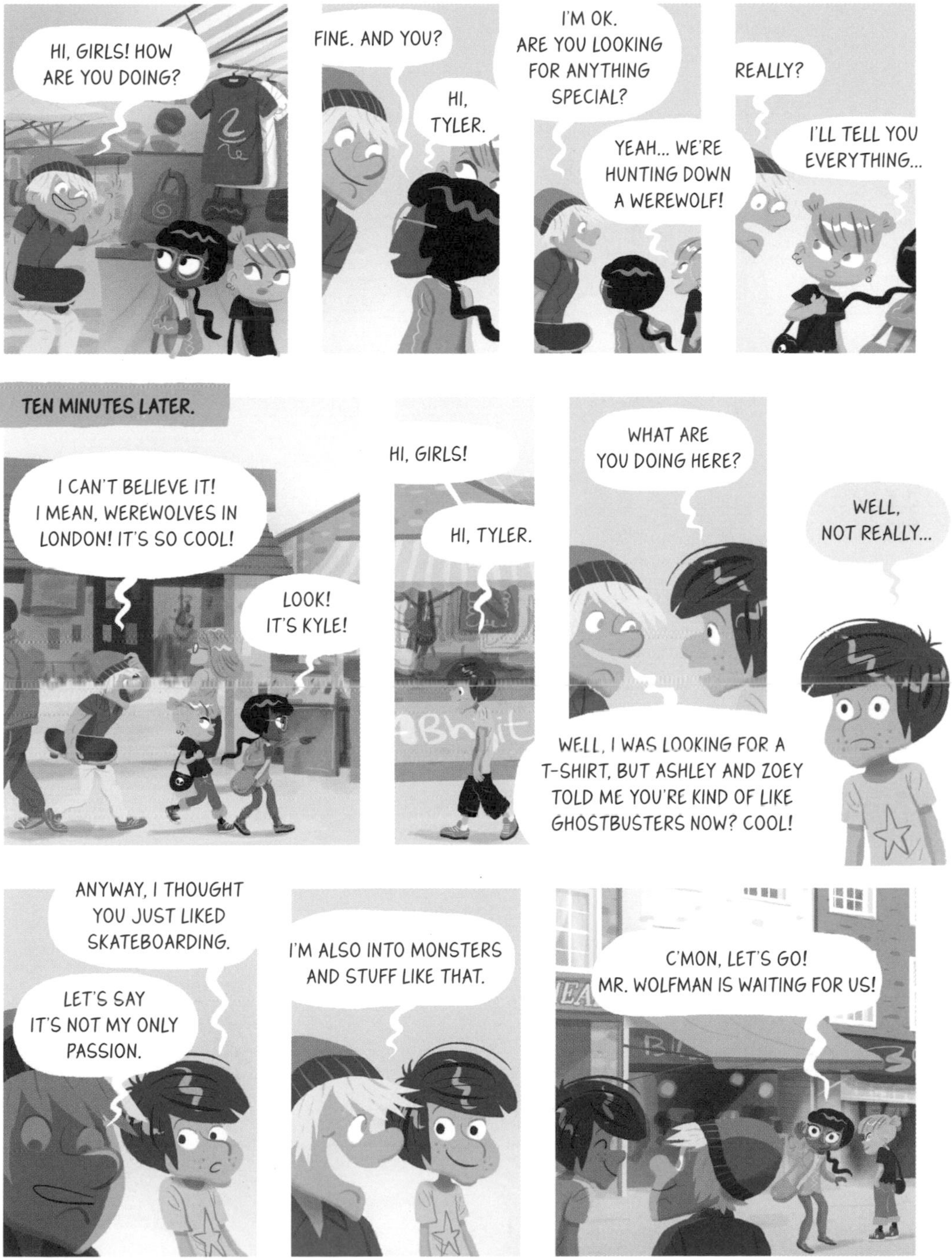
HI, GIRLS! HOW ARE YOU DOING?
FINE. AND YOU?
HI, TYLER.
I'M OK. ARE YOU LOOKING FOR ANYTHING SPECIAL?
YEAH... WE'RE HUNTING DOWN A WEREWOLF!
REALLY?
I'LL TELL YOU EVERYTHING...
TEN MINUTES LATER.
I CAN'T BELIEVE IT! I MEAN, WEREWOLVES IN LONDON! IT'S SO COOL!
LOOK! IT'S KYLE!
HI, GIRLS!
HI, TYLER.
WHAT ARE YOU DOING HERE?
WELL, NOT REALLY...
WELL, I WAS LOOKING FOR A T-SHIRT, BUT ASHLEY AND ZOEY TOLD ME YOU'RE KIND OF LIKE GHOSTBUSTERS NOW? COOL!
ANYWAY, I THOUGHT YOU JUST LIKED SKATEBOARDING.
LET'S SAY IT'S NOT MY ONLY PASSION.
I'M ALSO INTO MONSTERS AND STUFF LIKE THAT.
C'MON, LET'S GO! MR. WOLFMAN IS WAITING FOR US!

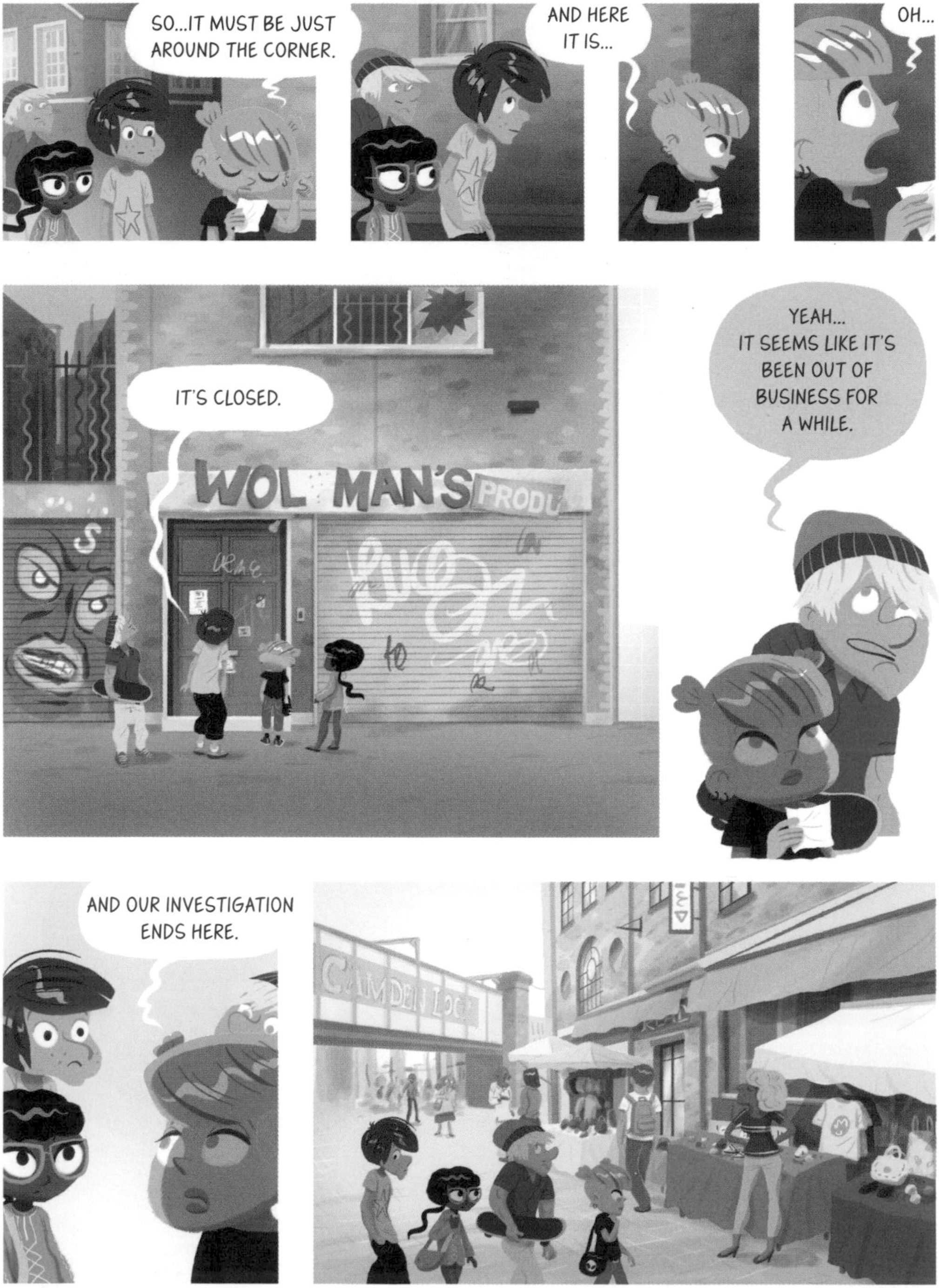
SO...IT MUST BE JUST AROUND THE CORNER.
AND HERE IT IS...
OH...
IT'S CLOSED.
WOL MAN'S PRODU
YEAH... IT SEEMS LIKE IT'S BEEN OUT OF BUSINESS FOR A WHILE.
AND OUR INVESTIGATION ENDS HERE.
CAMDEN LOCK

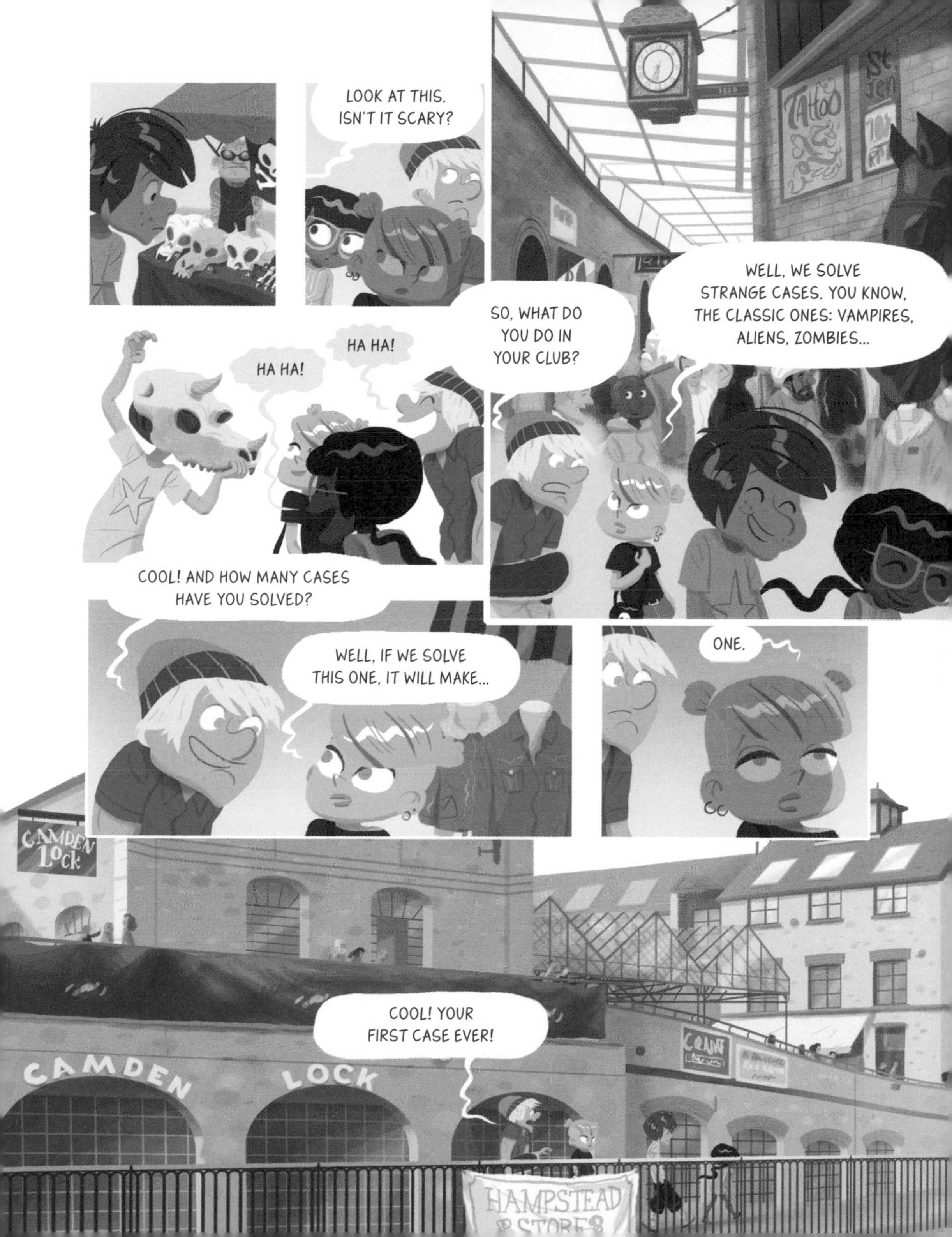
LOOK AT THIS.
ISN'T IT SCARY?
HA HA!
HA HA!
SO, WHAT DO
YOU DO IN
YOUR CLUB?
WELL, WE SOLVE
STRANGE CASES. YOU KNOW,
THE CLASSIC ONES: VAMPIRES,
ALIENS, ZOMBIES...
TATTOO
COOL! AND HOW MANY CASES
HAVE YOU SOLVED?
WELL, IF WE SOLVE
THIS ONE, IT WILL MAKE...
ONE.
CAMDEN LOCK
COOL! YOUR
FIRST CASE EVER!
CAMDEN
LOCK
HAMPSTEAD

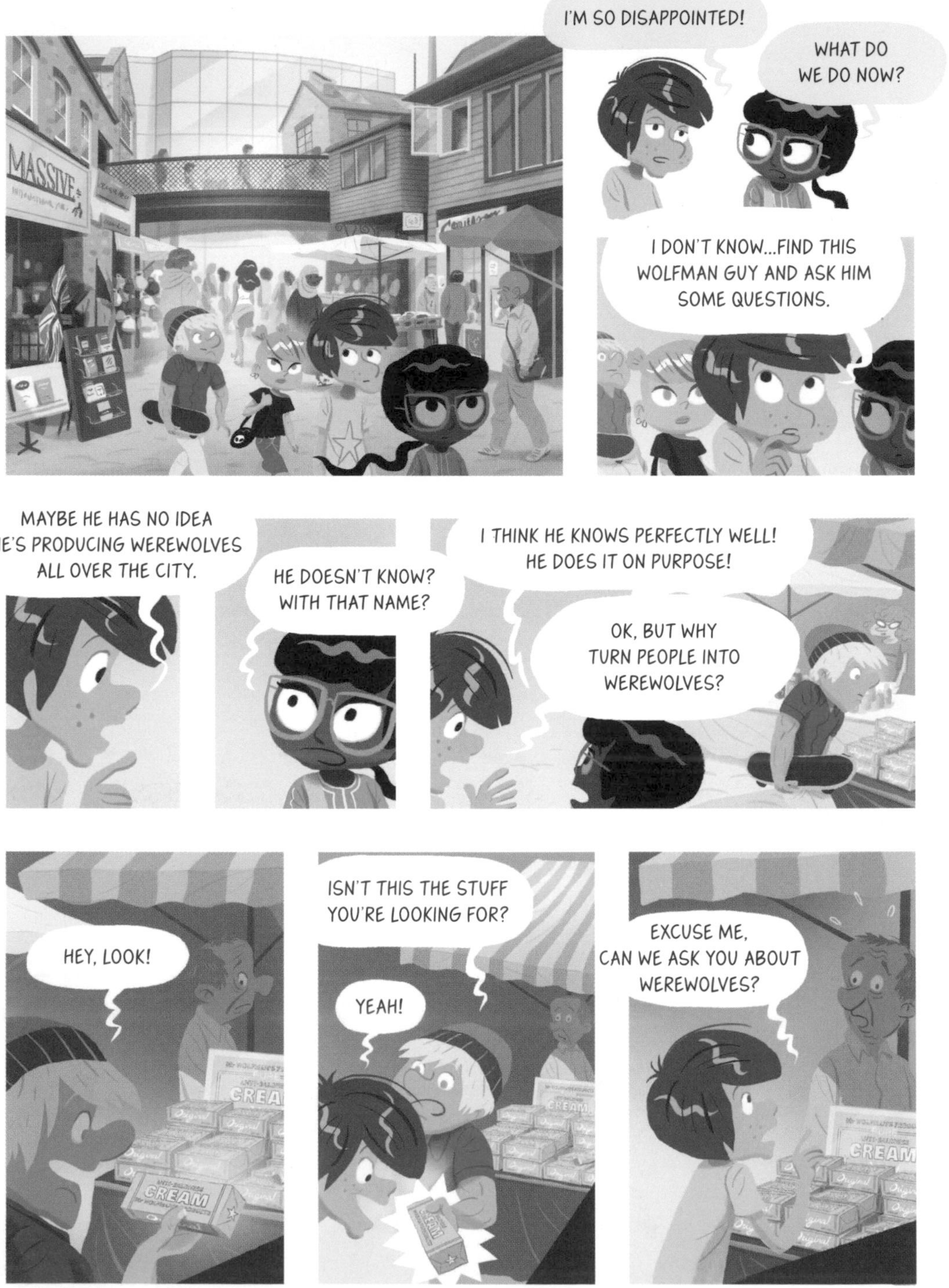
I'M SO DISAPPOINTED!
WHAT DO WE DO NOW?
I DON'T KNOW...FIND THIS WOLFMAN GUY AND ASK HIM SOME QUESTIONS.
MAYBE HE HAS NO IDEA HE'S PRODUCING WEREWOLVES ALL OVER THE CITY.
HE DOESN'T KNOW? WITH THAT NAME?
I THINK HE KNOWS PERFECTLY WELL! HE DOES IT ON PURPOSE!
OK, BUT WHY TURN PEOPLE INTO WEREWOLVES?
HEY, LOOK!
ISN'T THIS THE STUFF YOU'RE LOOKING FOR?
YEAH!
EXCUSE ME, CAN WE ASK YOU ABOUT WEREWOLVES?
MASSIVE
CREAM

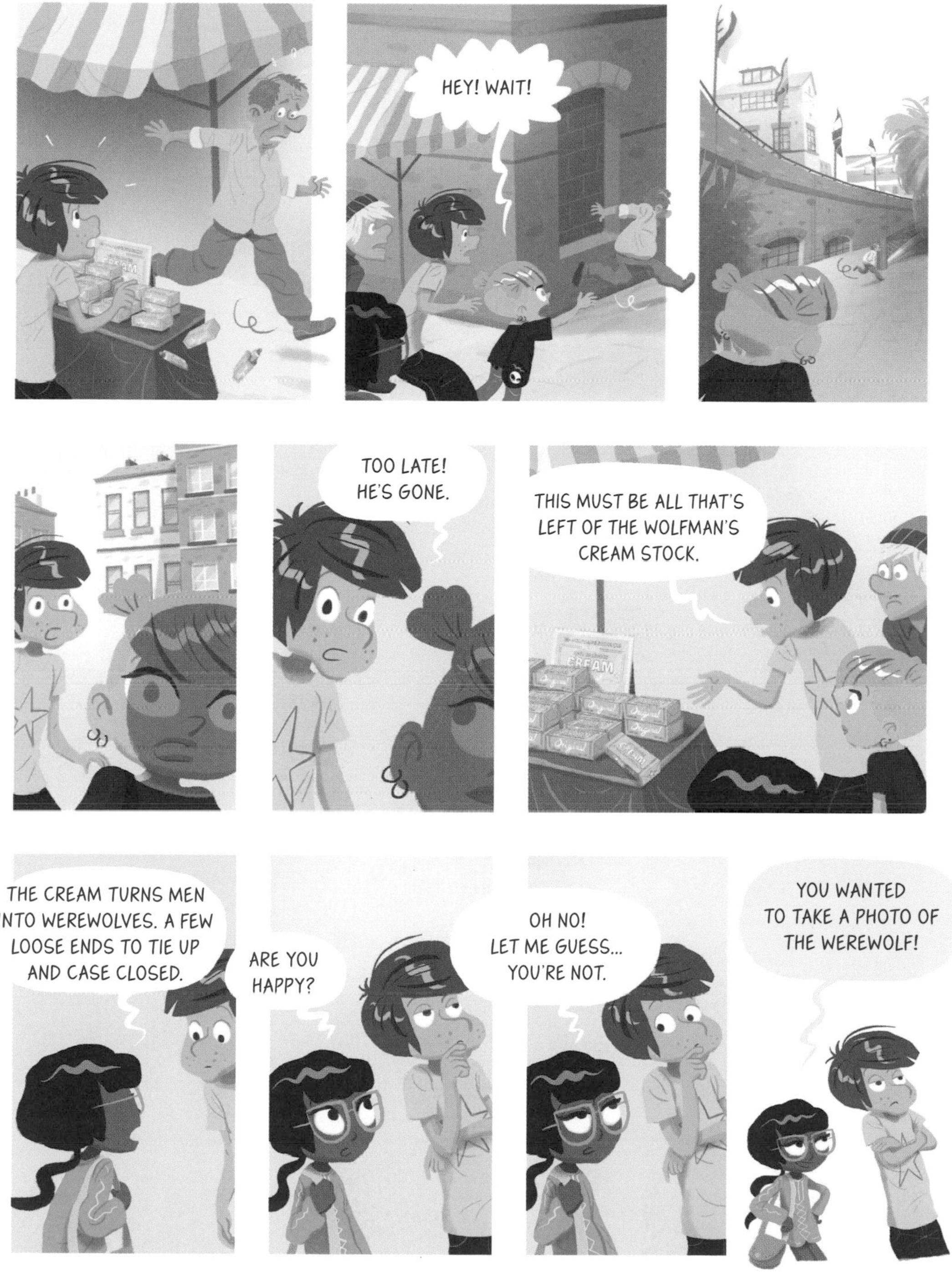
HEY! WAIT!
TOO LATE! HE'S GONE.
THIS MUST BE ALL THAT'S LEFT OF THE WOLFMAN'S CREAM STOCK.
THE CREAM TURNS MEN INTO WEREWOLVES. A FEW LOOSE ENDS TO TIE UP AND CASE CLOSED.
ARE YOU HAPPY?
OH NO! LET ME GUESS... YOU'RE NOT.
YOU WANTED TO TAKE A PHOTO OF THE WEREWOLF!

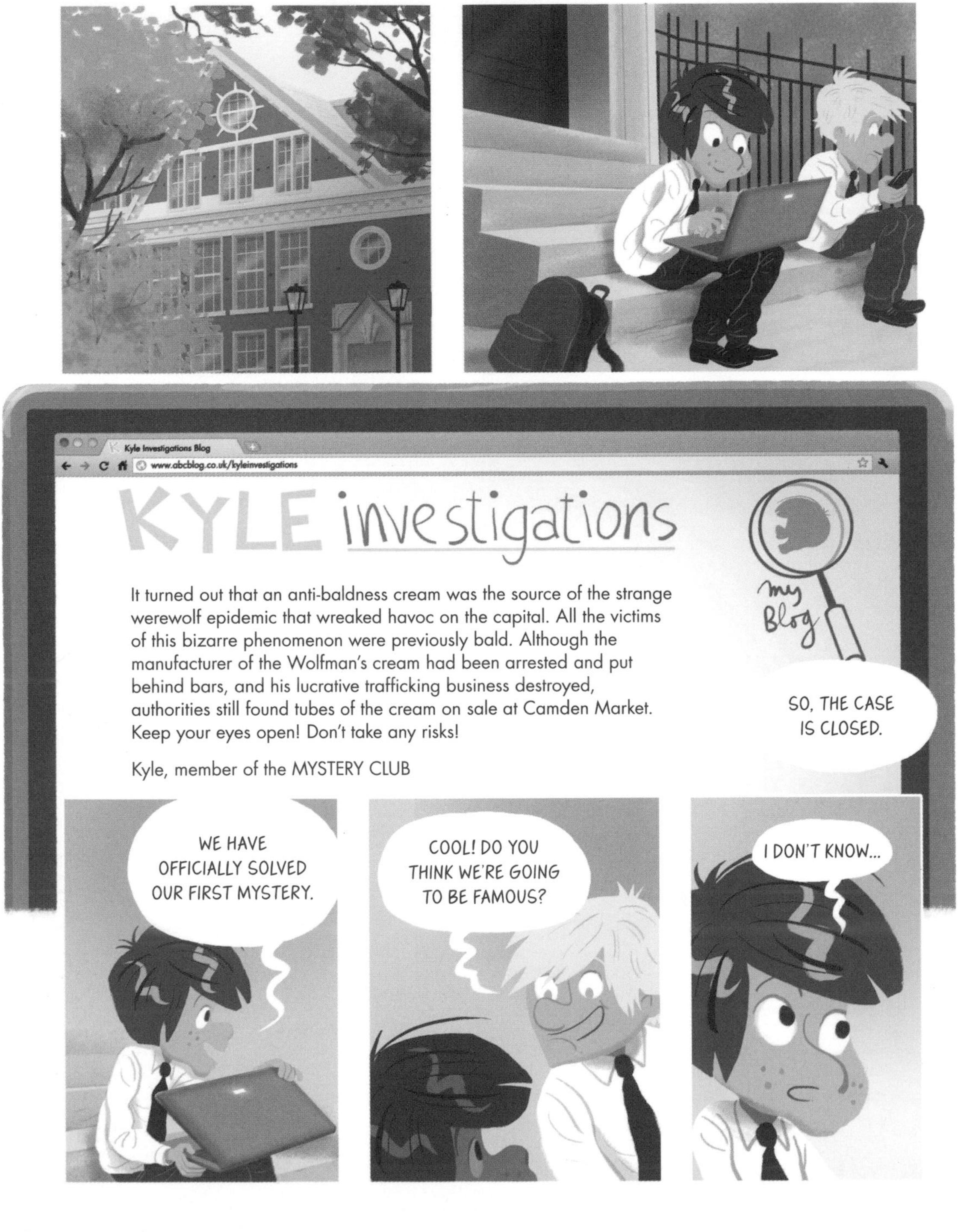
Kyle Investigations Blog
www.abcblog.co.uk/kyleinvestigations
KYLE investigations
It turned out that an anti-baldness cream was the source of the strange werewolf epidemic that wreaked havoc on the capital. All the victims of this bizarre phenomenon were previously bald. Although the manufacturer of the Wolfman's cream had been arrested and put behind bars, and his lucrative trafficking business destroyed, authorities still found tubes of the cream on sale at Camden Market. Keep your eyes open! Don't take any risks!
Kyle, member of the MYSTERY CLUB
my Blog
SO, THE CASE IS CLOSED.
WE HAVE OFFICIALLY SOLVED OUR FIRST MYSTERY.
COOL! DO YOU THINK WE'RE GOING TO BE FAMOUS?
I DON'T KNOW...

DING

OH, A MESSAGE!

WHAT'S GOING ON?

A NEWSPAPER AND A TV STATION WANT TO INTERVIEW US.

I TOLD YOU WE'D BE FAMOUS!

INDEX
.... 6
.... 11
.... 15
.... 16
.... 20
.... 21

since 2006

dia

TRIBUNE REVIEW
s.com

IOME
AMES!

Scoot to
page 35

formation

A GROUP OF KIDS
SOLVE THE WEREWOLF MYSTERY!

BY BETHANY HOFSTETTER
STAFF WRITER

YOUNG DETECTIVES CRACK
THE WEREWOLF ENIGMA!

...HAT UNHEALTHY

by GINNY SAND

GOT A MONSTER PROBLEM? CALL THE MYSTERY CLUB!

WE PUT THE MOT INTO M

MOT £25 INC. F RETE

£65

VEHICLE SERVICE & TEST
107 SOUTHLANDS Rd.
Off A21 next to Champions 460

The peppermint, camomile and Barrett, which has pathic medicine. The

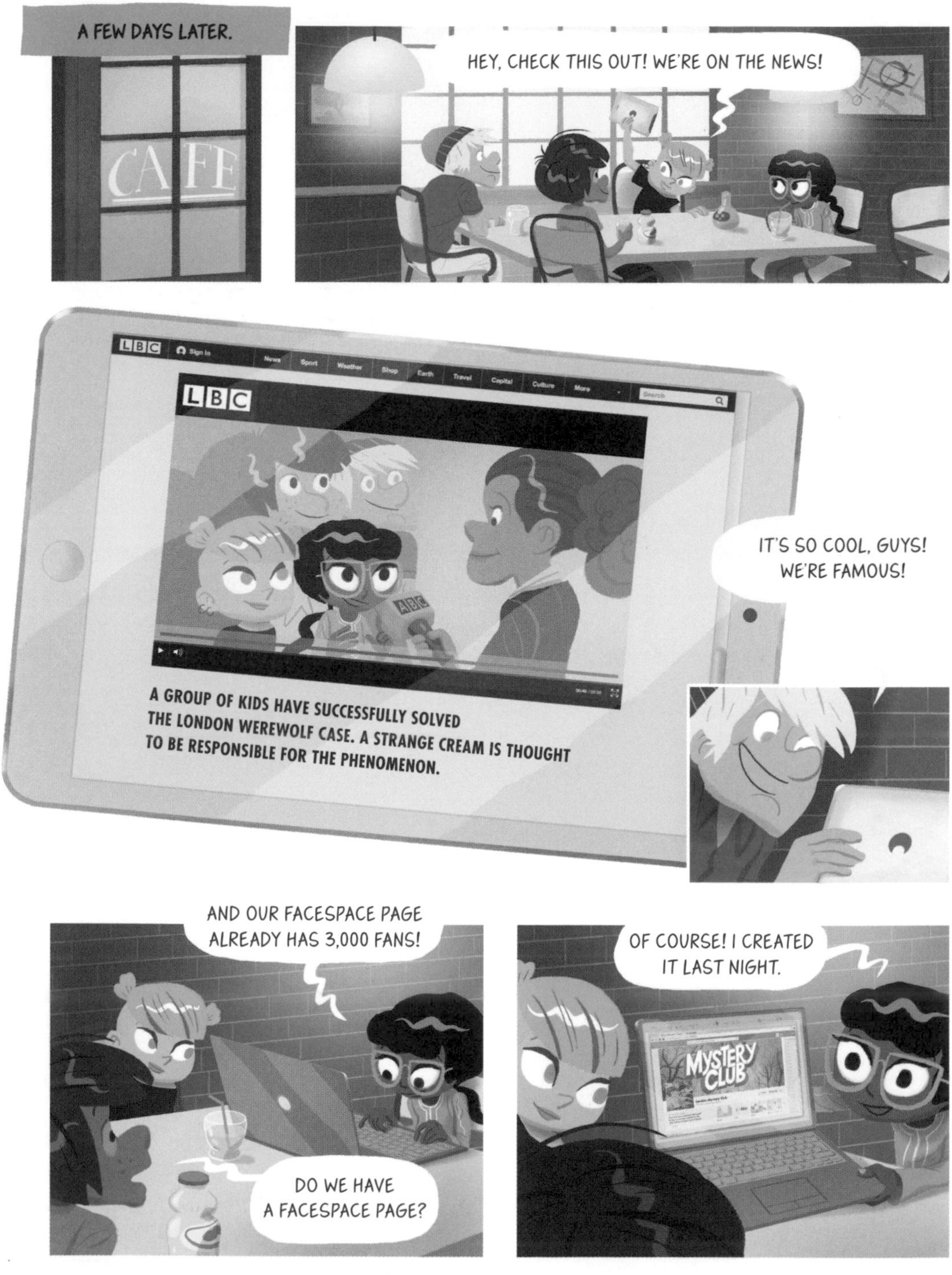
A FEW DAYS LATER.
CAFE
HEY, CHECK THIS OUT! WE'RE ON THE NEWS!
LBC
A GROUP OF KIDS HAVE SUCCESSFULLY SOLVED THE LONDON WEREWOLF CASE. A STRANGE CREAM IS THOUGHT TO BE RESPONSIBLE FOR THE PHENOMENON.
IT'S SO COOL, GUYS! WE'RE FAMOUS!
AND OUR FACESPACE PAGE ALREADY HAS 3,000 FANS!
DO WE HAVE A FACESPACE PAGE?
OF COURSE! I CREATED IT LAST NIGHT.
MYSTERY CLUB

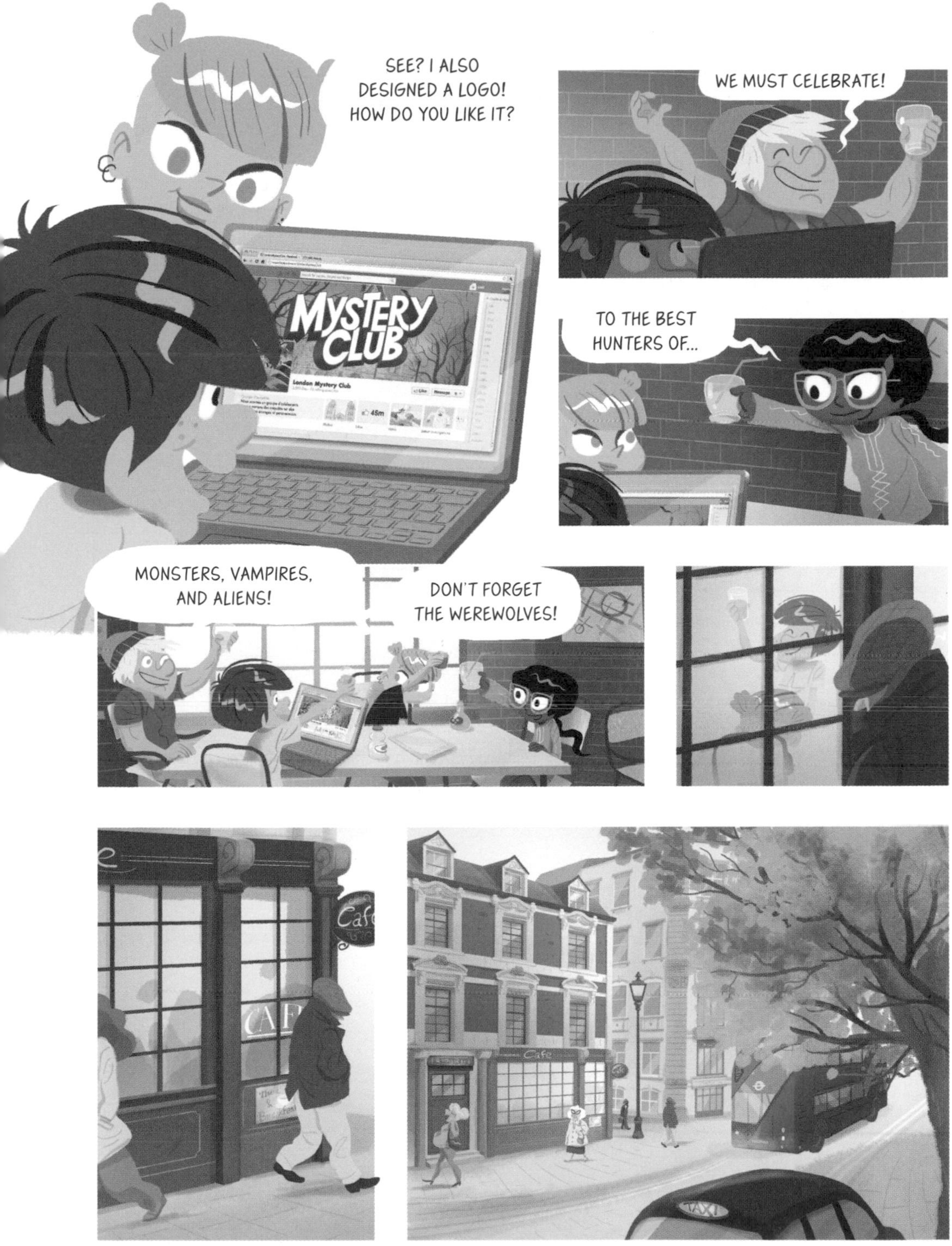

SEE? I ALSO DESIGNED A LOGO! HOW DO YOU LIKE IT?
MYSTERY CLUB
London Mystery Club
WE MUST CELEBRATE!
TO THE BEST HUNTERS OF...
MONSTERS, VAMPIRES, AND ALIENS!
DON'T FORGET THE WEREWOLVES!
Cafe
CAFE
Cafe
TAXI

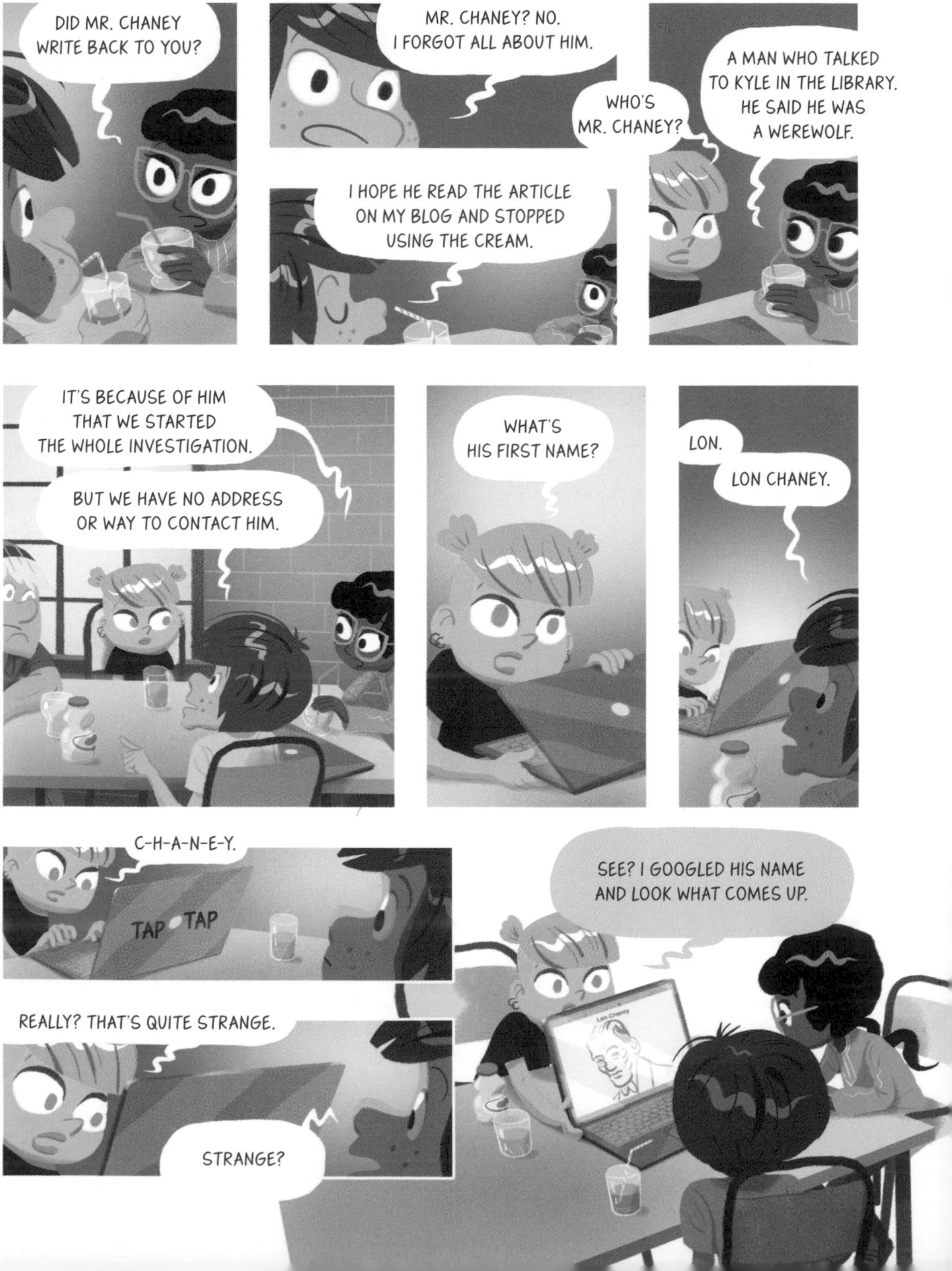
DID MR. CHANEY WRITE BACK TO YOU?
MR. CHANEY? NO. I FORGOT ALL ABOUT HIM.
I HOPE HE READ THE ARTICLE ON MY BLOG AND STOPPED USING THE CREAM.
WHO'S MR. CHANEY?
A MAN WHO TALKED TO KYLE IN THE LIBRARY. HE SAID HE WAS A WEREWOLF.
IT'S BECAUSE OF HIM THAT WE STARTED THE WHOLE INVESTIGATION.
BUT WE HAVE NO ADDRESS OR WAY TO CONTACT HIM.
WHAT'S HIS FIRST NAME?
LON.
LON CHANEY.
C-H-A-N-E-Y.
TAP TAP
REALLY? THAT'S QUITE STRANGE.
STRANGE?
SEE? I GOOGLED HIS NAME AND LOOK WHAT COMES UP.

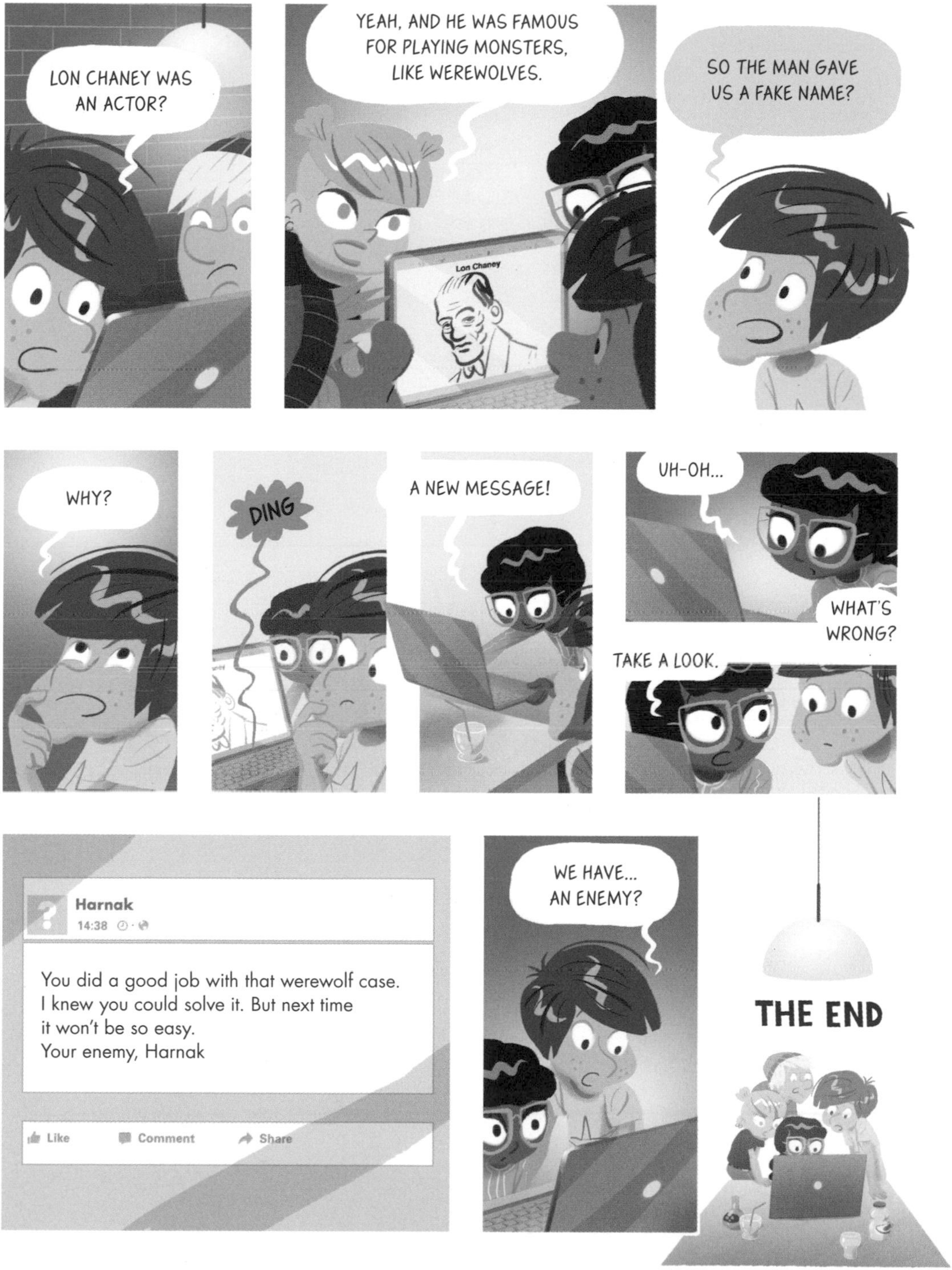
LON CHANEY WAS AN ACTOR?
YEAH, AND HE WAS FAMOUS FOR PLAYING MONSTERS, LIKE WEREWOLVES.
Lon Chaney
SO THE MAN GAVE US A FAKE NAME?
WHY?
DING
A NEW MESSAGE!
UH-OH...
WHAT'S WRONG?
TAKE A LOOK.
Harnak
14:38
You did a good job with that werewolf case.
I knew you could solve it. But next time
it won't be so easy.
Your enemy, Harnak
Like
Comment
Share
WE HAVE... AN ENEMY?
THE END

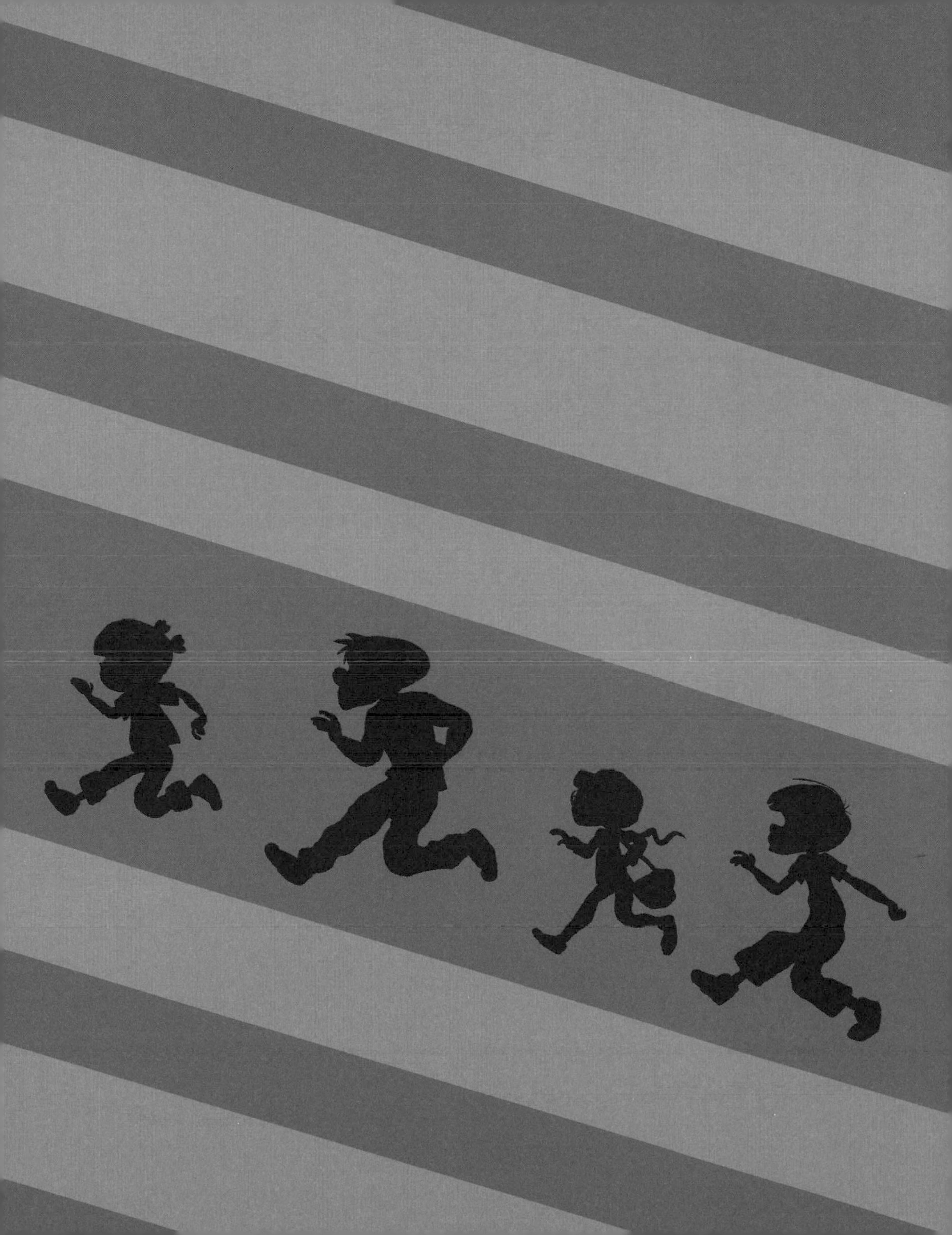

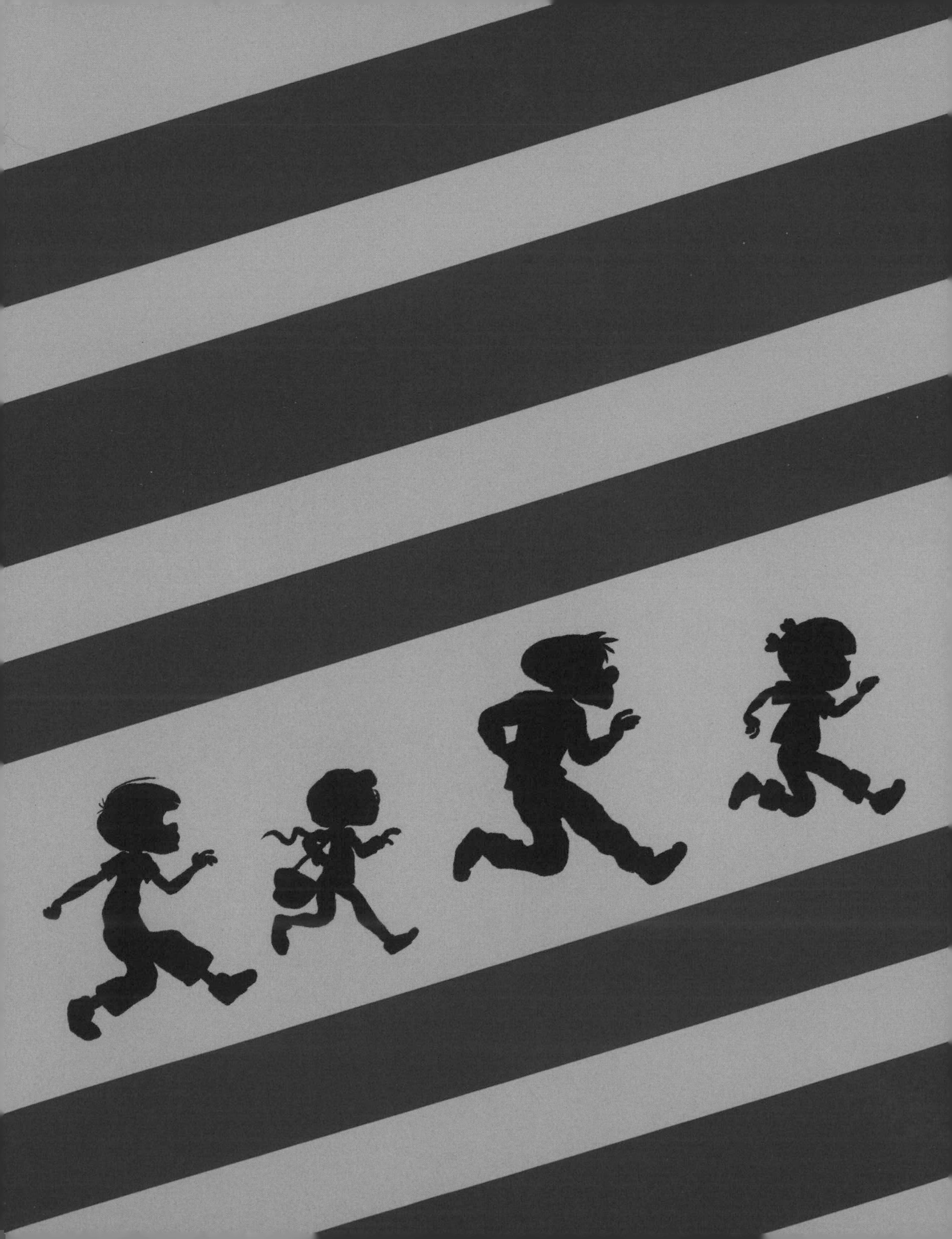

MUMMY MISCHIEF

by Davide Cali

Illustrated by AnnaLisa Ferrari

based on an original work by Yannick Robert

Houghton Mifflin Harcourt

Boston   New York

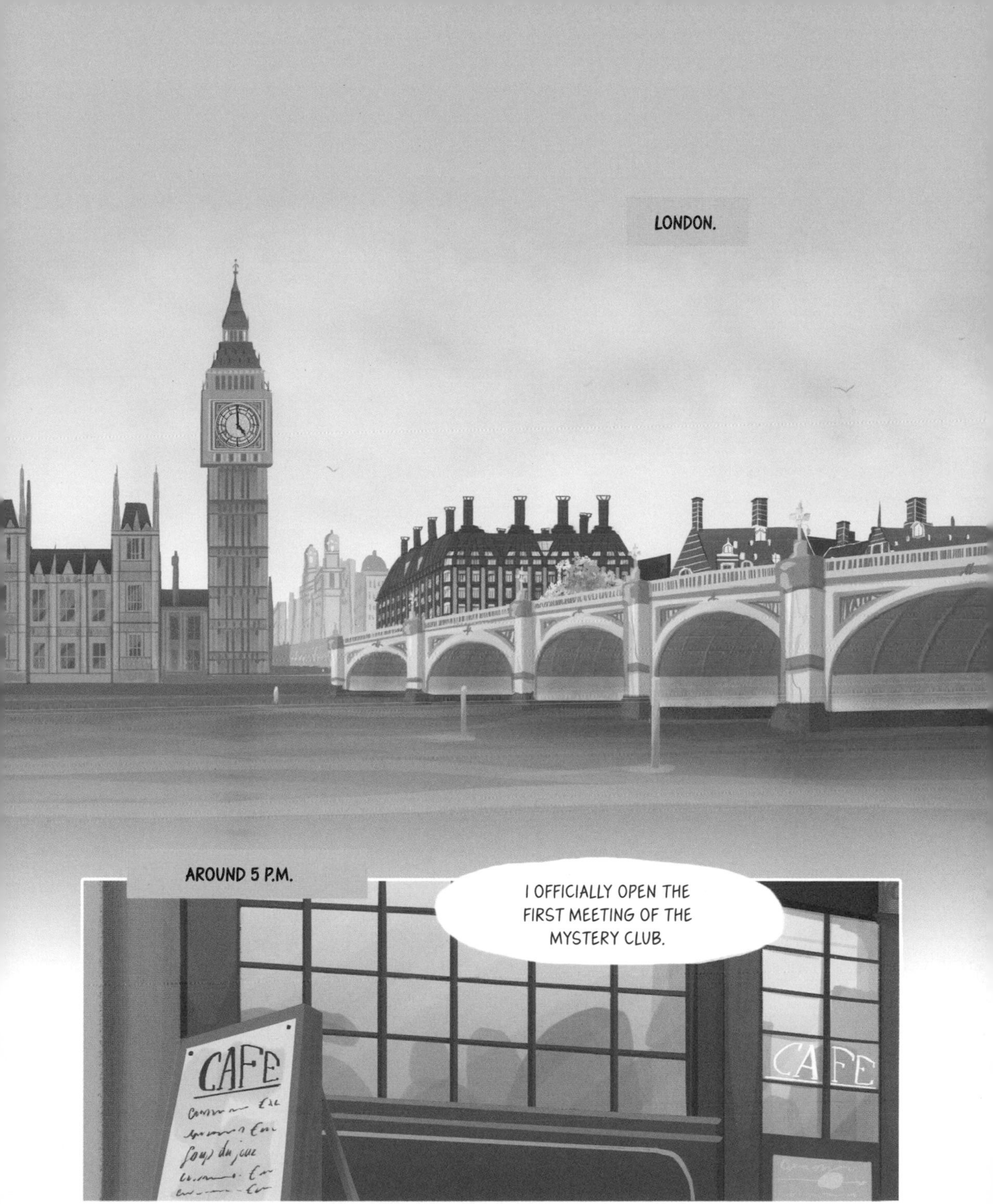
LONDON.
AROUND 5 P.M.
I OFFICIALLY OPEN THE FIRST MEETING OF THE MYSTERY CLUB.
CAFE
CAFE

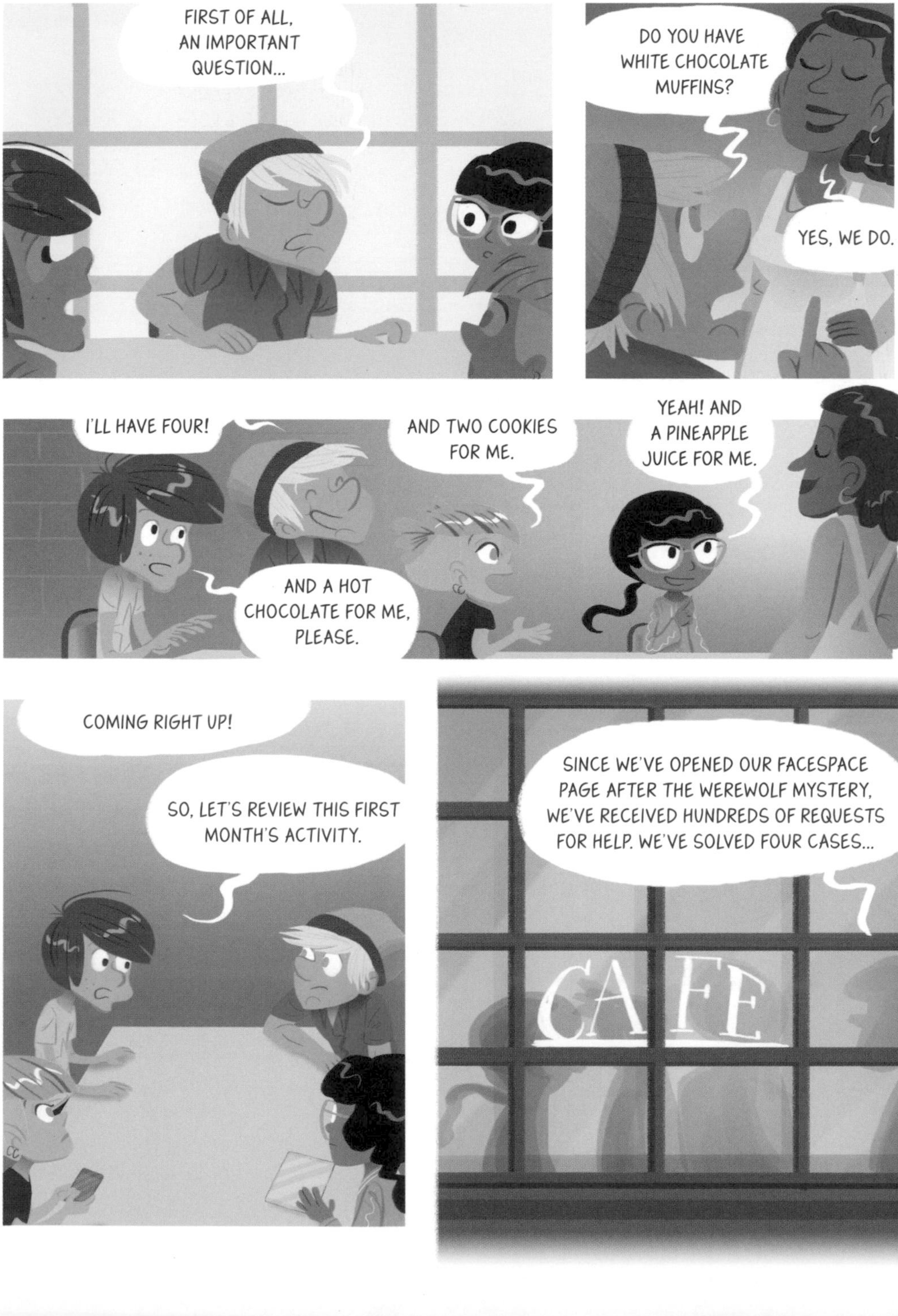
FIRST OF ALL, AN IMPORTANT QUESTION...
DO YOU HAVE WHITE CHOCOLATE MUFFINS?
YES, WE DO.
I'LL HAVE FOUR!
AND TWO COOKIES FOR ME.
YEAH! AND A PINEAPPLE JUICE FOR ME.
AND A HOT CHOCOLATE FOR ME, PLEASE.
COMING RIGHT UP!
SO, LET'S REVIEW THIS FIRST MONTH'S ACTIVITY.
SINCE WE'VE OPENED OUR FACESPACE PAGE AFTER THE WEREWOLF MYSTERY, WE'VE RECEIVED HUNDREDS OF REQUESTS FOR HELP. WE'VE SOLVED FOUR CASES...
CAFE

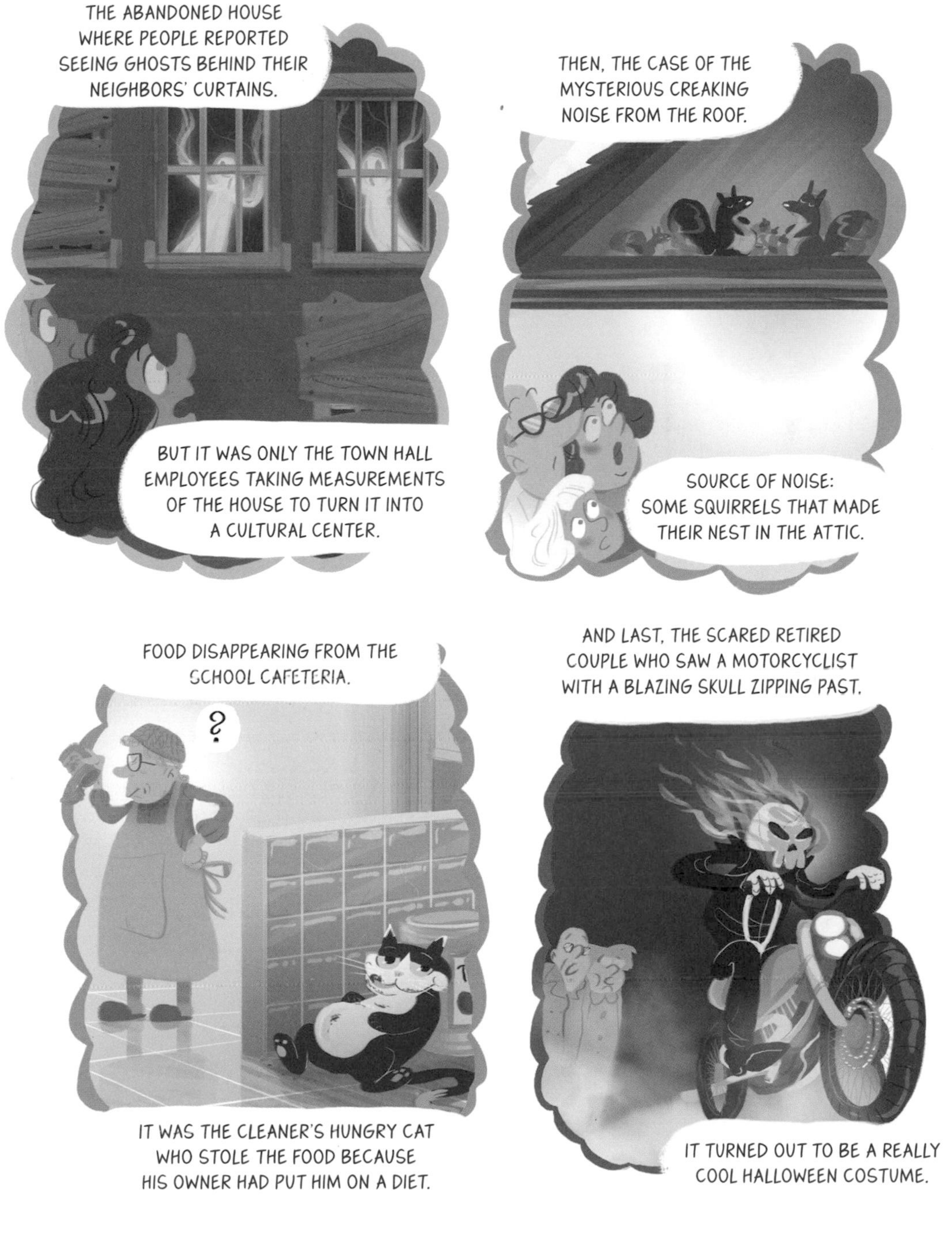
THE ABANDONED HOUSE WHERE PEOPLE REPORTED SEEING GHOSTS BEHIND THEIR NEIGHBORS' CURTAINS.
BUT IT WAS ONLY THE TOWN HALL EMPLOYEES TAKING MEASUREMENTS OF THE HOUSE TO TURN IT INTO A CULTURAL CENTER.
THEN, THE CASE OF THE MYSTERIOUS CREAKING NOISE FROM THE ROOF.
SOURCE OF NOISE: SOME SQUIRRELS THAT MADE THEIR NEST IN THE ATTIC.
FOOD DISAPPEARING FROM THE SCHOOL CAFETERIA.
?
IT WAS THE CLEANER'S HUNGRY CAT WHO STOLE THE FOOD BECAUSE HIS OWNER HAD PUT HIM ON A DIET.
AND LAST, THE SCARED RETIRED COUPLE WHO SAW A MOTORCYCLIST WITH A BLAZING SKULL ZIPPING PAST.
IT TURNED OUT TO BE A REALLY COOL HALLOWEEN COSTUME.

NOW WE REALLY NEED A NEW MYSTERY TO SOLVE.

A REAL ONE THIS TIME!

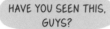

HAVE YOU SEEN THIS, GUYS?

A MUMMY ON THE SUBWAY?

YESTERDAY, SEVERAL PASSENGERS CALLED SCOTLAND YARD TO REPORT THE PRESENCE OF A MUMMY ON THE SUBWAY. HOAX OR REALITY?

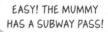

GOOD CATCH, ZOEY!

HOW IS IT POSSIBLE?

EASY! THE MUMMY HAS A SUBWAY PASS!

THEY SAY THAT THE MUMMY HAS BEEN SPOTTED IN SEVERAL NORTHERN LINE STATIONS.

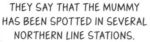

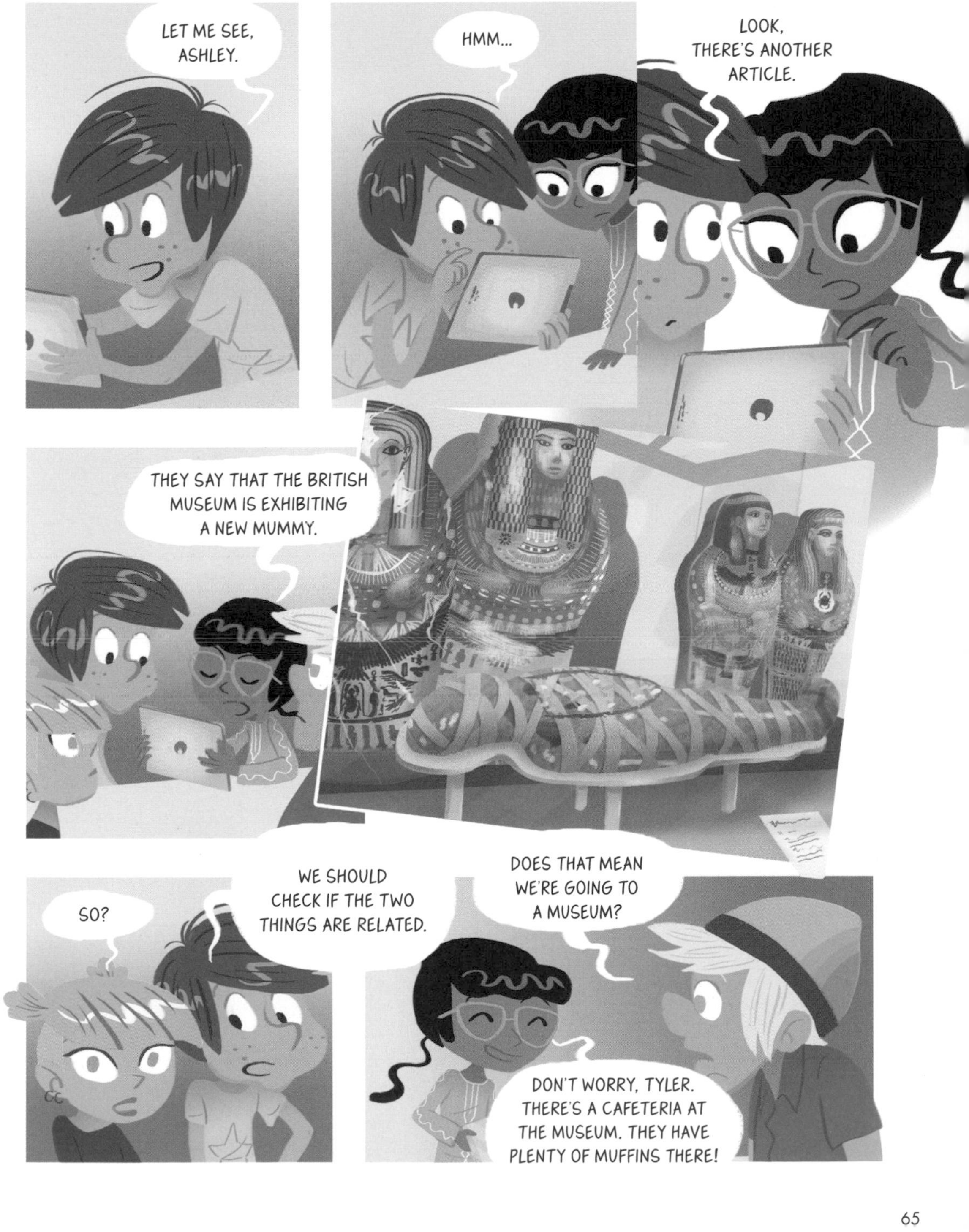
LET ME SEE, ASHLEY.
HMM...
LOOK, THERE'S ANOTHER ARTICLE.
THEY SAY THAT THE BRITISH MUSEUM IS EXHIBITING A NEW MUMMY.
SO?
WE SHOULD CHECK IF THE TWO THINGS ARE RELATED.
DOES THAT MEAN WE'RE GOING TO A MUSEUM?
DON'T WORRY, TYLER. THERE'S A CAFETERIA AT THE MUSEUM. THEY HAVE PLENTY OF MUFFINS THERE!

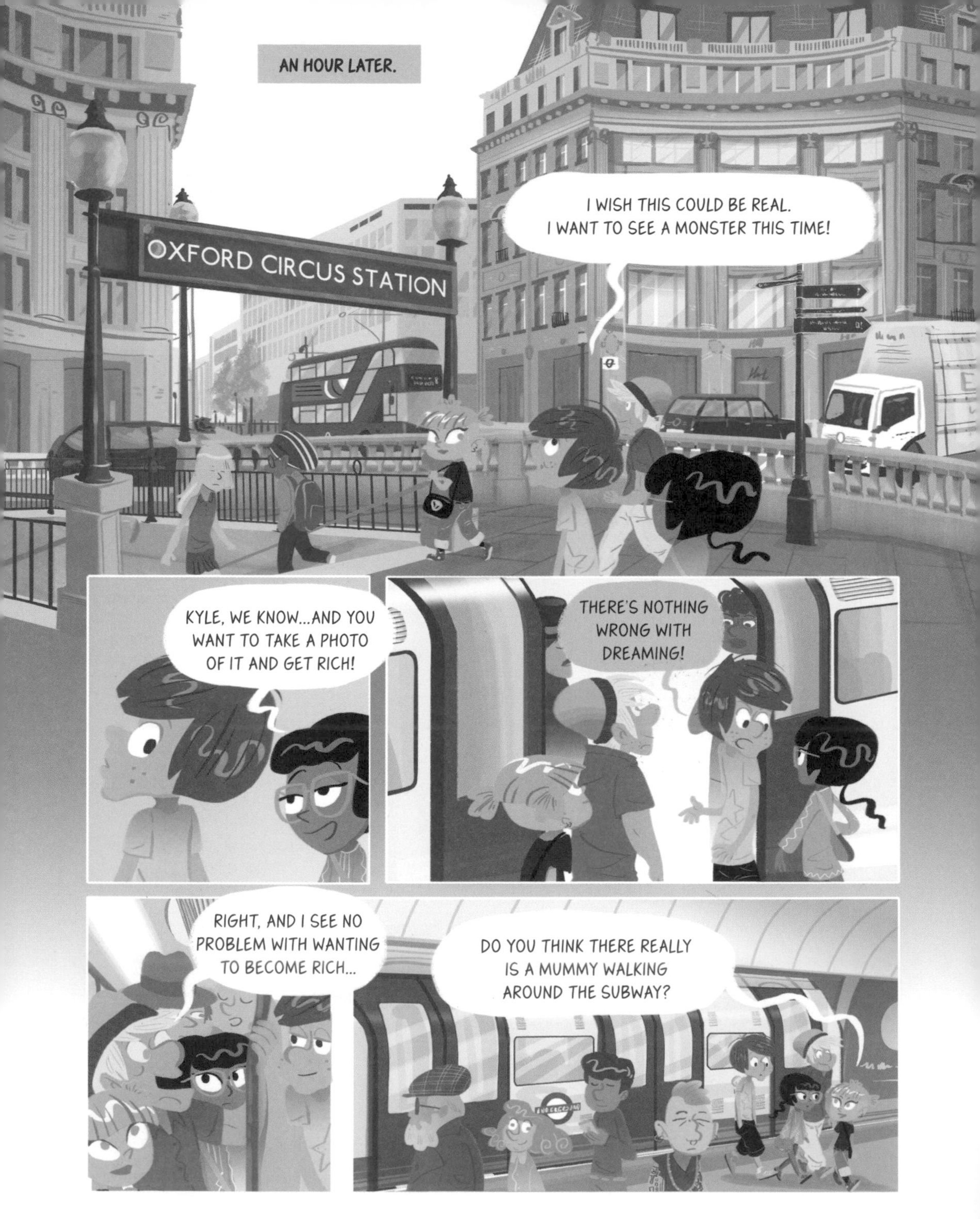
AN HOUR LATER.
OXFORD CIRCUS STATION
I WISH THIS COULD BE REAL. I WANT TO SEE A MONSTER THIS TIME!
KYLE, WE KNOW...AND YOU WANT TO TAKE A PHOTO OF IT AND GET RICH!
THERE'S NOTHING WRONG WITH DREAMING!
RIGHT, AND I SEE NO PROBLEM WITH WANTING TO BECOME RICH...
DO YOU THINK THERE REALLY IS A MUMMY WALKING AROUND THE SUBWAY?

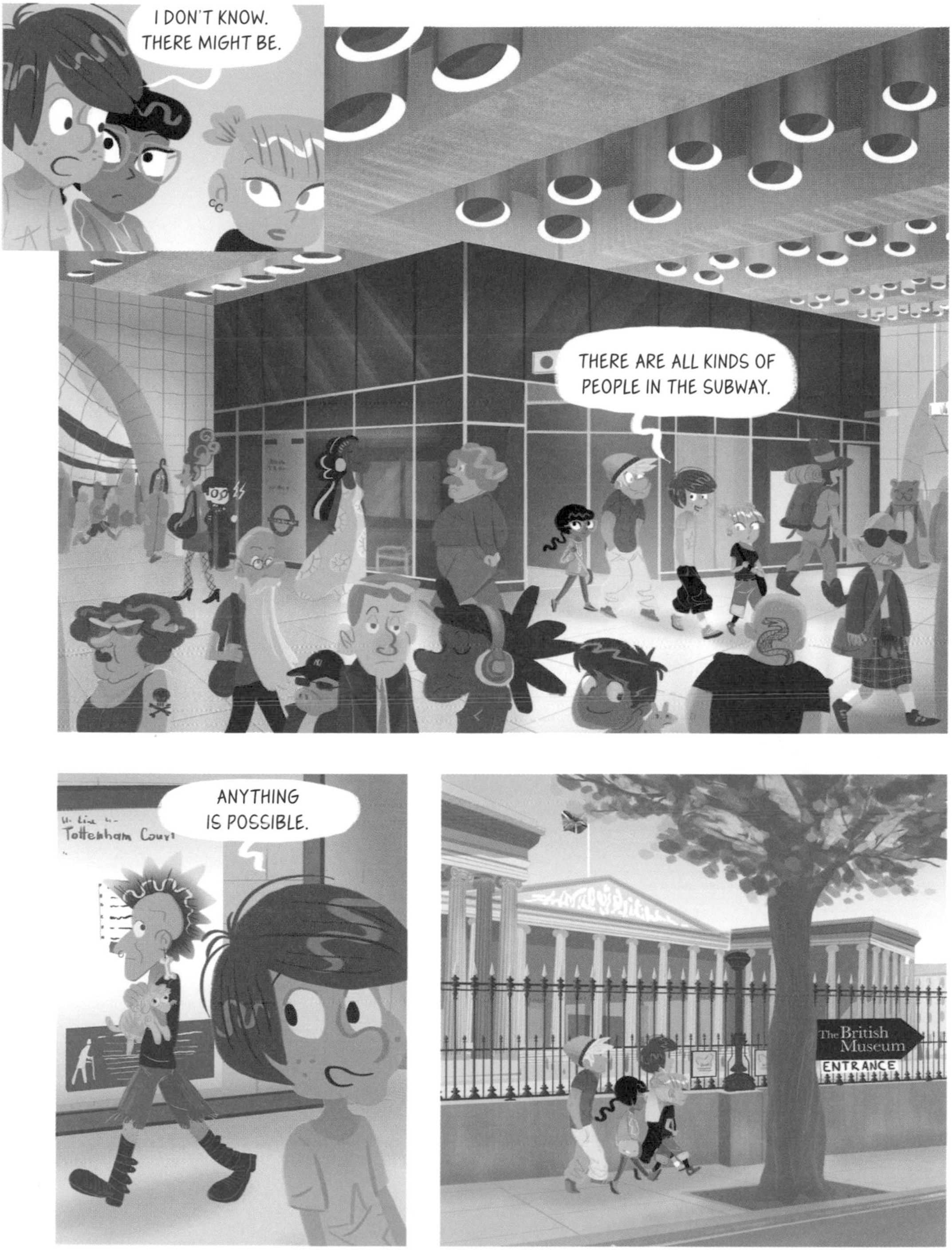
I DON'T KNOW. THERE MIGHT BE.
THERE ARE ALL KINDS OF PEOPLE IN THE SUBWAY.
ANYTHING IS POSSIBLE.
Tottenham Cour
The British Museum
ENTRANCE

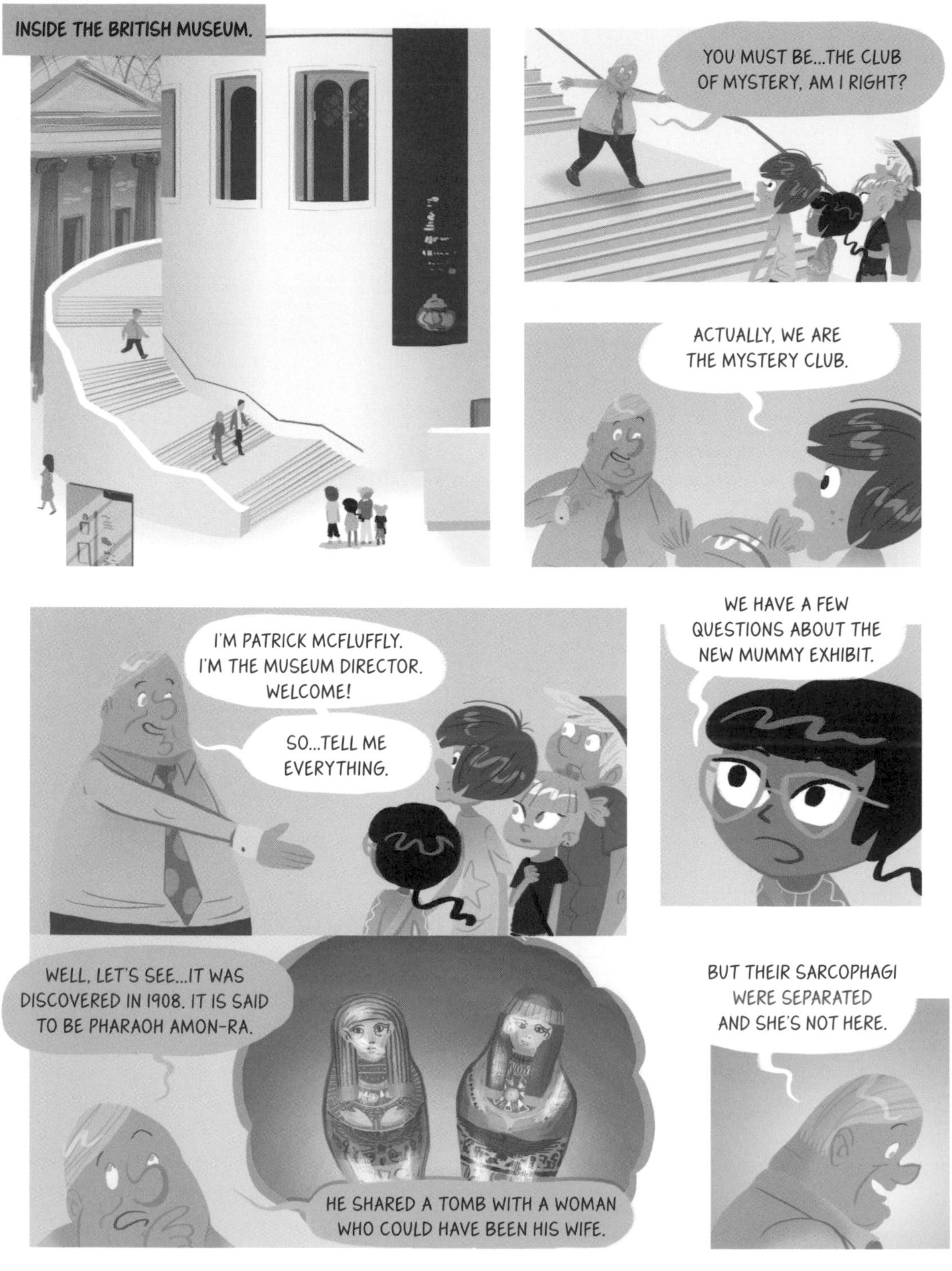
INSIDE THE BRITISH MUSEUM.
YOU MUST BE...THE CLUB OF MYSTERY, AM I RIGHT?
ACTUALLY, WE ARE THE MYSTERY CLUB.
I'M PATRICK MCFLUFFLY. I'M THE MUSEUM DIRECTOR. WELCOME!
SO...TELL ME EVERYTHING.
WE HAVE A FEW QUESTIONS ABOUT THE NEW MUMMY EXHIBIT.
WELL, LET'S SEE...IT WAS DISCOVERED IN 1908. IT IS SAID TO BE PHARAOH AMON-RA.
HE SHARED A TOMB WITH A WOMAN WHO COULD HAVE BEEN HIS WIFE.
BUT THEIR SARCOPHAGI WERE SEPARATED AND SHE'S NOT HERE.

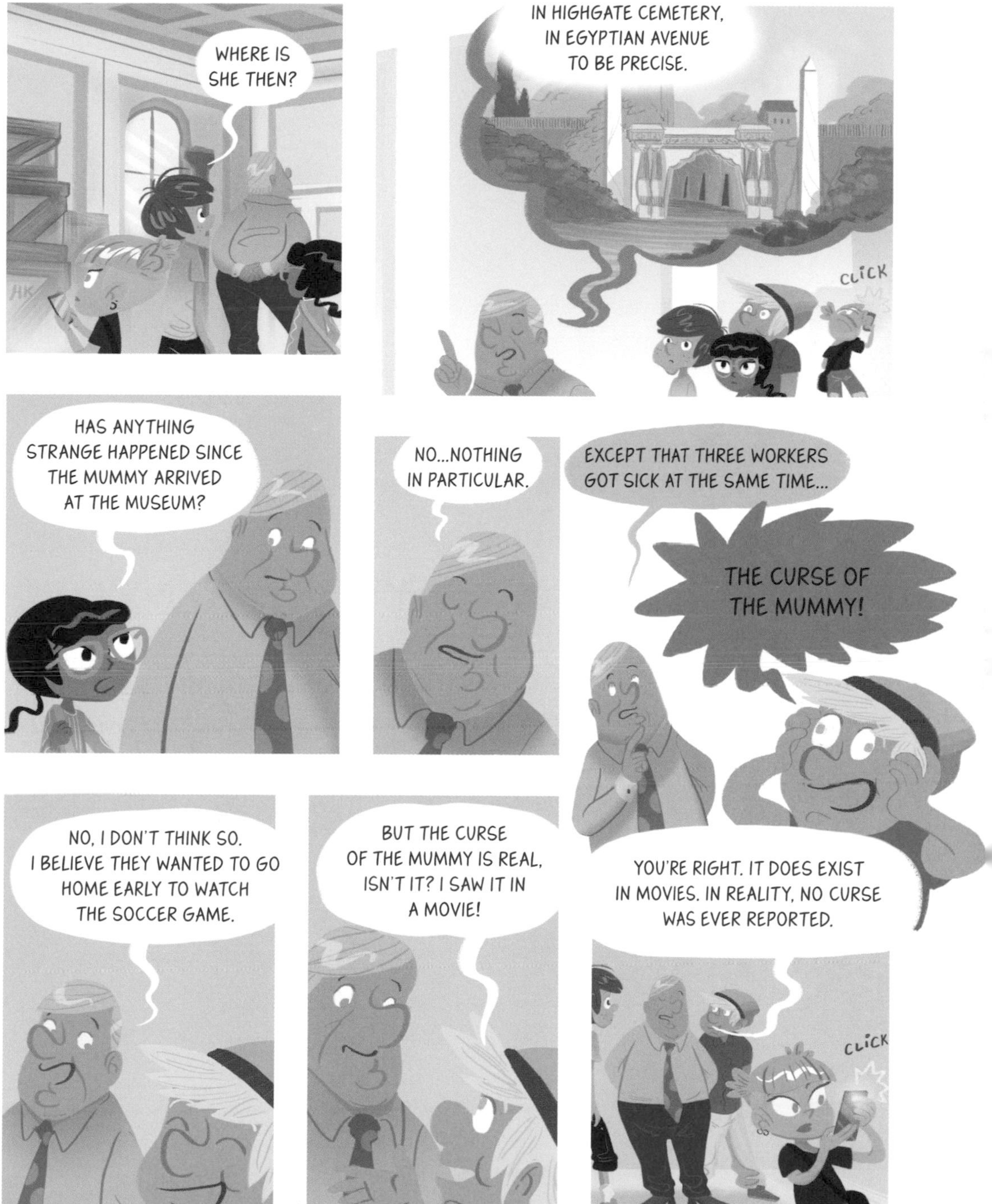
WHERE IS SHE THEN?
IN HIGHGATE CEMETERY, IN EGYPTIAN AVENUE TO BE PRECISE.
CLICK
HAS ANYTHING STRANGE HAPPENED SINCE THE MUMMY ARRIVED AT THE MUSEUM?
NO...NOTHING IN PARTICULAR.
EXCEPT THAT THREE WORKERS GOT SICK AT THE SAME TIME...
THE CURSE OF THE MUMMY!
NO, I DON'T THINK SO. I BELIEVE THEY WANTED TO GO HOME EARLY TO WATCH THE SOCCER GAME.
BUT THE CURSE OF THE MUMMY IS REAL, ISN'T IT? I SAW IT IN A MOVIE!
YOU'RE RIGHT. IT DOES EXIST IN MOVIES. IN REALITY, NO CURSE WAS EVER REPORTED.
CLICK

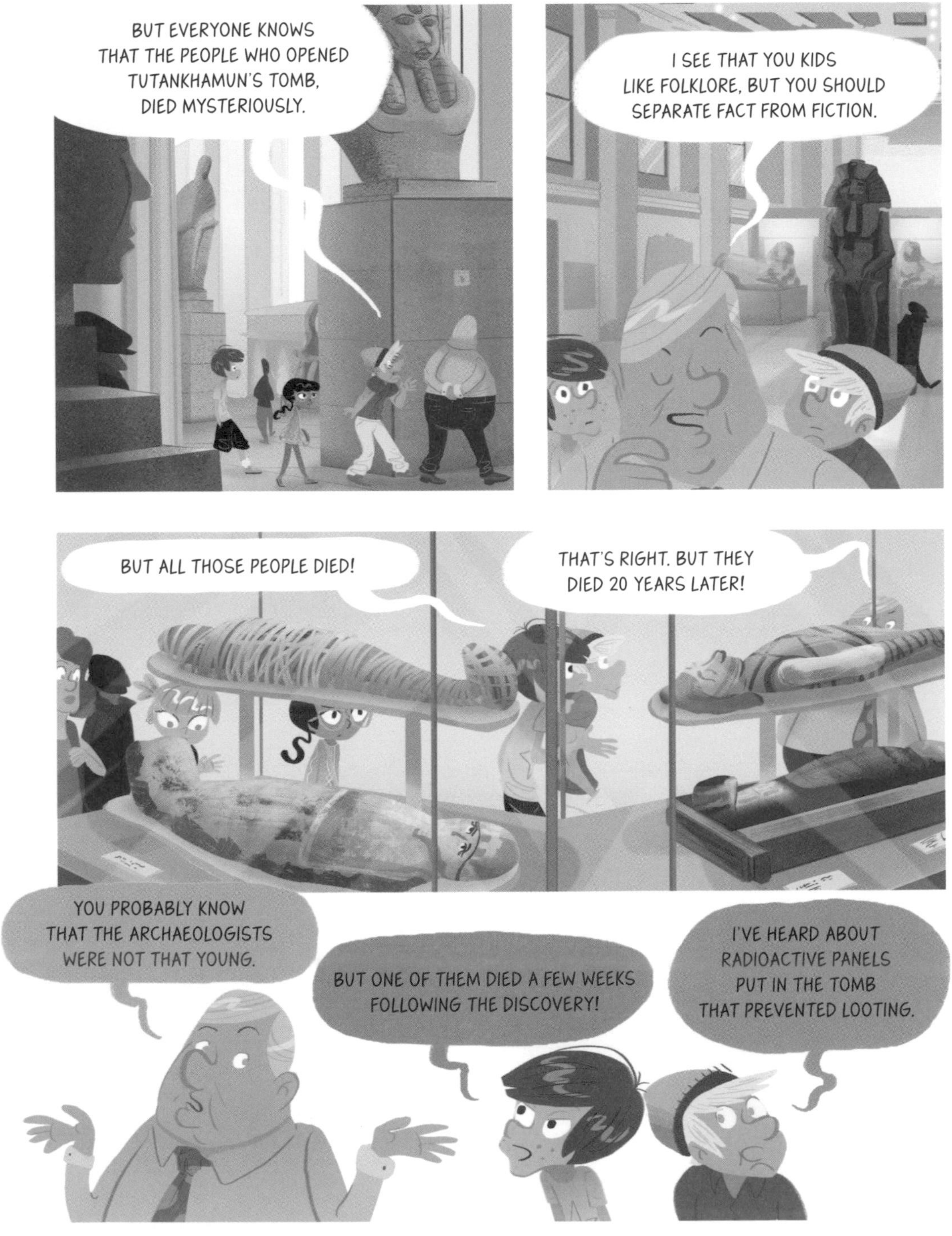
BUT EVERYONE KNOWS THAT THE PEOPLE WHO OPENED TUTANKHAMUN'S TOMB, DIED MYSTERIOUSLY.
I SEE THAT YOU KIDS LIKE FOLKLORE, BUT YOU SHOULD SEPARATE FACT FROM FICTION.
BUT ALL THOSE PEOPLE DIED!
THAT'S RIGHT. BUT THEY DIED 20 YEARS LATER!
YOU PROBABLY KNOW THAT THE ARCHAEOLOGISTS WERE NOT THAT YOUNG.
BUT ONE OF THEM DIED A FEW WEEKS FOLLOWING THE DISCOVERY!
I'VE HEARD ABOUT RADIOACTIVE PANELS PUT IN THE TOMB THAT PREVENTED LOOTING.

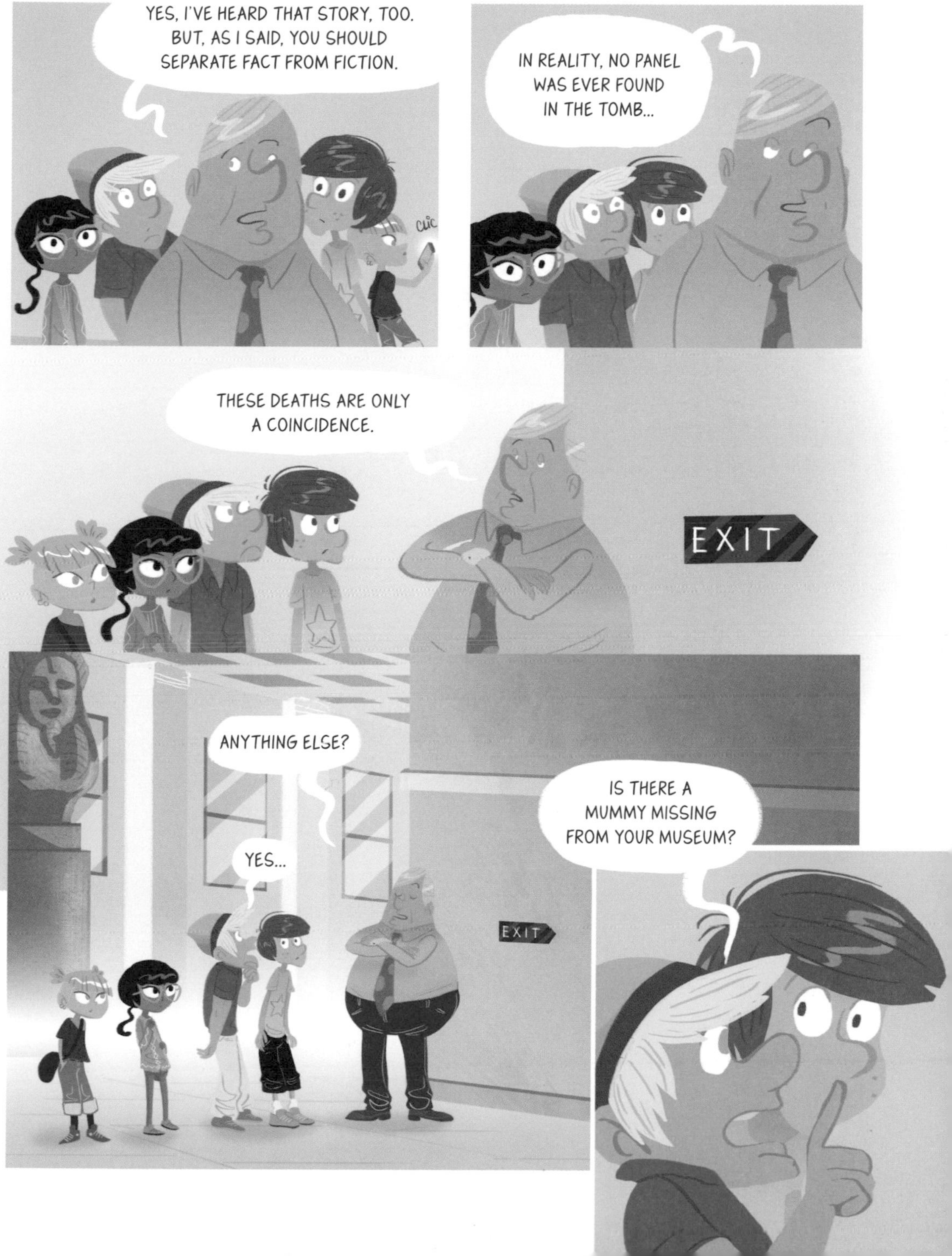
YES, I'VE HEARD THAT STORY, TOO. BUT, AS I SAID, YOU SHOULD SEPARATE FACT FROM FICTION.
CLIC
IN REALITY, NO PANEL WAS EVER FOUND IN THE TOMB...
THESE DEATHS ARE ONLY A COINCIDENCE.
EXIT
ANYTHING ELSE?
YES...
EXIT
IS THERE A MUMMY MISSING FROM YOUR MUSEUM?

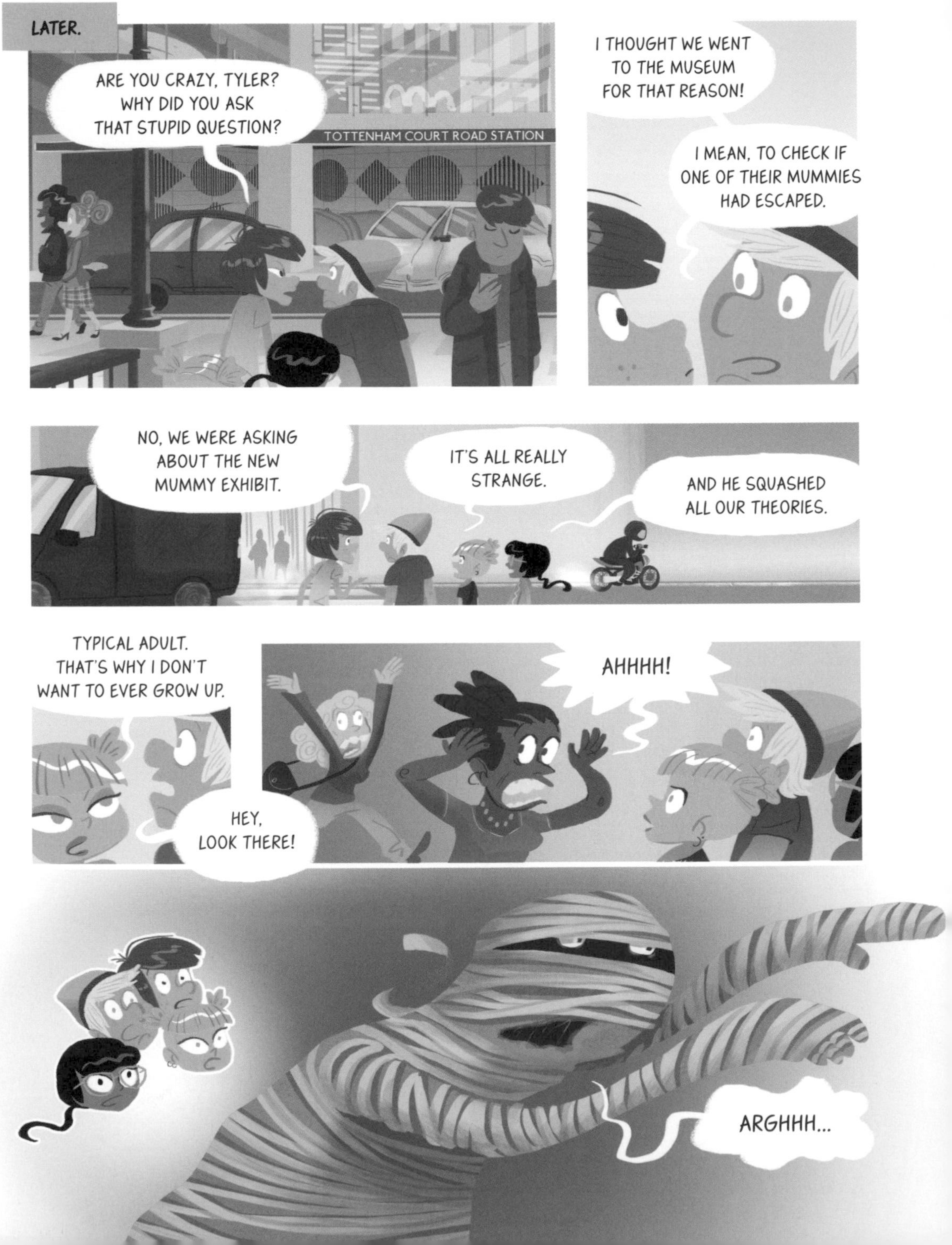
LATER.
ARE YOU CRAZY, TYLER? WHY DID YOU ASK THAT STUPID QUESTION?
TOTTENHAM COURT ROAD STATION
I THOUGHT WE WENT TO THE MUSEUM FOR THAT REASON!
I MEAN, TO CHECK IF ONE OF THEIR MUMMIES HAD ESCAPED.
NO, WE WERE ASKING ABOUT THE NEW MUMMY EXHIBIT.
IT'S ALL REALLY STRANGE.
AND HE SQUASHED ALL OUR THEORIES.
TYPICAL ADULT. THAT'S WHY I DON'T WANT TO EVER GROW UP.
HEY, LOOK THERE!
AHHHH!
ARGHHH...

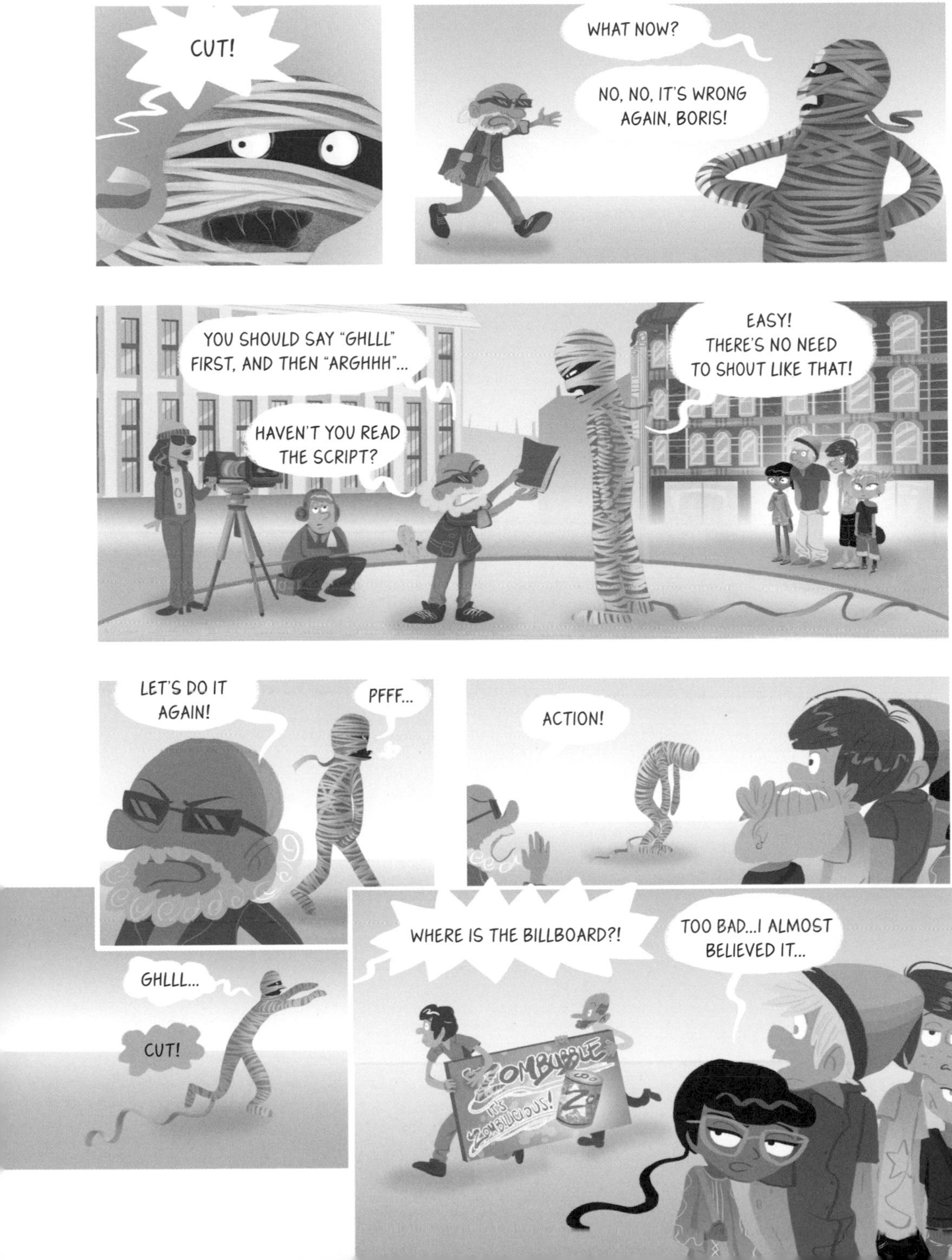
CUT!
WHAT NOW?
NO, NO, IT'S WRONG AGAIN, BORIS!
YOU SHOULD SAY "GHLLL" FIRST, AND THEN "ARGHHH"...
HAVEN'T YOU READ THE SCRIPT?
EASY! THERE'S NO NEED TO SHOUT LIKE THAT!
LET'S DO IT AGAIN!
PFFF...
ACTION!
GHLLL...
CUT!
WHERE IS THE BILLBOARD?!
TOO BAD...I ALMOST BELIEVED IT...
ZOMBUBBLE
IT'S ZOMBILICIOUS!

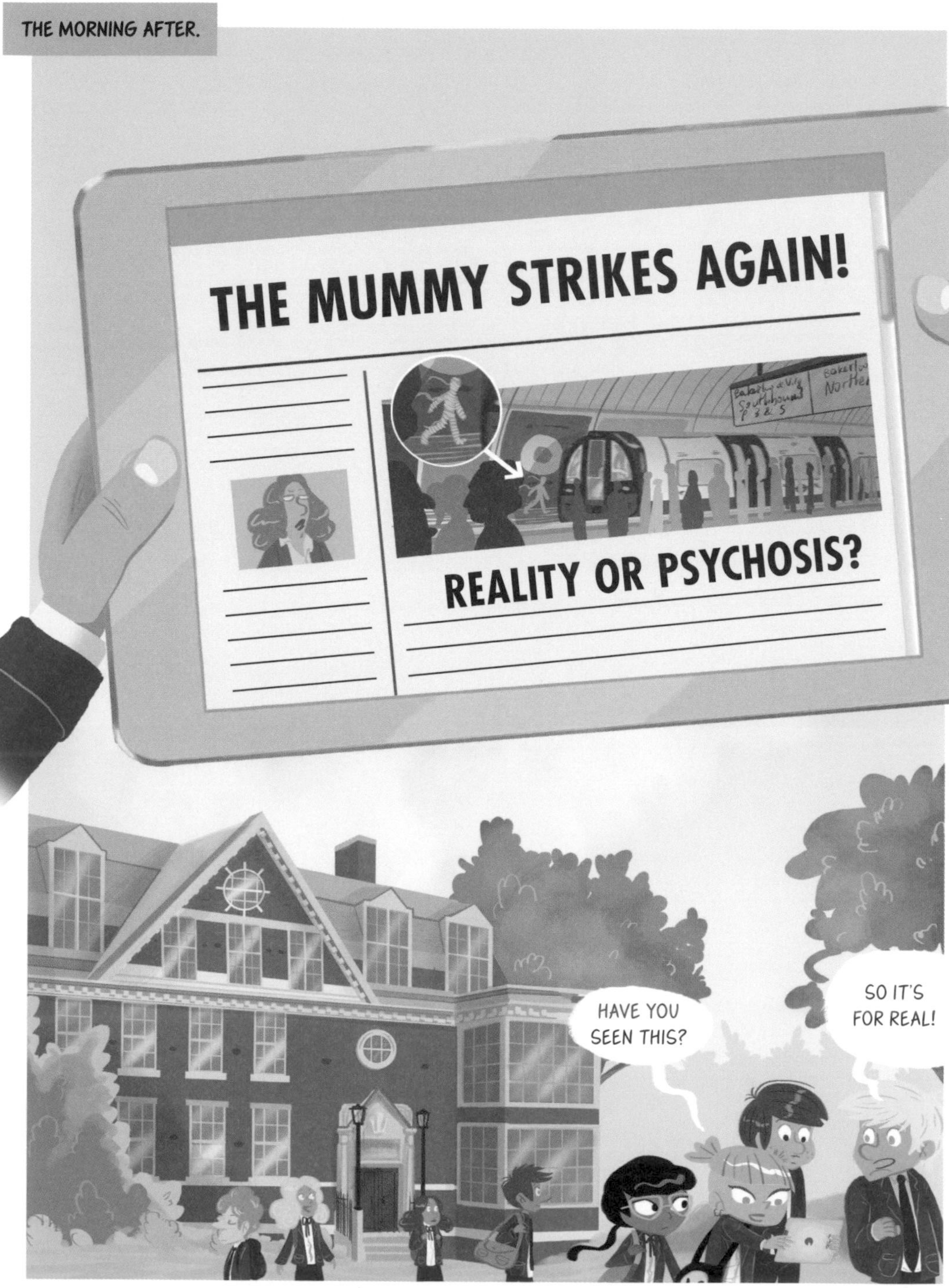
THE MORNING AFTER.
THE MUMMY STRIKES AGAIN!
REALITY OR PSYCHOSIS?
HAVE YOU SEEN THIS?
SO IT'S FOR REAL!

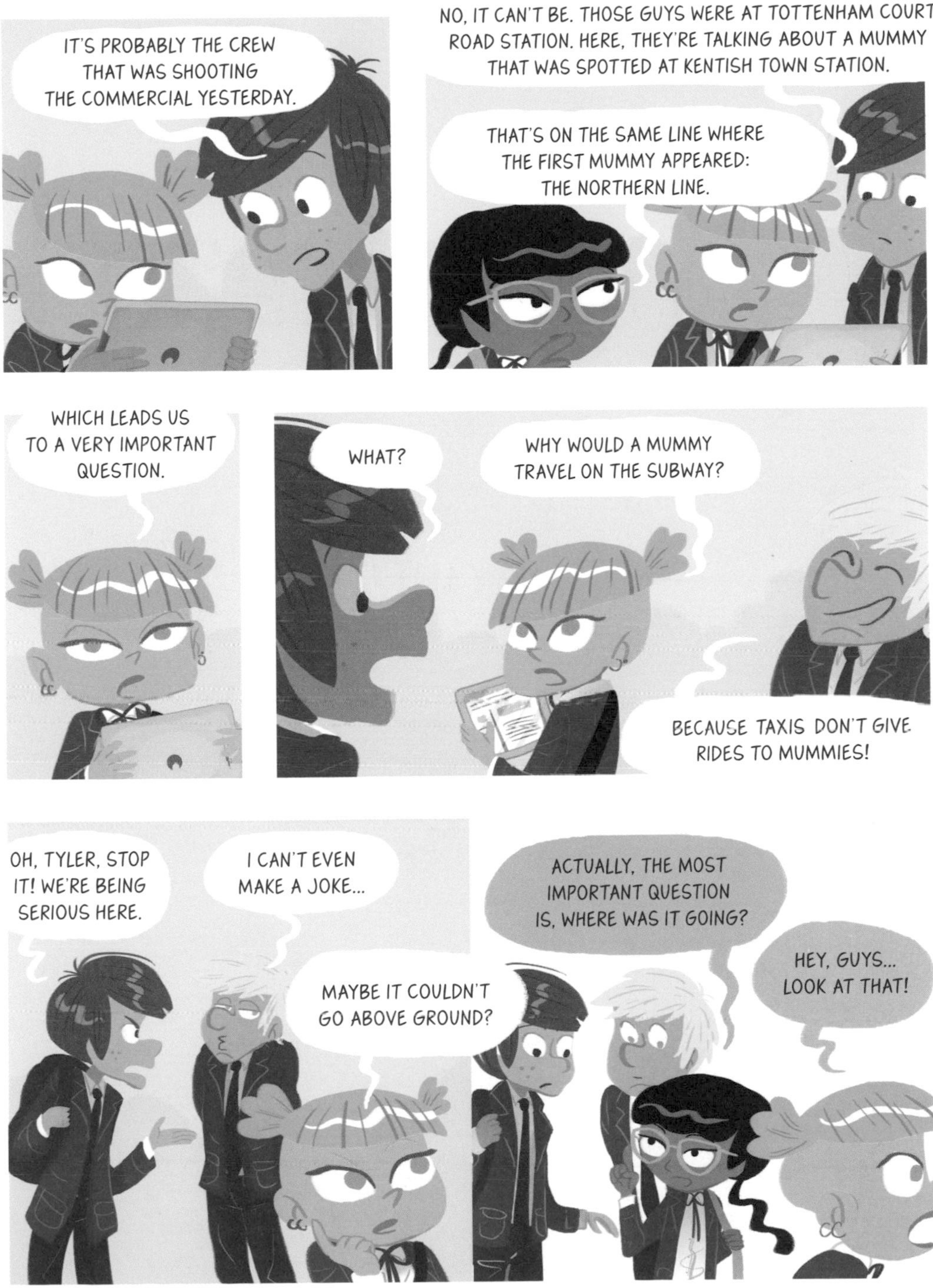
IT'S PROBABLY THE CREW THAT WAS SHOOTING THE COMMERCIAL YESTERDAY.
NO, IT CAN'T BE. THOSE GUYS WERE AT TOTTENHAM COURT ROAD STATION. HERE, THEY'RE TALKING ABOUT A MUMMY THAT WAS SPOTTED AT KENTISH TOWN STATION.
THAT'S ON THE SAME LINE WHERE THE FIRST MUMMY APPEARED: THE NORTHERN LINE.
WHICH LEADS US TO A VERY IMPORTANT QUESTION.
WHAT?
WHY WOULD A MUMMY TRAVEL ON THE SUBWAY?
BECAUSE TAXIS DON'T GIVE RIDES TO MUMMIES!
OH, TYLER, STOP IT! WE'RE BEING SERIOUS HERE.
I CAN'T EVEN MAKE A JOKE...
MAYBE IT COULDN'T GO ABOVE GROUND?
ACTUALLY, THE MOST IMPORTANT QUESTION IS, WHERE WAS IT GOING?
HEY, GUYS... LOOK AT THAT!

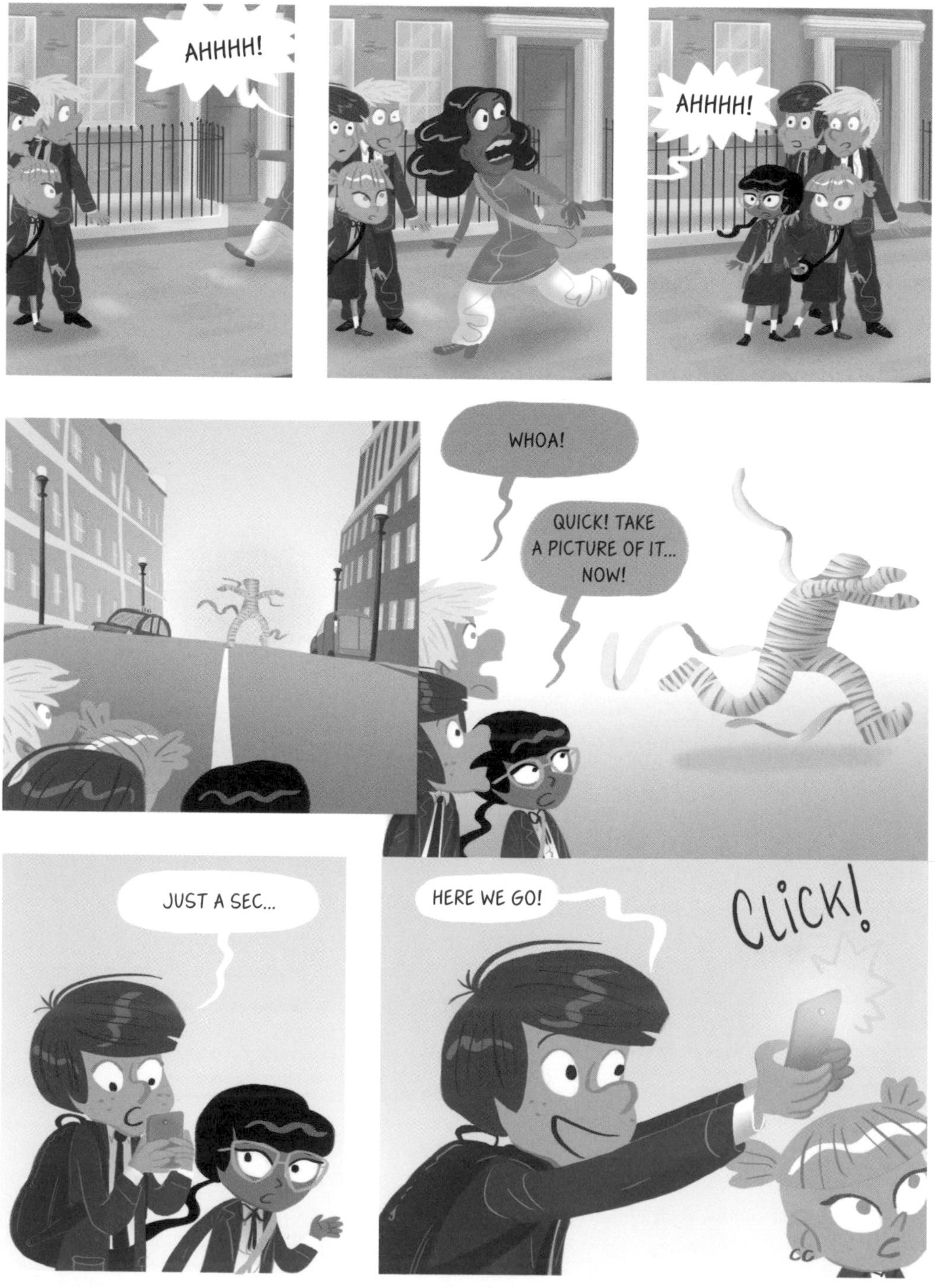
AHHHH!
AHHHH!
WHOA!
QUICK! TAKE A PICTURE OF IT... NOW!
JUST A SEC...
HERE WE GO!
CLICK!

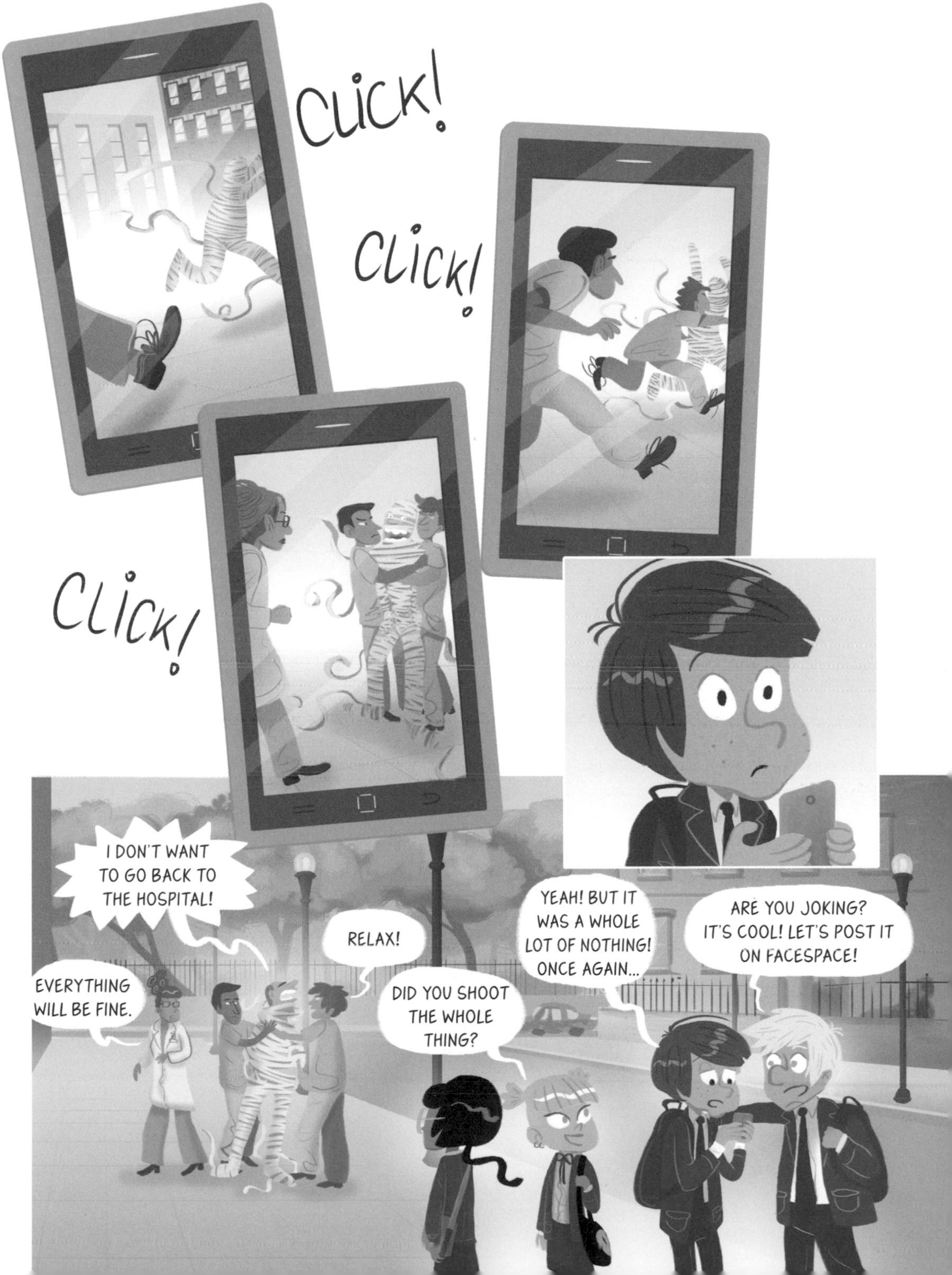
CLICK!
CLICK!
CLICK!
I DON'T WANT TO GO BACK TO THE HOSPITAL!
EVERYTHING WILL BE FINE.
RELAX!
DID YOU SHOOT THE WHOLE THING?
YEAH! BUT IT WAS A WHOLE LOT OF NOTHING! ONCE AGAIN...
ARE YOU JOKING? IT'S COOL! LET'S POST IT ON FACESPACE!

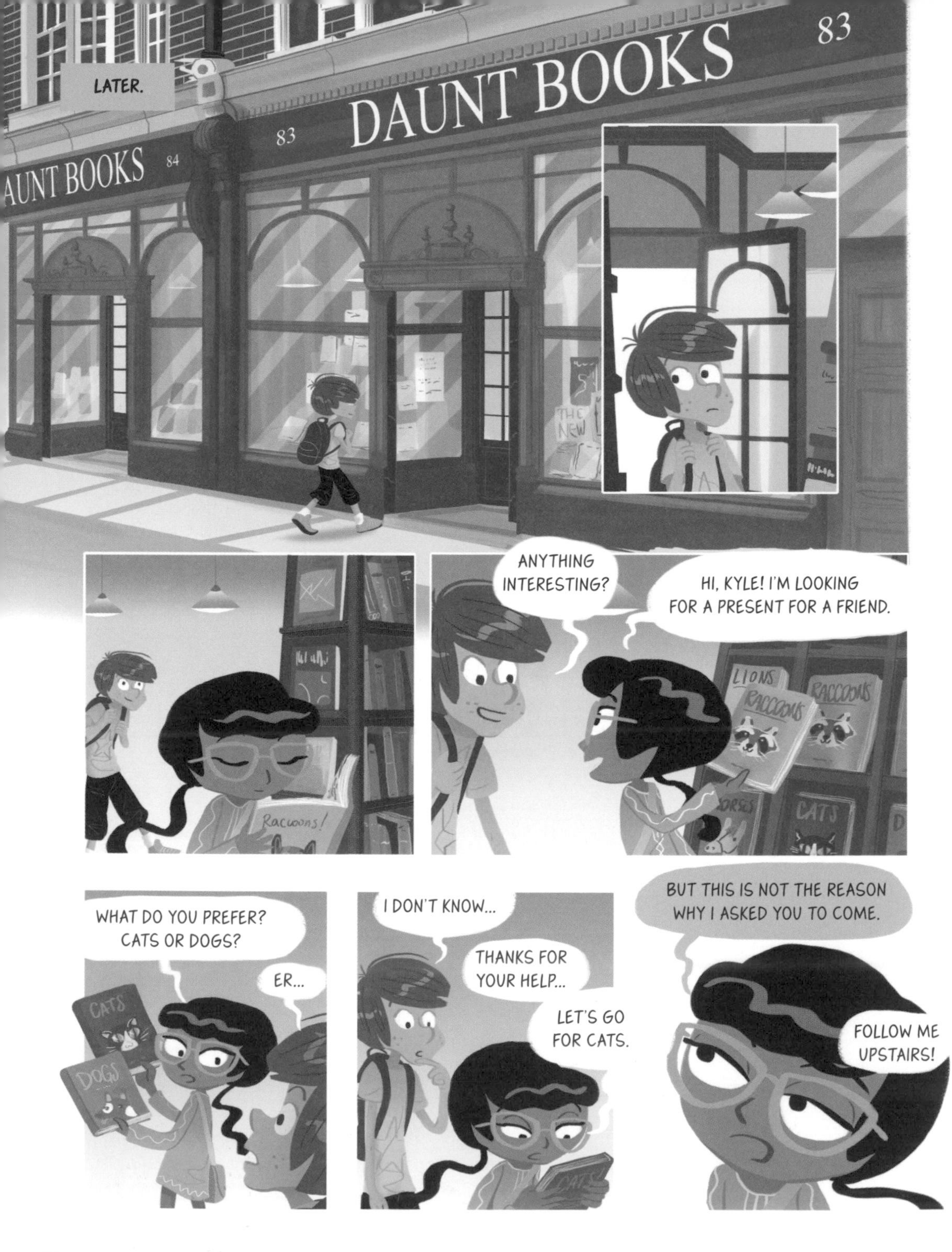
LATER.
DAUNT BOOKS 83
83 DAUNT BOOKS
AUNT BOOKS 84
ANYTHING INTERESTING?
HI, KYLE! I'M LOOKING FOR A PRESENT FOR A FRIEND.
Racoons!
LIONS
RACCOONS
RACCOONS
CATS
WHAT DO YOU PREFER? CATS OR DOGS?
ER...
CATS
DOGS
I DON'T KNOW...
THANKS FOR YOUR HELP...
LET'S GO FOR CATS.
BUT THIS IS NOT THE REASON WHY I ASKED YOU TO COME.
FOLLOW ME UPSTAIRS!

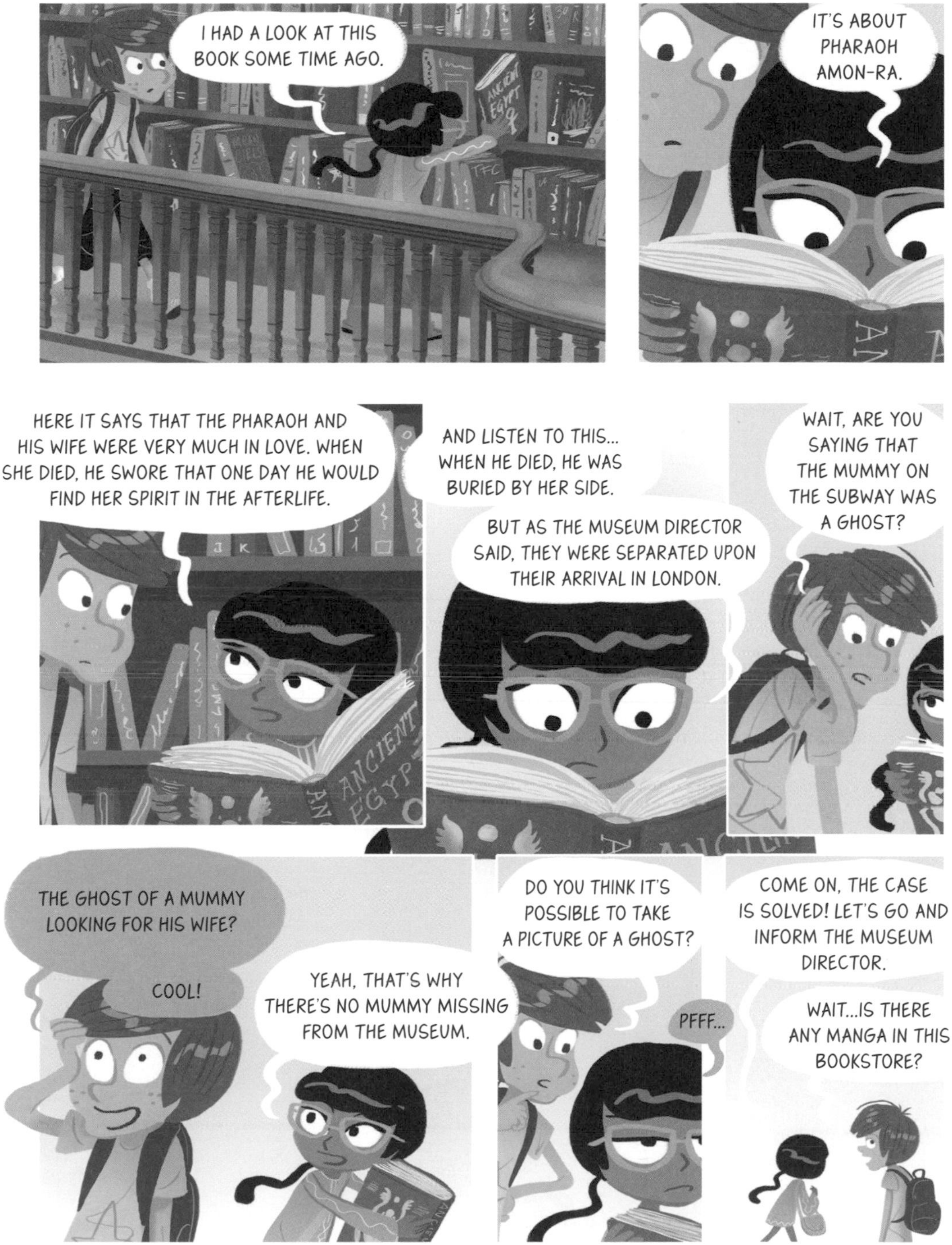
I HAD A LOOK AT THIS BOOK SOME TIME AGO.
IT'S ABOUT PHARAOH AMON-RA.
HERE IT SAYS THAT THE PHARAOH AND HIS WIFE WERE VERY MUCH IN LOVE. WHEN SHE DIED, HE SWORE THAT ONE DAY HE WOULD FIND HER SPIRIT IN THE AFTERLIFE.
AND LISTEN TO THIS... WHEN HE DIED, HE WAS BURIED BY HER SIDE.
BUT AS THE MUSEUM DIRECTOR SAID, THEY WERE SEPARATED UPON THEIR ARRIVAL IN LONDON.
WAIT, ARE YOU SAYING THAT THE MUMMY ON THE SUBWAY WAS A GHOST?
THE GHOST OF A MUMMY LOOKING FOR HIS WIFE?
COOL!
YEAH, THAT'S WHY THERE'S NO MUMMY MISSING FROM THE MUSEUM.
DO YOU THINK IT'S POSSIBLE TO TAKE A PICTURE OF A GHOST?
PFFF...
COME ON, THE CASE IS SOLVED! LET'S GO AND INFORM THE MUSEUM DIRECTOR.
WAIT...IS THERE ANY MANGA IN THIS BOOKSTORE?

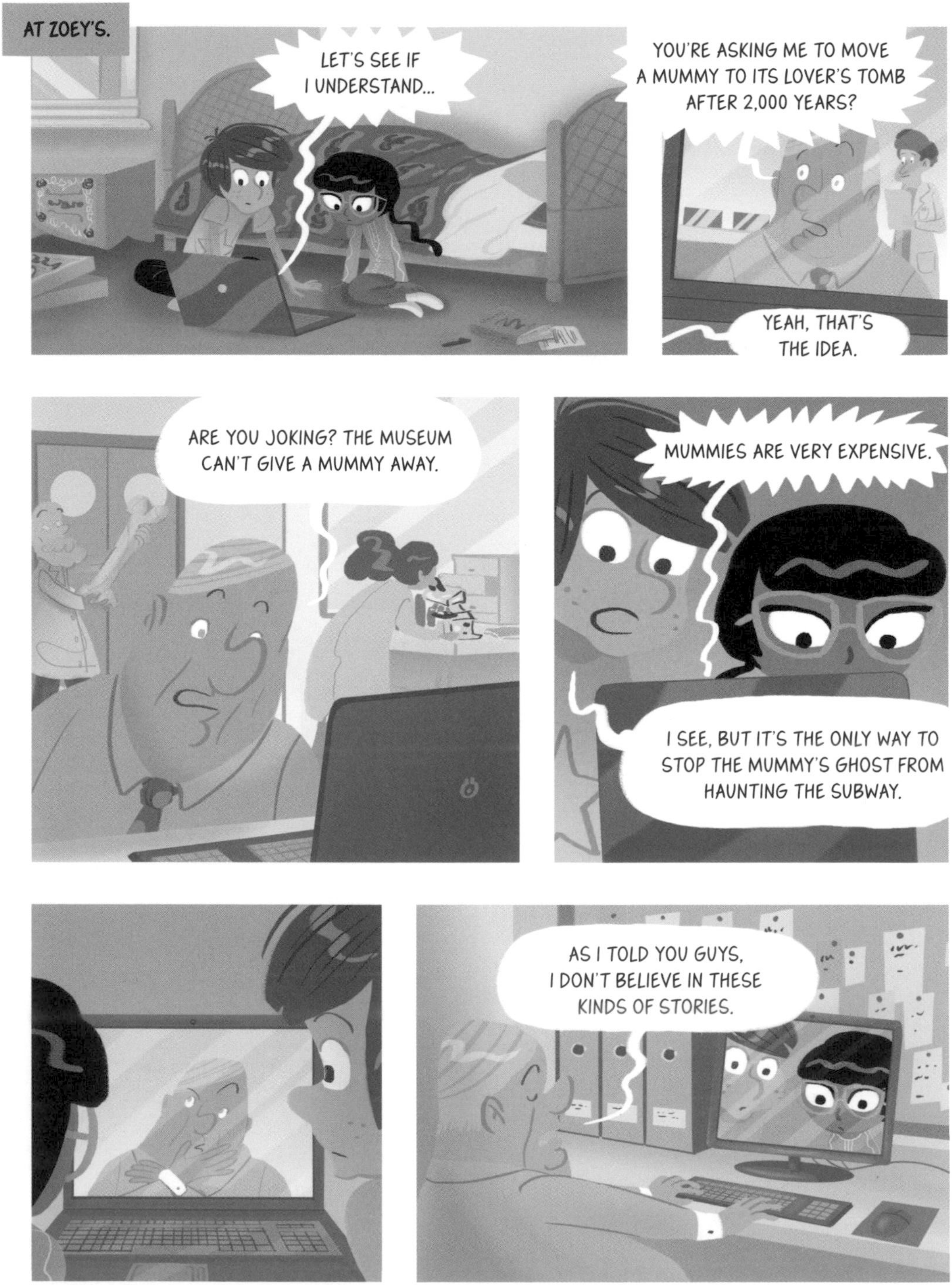
AT ZOEY'S.
LET'S SEE IF I UNDERSTAND...
YOU'RE ASKING ME TO MOVE A MUMMY TO ITS LOVER'S TOMB AFTER 2,000 YEARS?
YEAH, THAT'S THE IDEA.
ARE YOU JOKING? THE MUSEUM CAN'T GIVE A MUMMY AWAY.
MUMMIES ARE VERY EXPENSIVE.
I SEE, BUT IT'S THE ONLY WAY TO STOP THE MUMMY'S GHOST FROM HAUNTING THE SUBWAY.
AS I TOLD YOU GUYS, I DON'T BELIEVE IN THESE KINDS OF STORIES.

ANYWAY, TO BE HONEST, THIS NEWS DOESN'T BOTHER ME AT ALL. IT WILL PROBABLY BRING SOME PUBLICITY TO THE MUSEUM.

THANKS FOR CALLING. YOU ARE SMART KIDS AND I WISH LUCK TO YOUR MYSTERY CLUB.

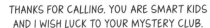

CLICK

LOG OUT

THIS IS SO BAD! WE ALMOST SOLVED THE CASE!

LOG OUT

DON'T WORRY! YOU CAN ALWAYS TRY TO TAKE A PICTURE OF THE GHOST.

TO MAKE YOU FEEL BETTER, I'LL LET YOU HAVE THE LAST SLICE OF PIZZA!

REALLY? THANKS, ZOEY...

HERE YOU GO!

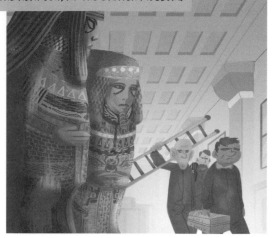

THE NEXT DAY, AT THE BRITISH MUSEUM.
?
WHO OPENED THIS SARCOPHAGUS?
I HAVE NO IDEA...
HOW STRANGE, WHERE HAS THE MUMMY GONE?
MEANWHILE IN ANOTHER HALL.
IN THIS SECTION, YOU CAN ADMIRE THE GREATEST ARCHAEOLOGICAL DISCOVERIES FROM EGYPT...
OH MY GOSH!
THIS IS WHAT HAPPENED THIS MORNING.
THAT'S WHY I CALLED YOU BACK SO URGENTLY.

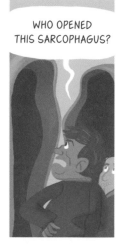

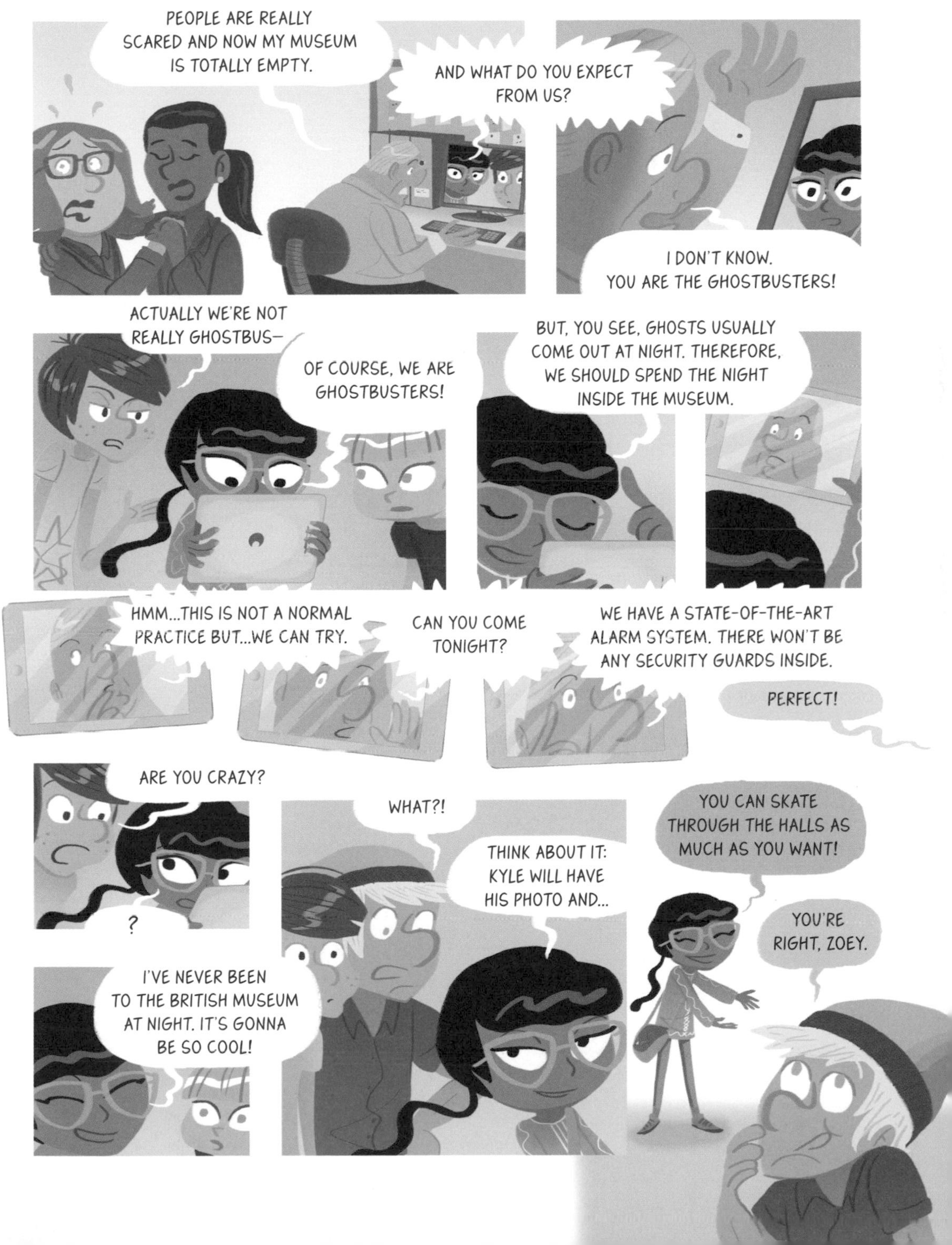
PEOPLE ARE REALLY SCARED AND NOW MY MUSEUM IS TOTALLY EMPTY.
AND WHAT DO YOU EXPECT FROM US?
I DON'T KNOW. YOU ARE THE GHOSTBUSTERS!
ACTUALLY WE'RE NOT REALLY GHOSTBUS—
OF COURSE, WE ARE GHOSTBUSTERS!
BUT, YOU SEE, GHOSTS USUALLY COME OUT AT NIGHT. THEREFORE, WE SHOULD SPEND THE NIGHT INSIDE THE MUSEUM.
HMM...THIS IS NOT A NORMAL PRACTICE BUT...WE CAN TRY.
CAN YOU COME TONIGHT?
WE HAVE A STATE-OF-THE-ART ALARM SYSTEM. THERE WON'T BE ANY SECURITY GUARDS INSIDE.
PERFECT!
ARE YOU CRAZY?
?
WHAT?!
THINK ABOUT IT: KYLE WILL HAVE HIS PHOTO AND...
YOU CAN SKATE THROUGH THE HALLS AS MUCH AS YOU WANT!
YOU'RE RIGHT, ZOEY.
I'VE NEVER BEEN TO THE BRITISH MUSEUM AT NIGHT. IT'S GONNA BE SO COOL!

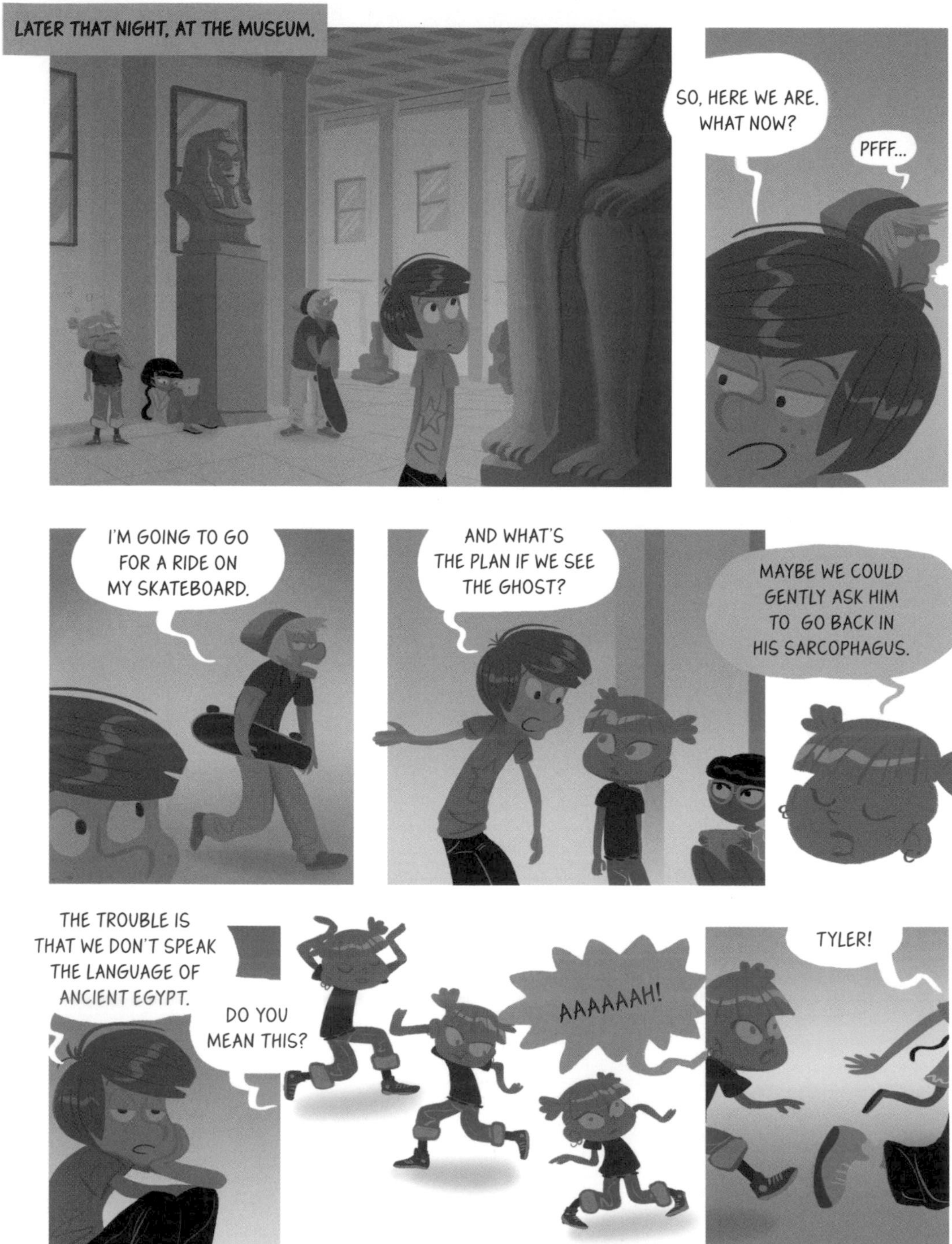
LATER THAT NIGHT, AT THE MUSEUM.
SO, HERE WE ARE. WHAT NOW?
PFFF...
I'M GOING TO GO FOR A RIDE ON MY SKATEBOARD.
AND WHAT'S THE PLAN IF WE SEE THE GHOST?
MAYBE WE COULD GENTLY ASK HIM TO GO BACK IN HIS SARCOPHAGUS.
THE TROUBLE IS THAT WE DON'T SPEAK THE LANGUAGE OF ANCIENT EGYPT.
DO YOU MEAN THIS?
AAAAAAH!
TYLER!

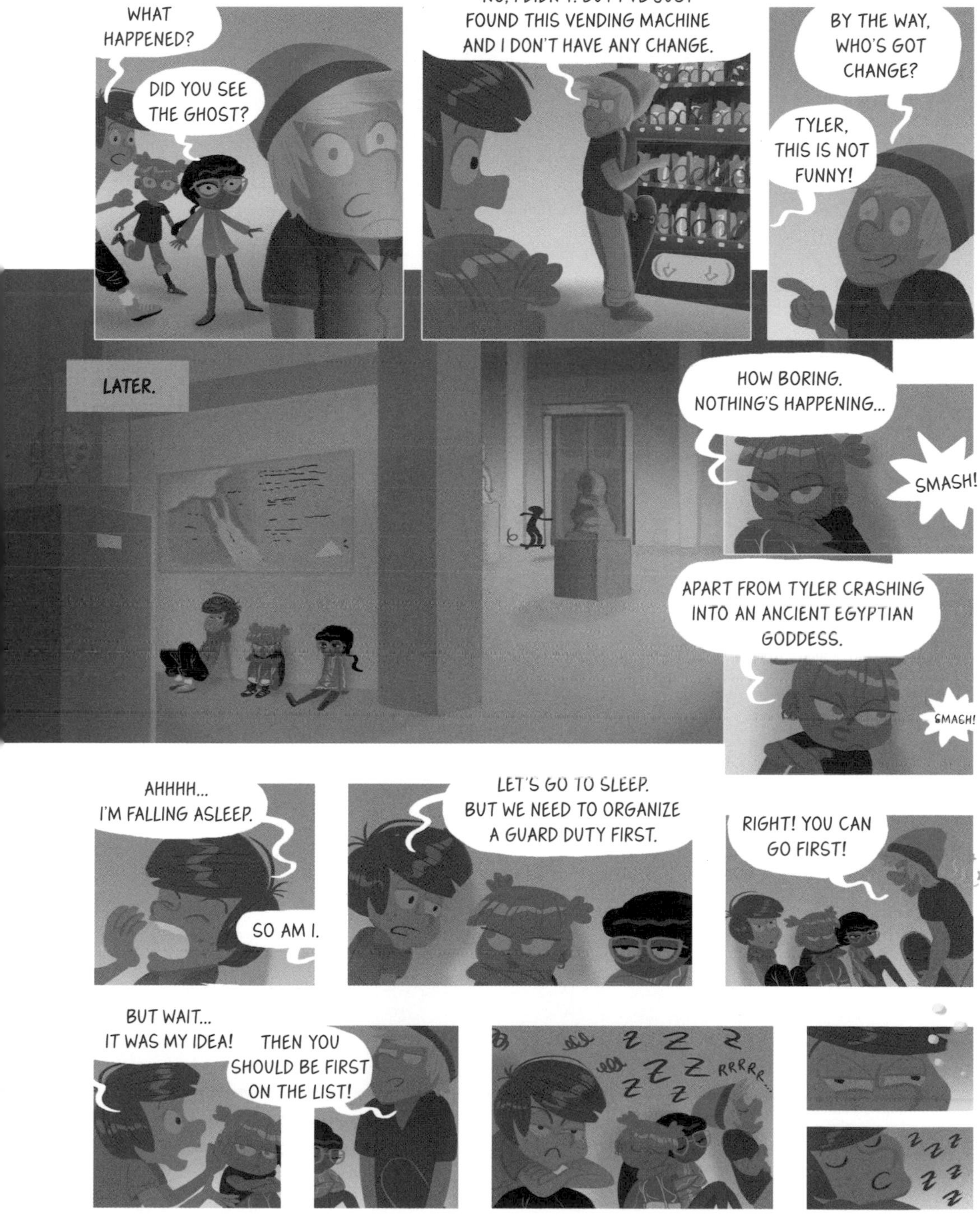

WHAT HAPPENED?
DID YOU SEE THE GHOST?
NO, I DIDN'T. BUT I'VE JUST FOUND THIS VENDING MACHINE AND I DON'T HAVE ANY CHANGE.
BY THE WAY, WHO'S GOT CHANGE?
TYLER, THIS IS NOT FUNNY!
LATER.
HOW BORING. NOTHING'S HAPPENING...
SMASH!
APART FROM TYLER CRASHING INTO AN ANCIENT EGYPTIAN GODDESS.
SMASH!
AHHHH... I'M FALLING ASLEEP.
SO AM I.
LET'S GO TO SLEEP. BUT WE NEED TO ORGANIZE A GUARD DUTY FIRST.
RIGHT! YOU CAN GO FIRST!
BUT WAIT... IT WAS MY IDEA!
THEN YOU SHOULD BE FIRST ON THE LIST!
Z Z Z Z Z Z Z RRRRR...
Z Z Z Z Z

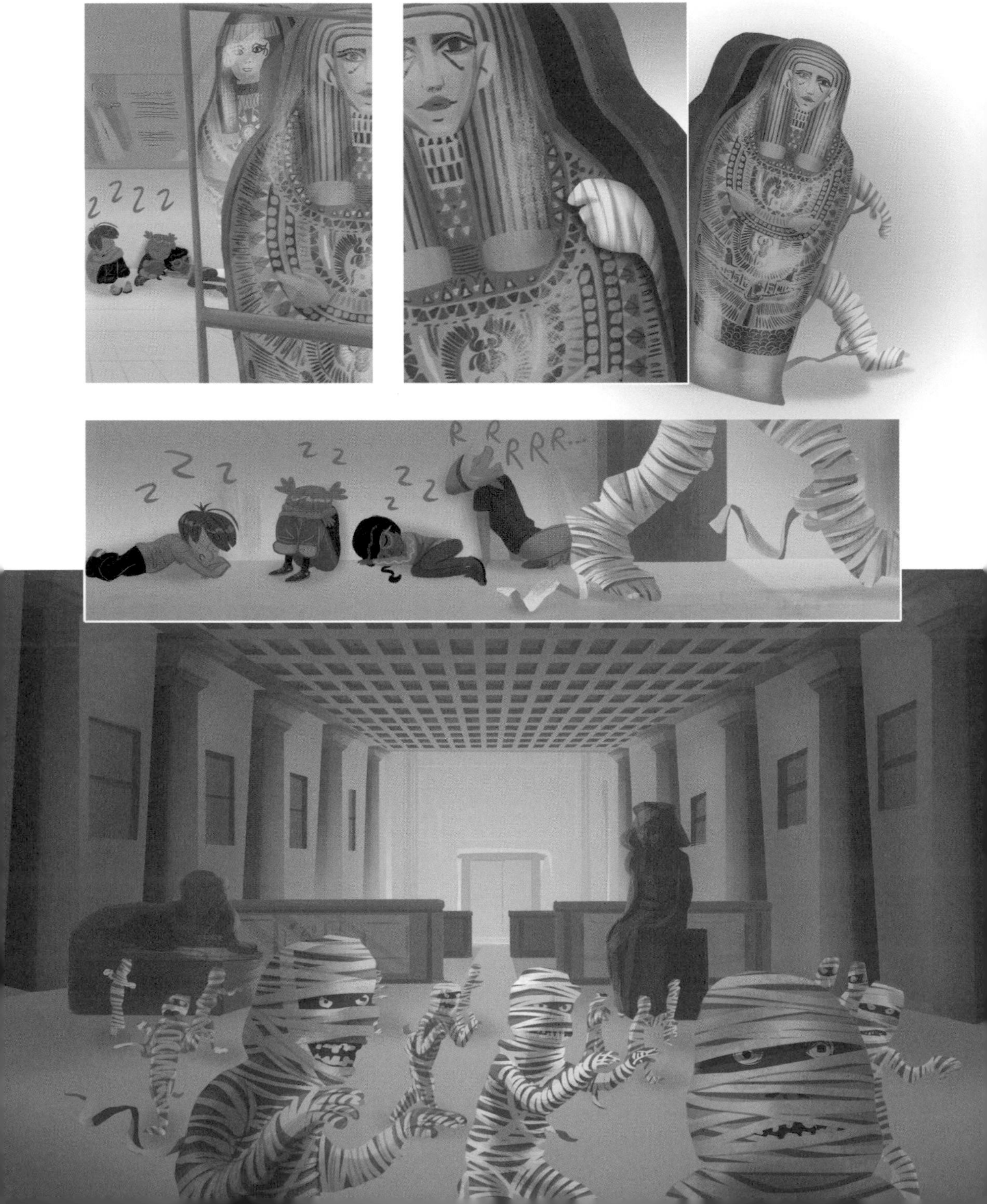
ZZZZ
ZZZ
ZZ
ZZZZ
RRRRR...

HEY, GUYS...

WAKE UP!

I THINK WE HAVE A MAJOR PROBLEM HERE.

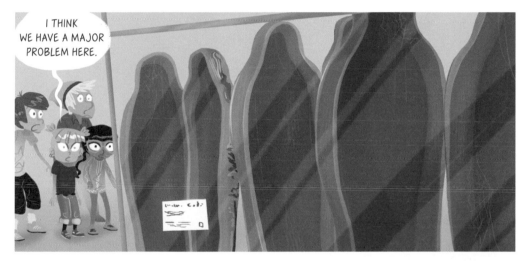

WHAT HAPPENED?

I CAN'T BELIEVE IT! THE MUMMIES HAVE COME BACK TO LIFE... FOR REAL!

THEY MUST HAVE GONE OUT THAT WAY!

FREEZE!

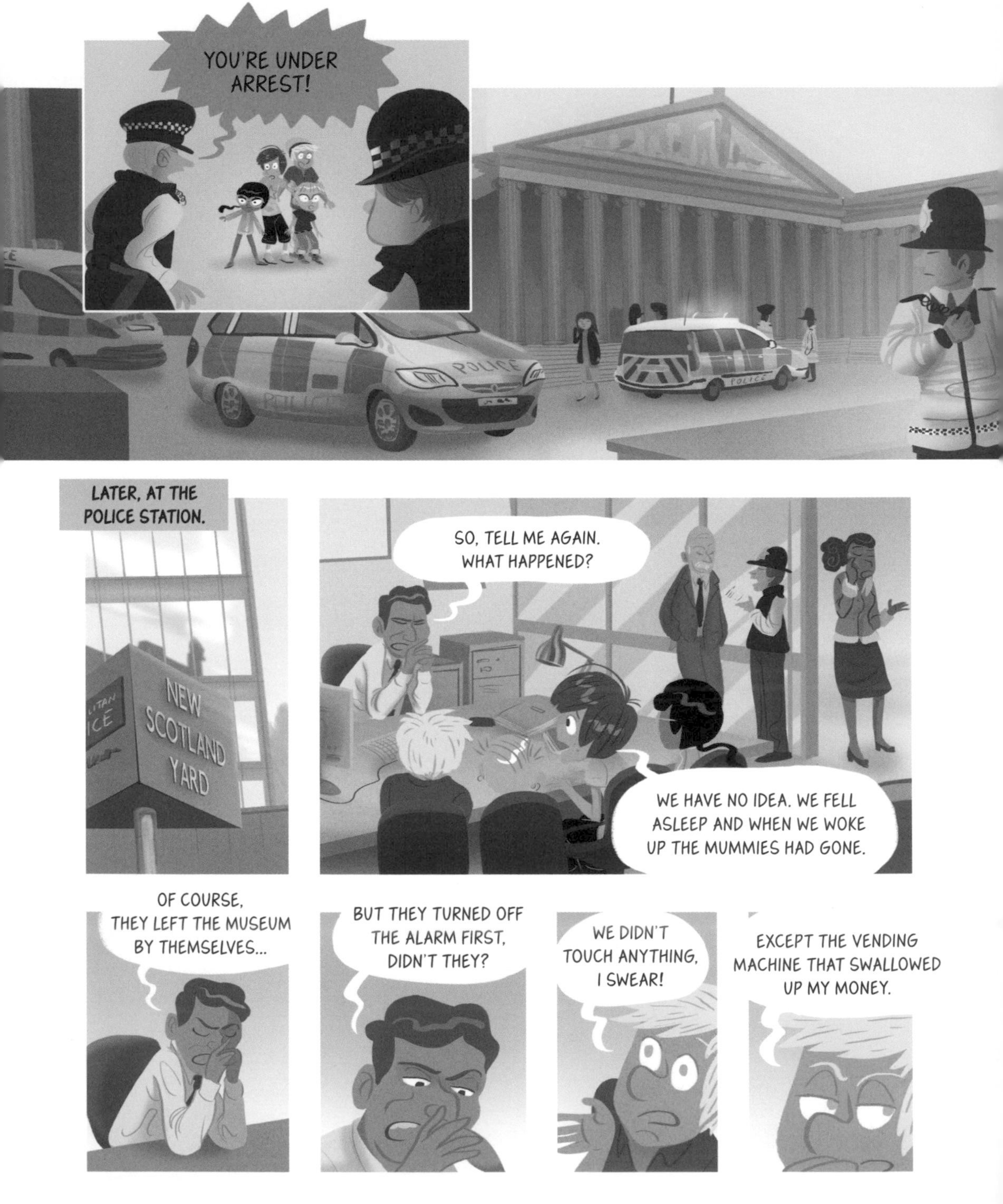
YOU'RE UNDER ARREST!
POLICE
POLICE
LATER, AT THE POLICE STATION.
NEW SCOTLAND YARD
SO, TELL ME AGAIN. WHAT HAPPENED?
WE HAVE NO IDEA. WE FELL ASLEEP AND WHEN WE WOKE UP THE MUMMIES HAD GONE.
OF COURSE, THEY LEFT THE MUSEUM BY THEMSELVES...
BUT THEY TURNED OFF THE ALARM FIRST, DIDN'T THEY?
WE DIDN'T TOUCH ANYTHING, I SWEAR!
EXCEPT THE VENDING MACHINE THAT SWALLOWED UP MY MONEY.

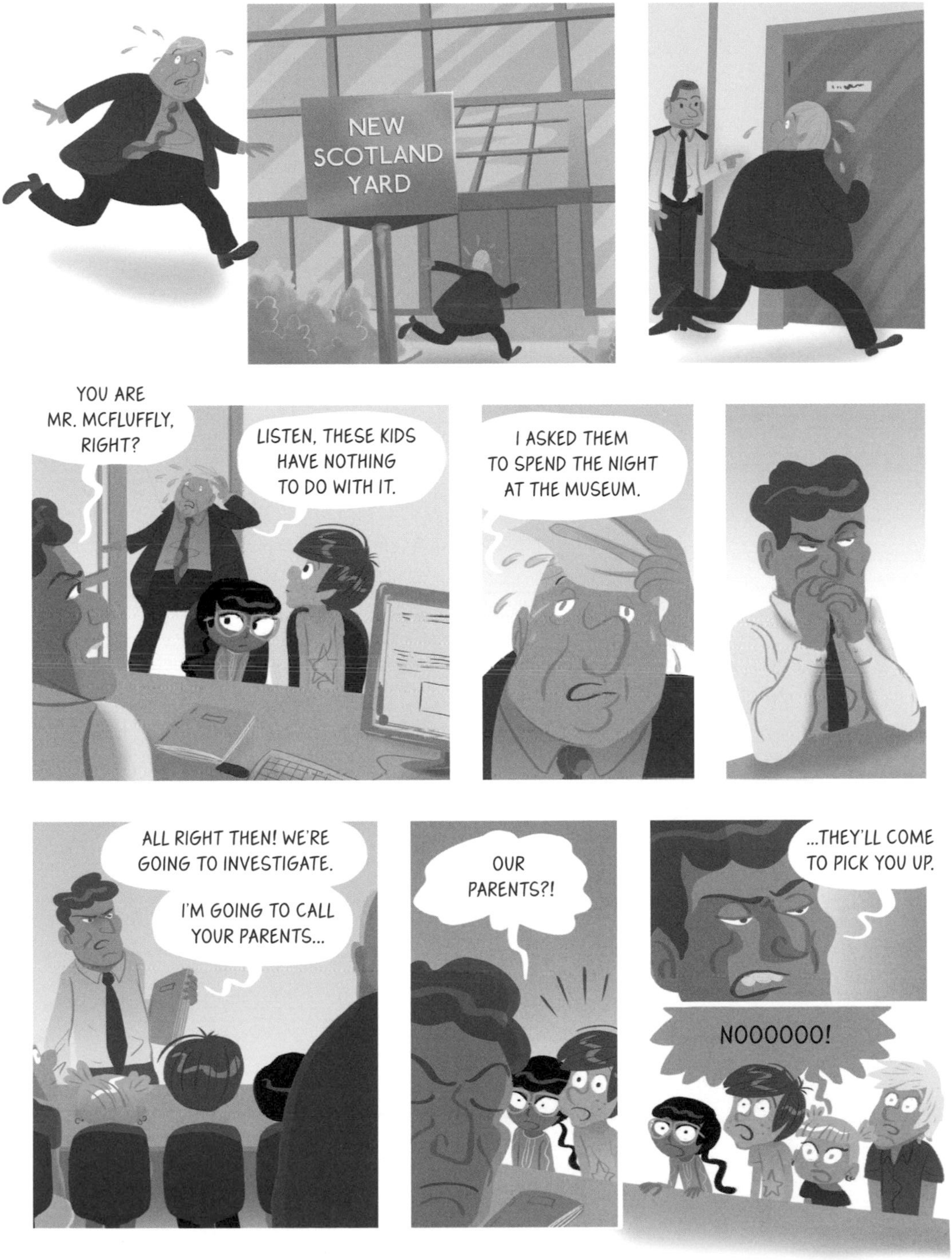
NEW SCOTLAND YARD
YOU ARE MR. MCFLUFFLY, RIGHT?
LISTEN, THESE KIDS HAVE NOTHING TO DO WITH IT.
I ASKED THEM TO SPEND THE NIGHT AT THE MUSEUM.
ALL RIGHT THEN! WE'RE GOING TO INVESTIGATE.
I'M GOING TO CALL YOUR PARENTS...
OUR PARENTS?!
...THEY'LL COME TO PICK YOU UP.
NOOOOOO!

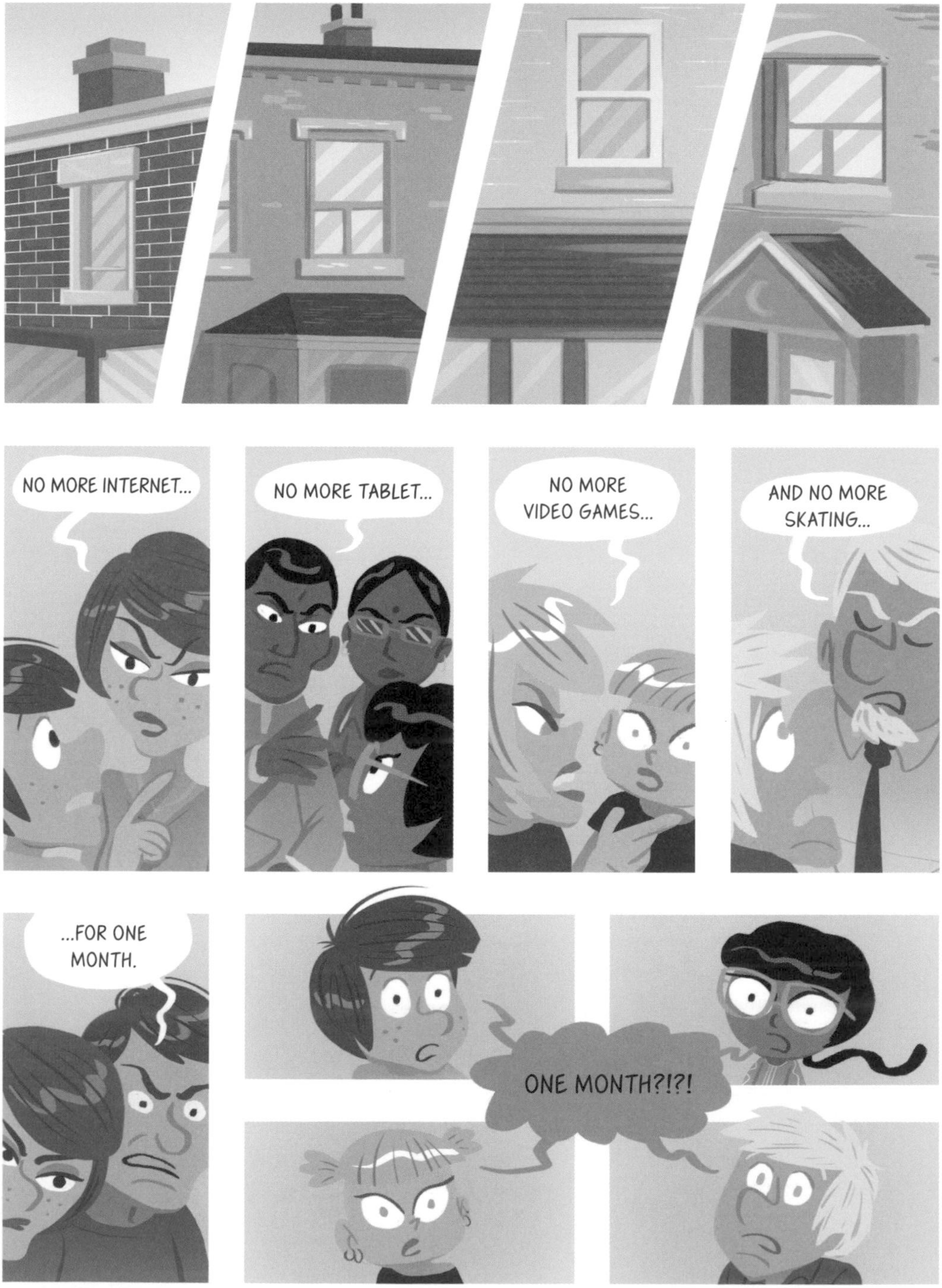
NO MORE INTERNET...
NO MORE TABLET...
NO MORE VIDEO GAMES...
AND NO MORE SKATING...
...FOR ONE MONTH.
ONE MONTH?!?!

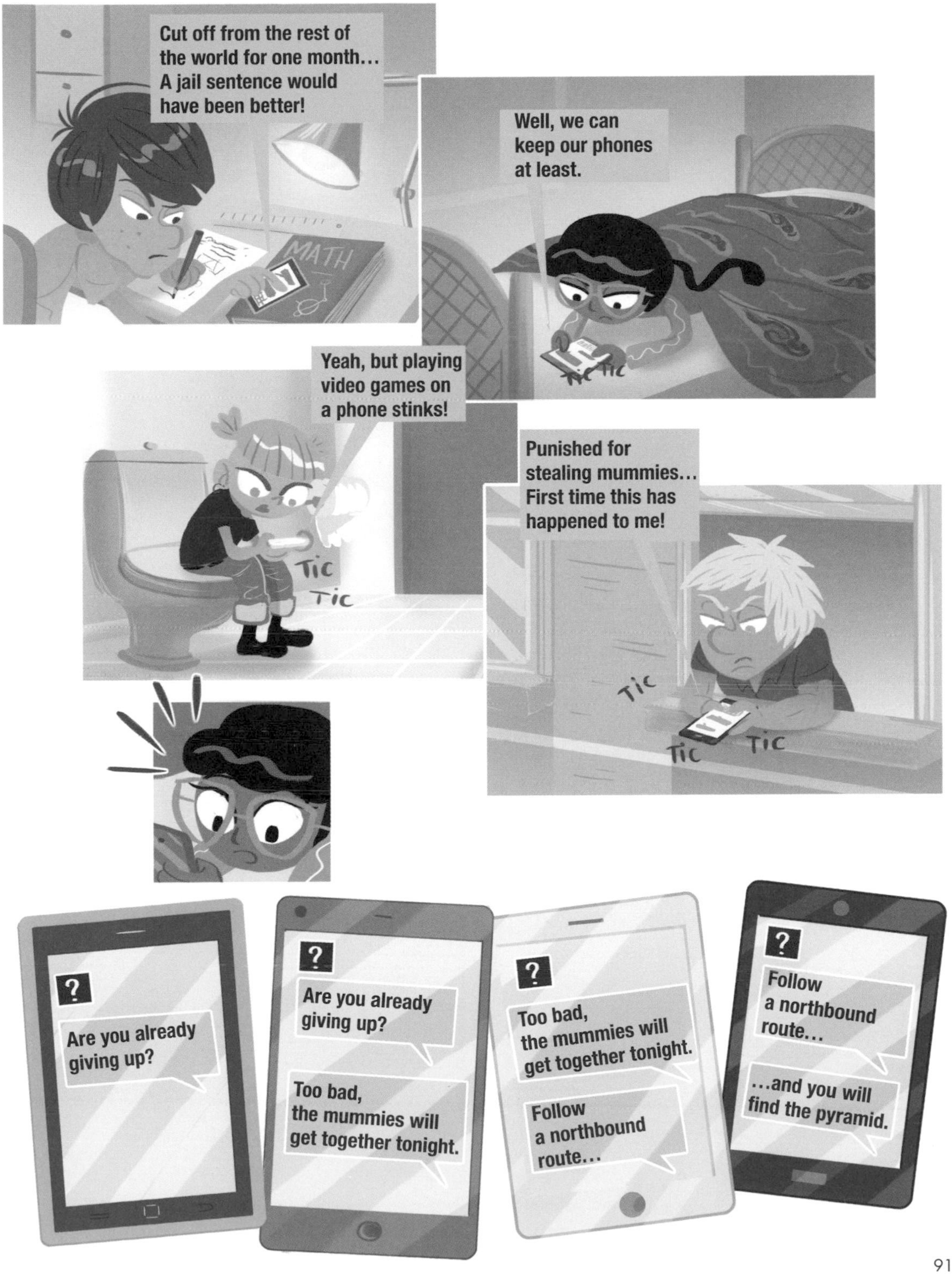
Cut off from the rest of the world for one month... A jail sentence would have been better!
MATH
Well, we can keep our phones at least.
TIC TIC
Yeah, but playing video games on a phone stinks!
TIC
TIC
Punished for stealing mummies... First time this has happened to me!
TIC
TIC
TIC
?
Are you already giving up?
?
Are you already giving up?
Too bad, the mummies will get together tonight.
?
Too bad, the mummies will get together tonight.
Follow a northbound route...
?
Follow a northbound route...
...and you will find the pyramid.

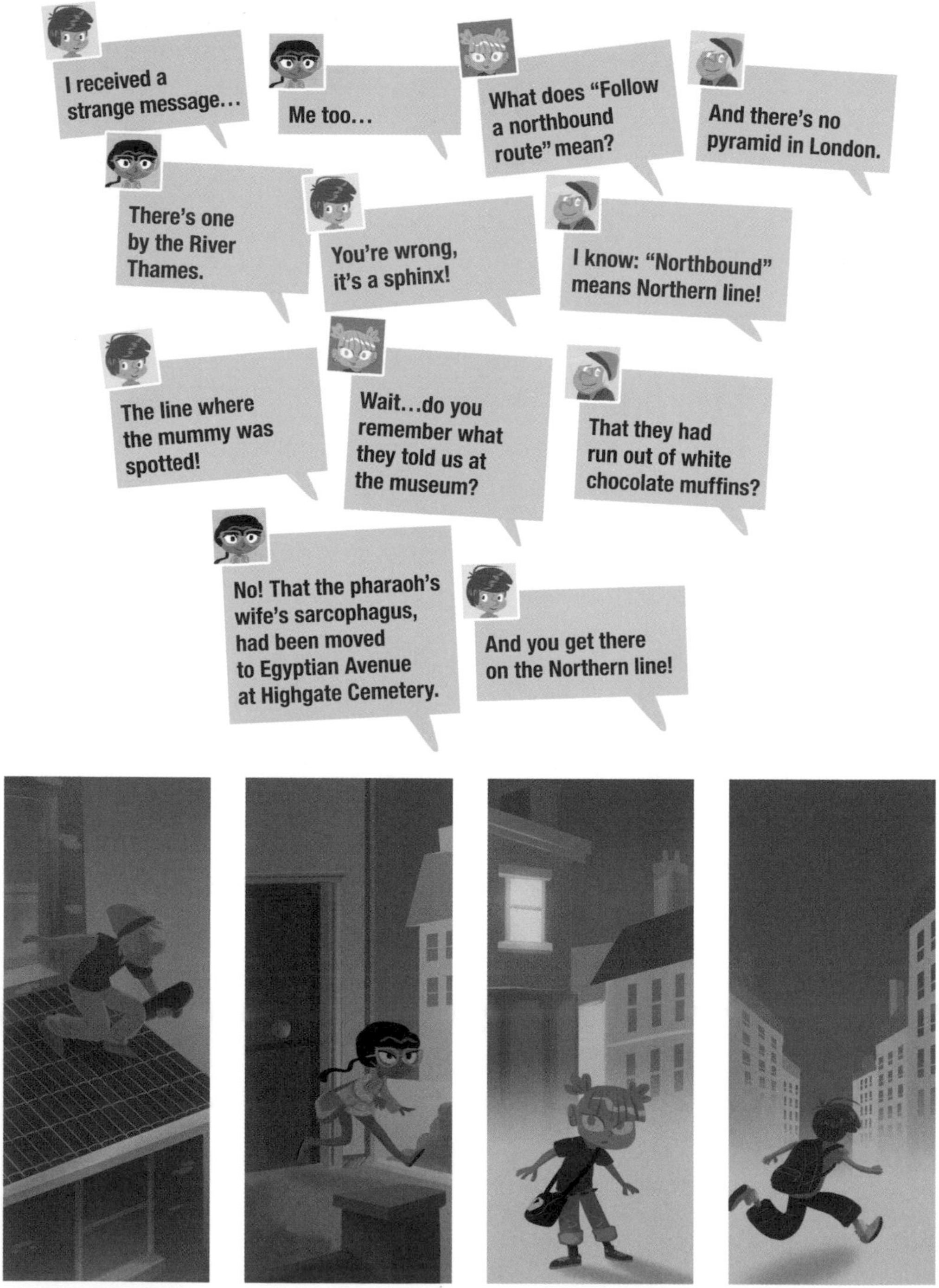
I received a strange message...
Me too...
What does "Follow a northbound route" mean?
And there's no pyramid in London.
There's one by the River Thames.
You're wrong, it's a sphinx!
I know: "Northbound" means Northern line!
The line where the mummy was spotted!
Wait...do you remember what they told us at the museum?
That they had run out of white chocolate muffins?
No! That the pharaoh's wife's sarcophagus, had been moved to Egyptian Avenue at Highgate Cemetery.
And you get there on the Northern line!

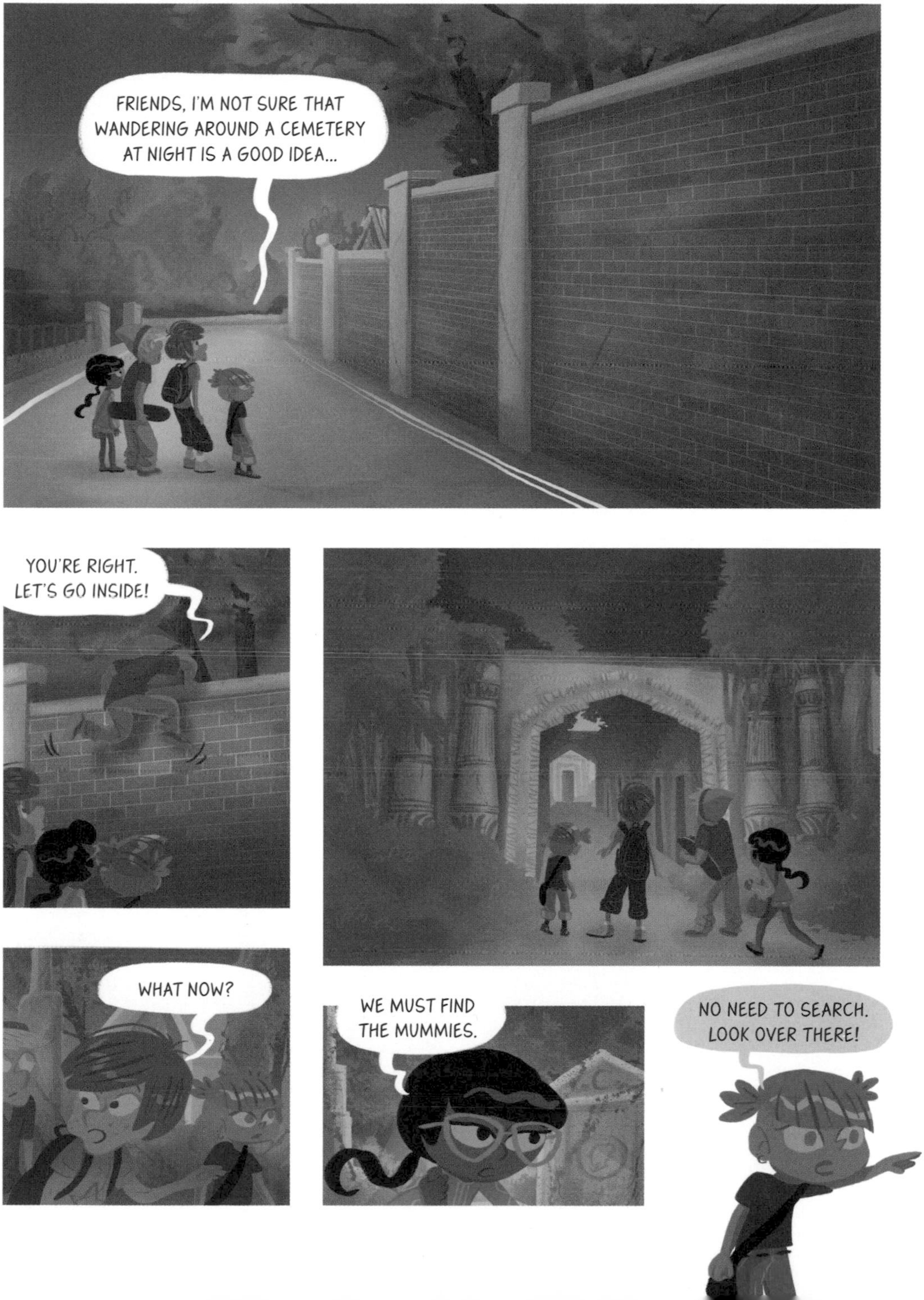
FRIENDS, I'M NOT SURE THAT WANDERING AROUND A CEMETERY AT NIGHT IS A GOOD IDEA...
YOU'RE RIGHT. LET'S GO INSIDE!
WHAT NOW?
WE MUST FIND THE MUMMIES.
NO NEED TO SEARCH. LOOK OVER THERE!

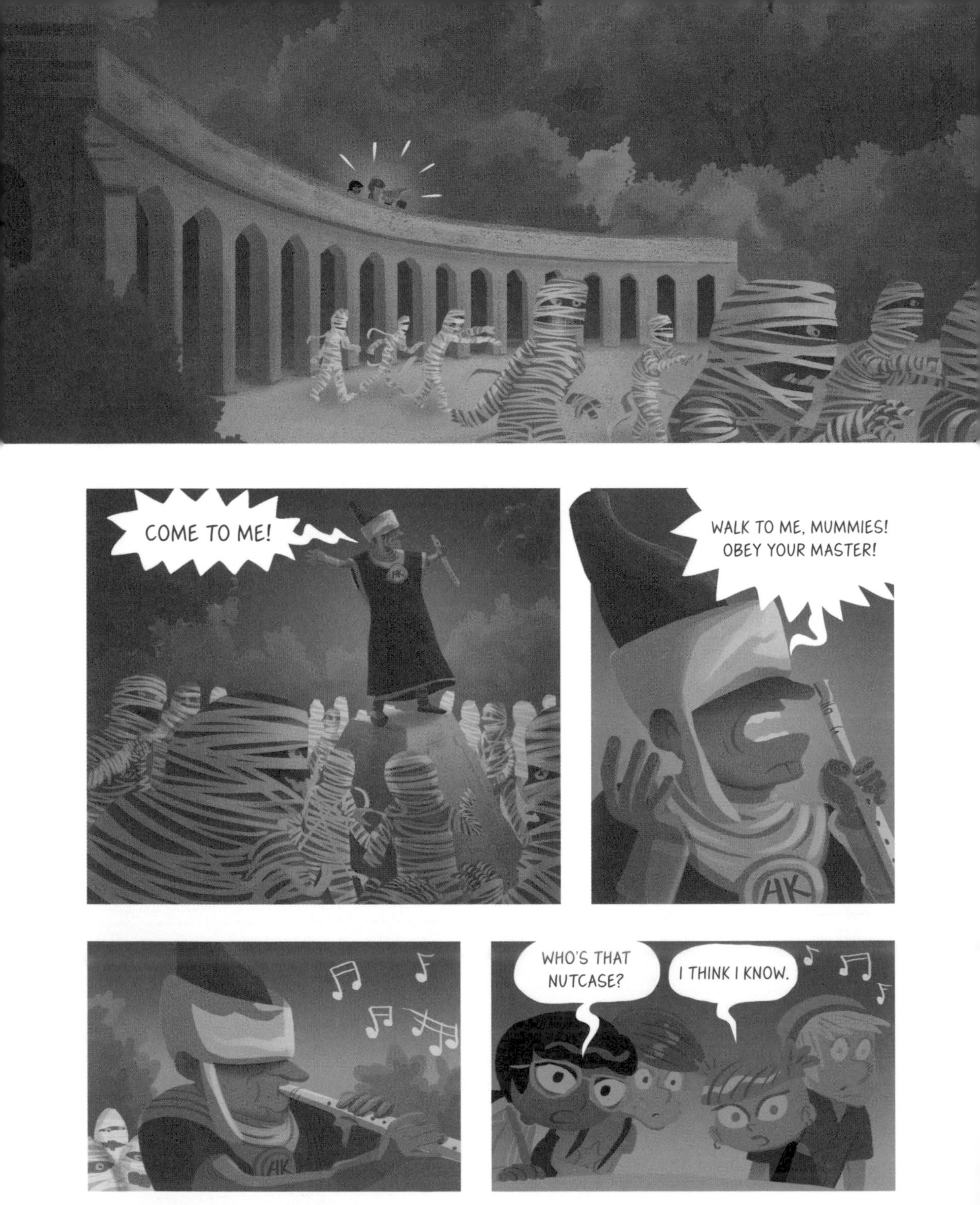
COME TO ME!
WALK TO ME, MUMMIES! OBEY YOUR MASTER!
WHO'S THAT NUTCASE?
I THINK I KNOW.

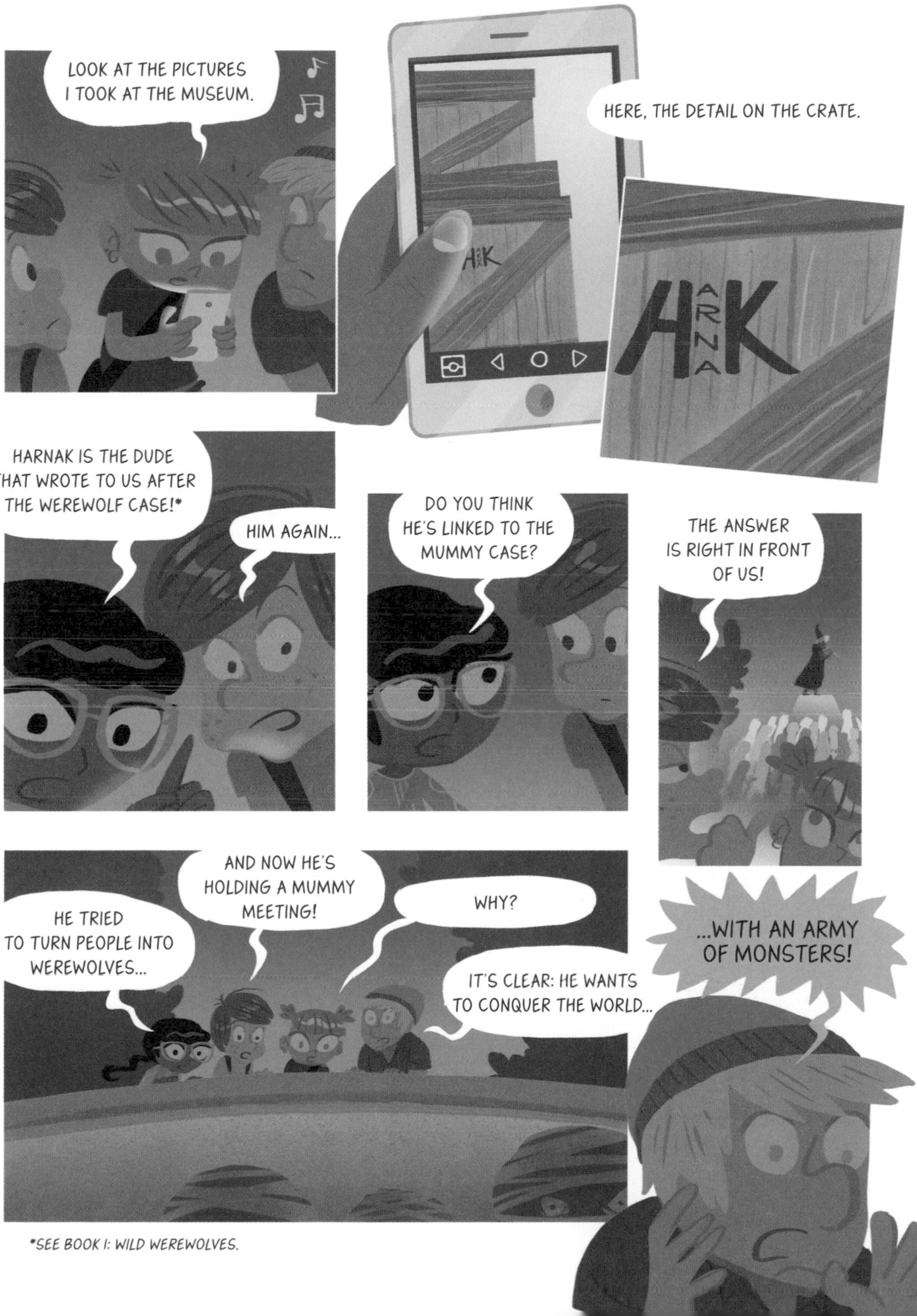
LOOK AT THE PICTURES I TOOK AT THE MUSEUM.
HERE, THE DETAIL ON THE CRATE.
HARNAK IS THE DUDE THAT WROTE TO US AFTER THE WEREWOLF CASE!*
HIM AGAIN...
DO YOU THINK HE'S LINKED TO THE MUMMY CASE?
THE ANSWER IS RIGHT IN FRONT OF US!
HE TRIED TO TURN PEOPLE INTO WEREWOLVES...
AND NOW HE'S HOLDING A MUMMY MEETING!
WHY?
IT'S CLEAR: HE WANTS TO CONQUER THE WORLD...
...WITH AN ARMY OF MONSTERS!

*SEE BOOK 1: WILD WEREWOLVES.

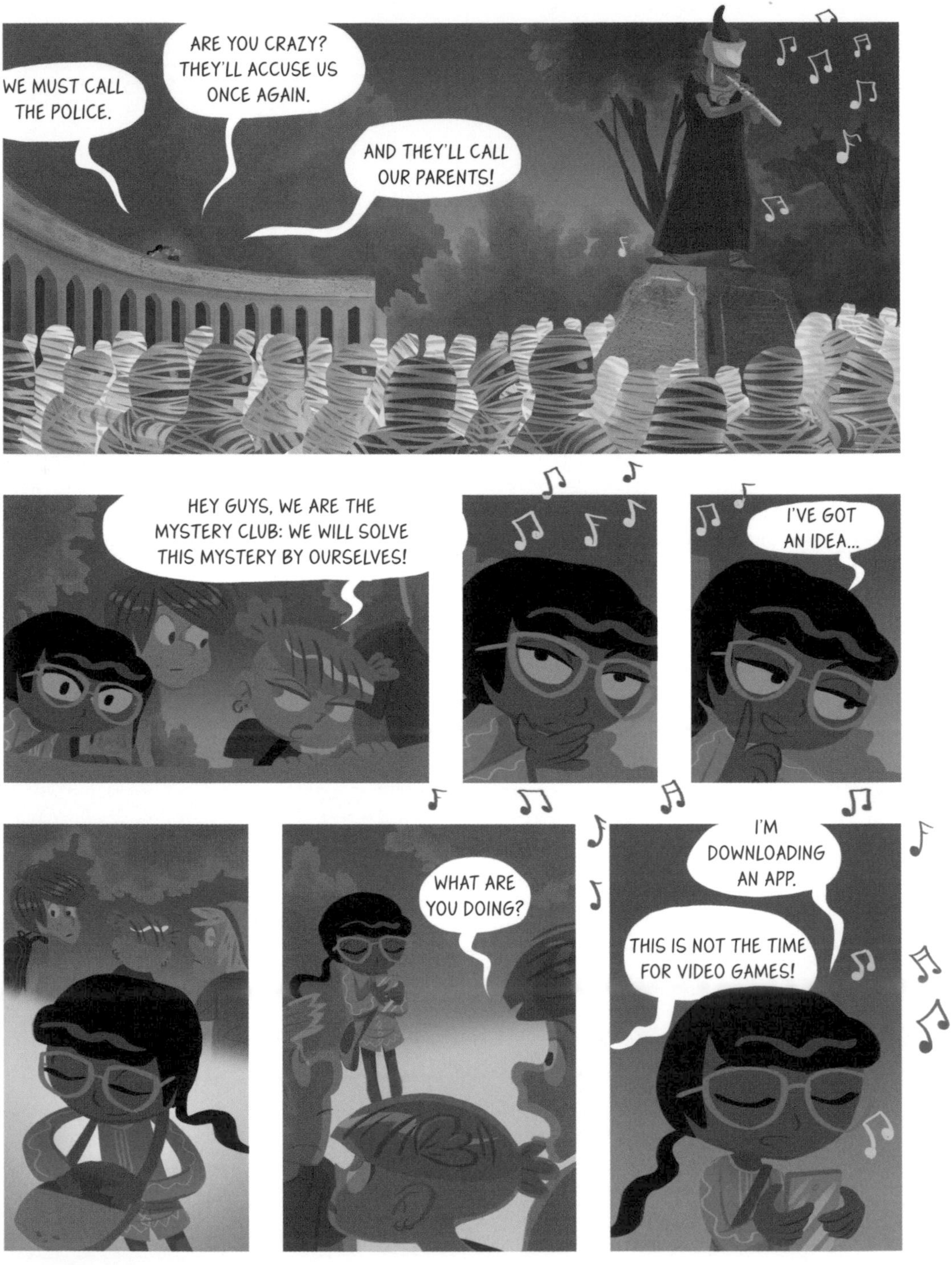
WE MUST CALL THE POLICE.
ARE YOU CRAZY? THEY'LL ACCUSE US ONCE AGAIN.
AND THEY'LL CALL OUR PARENTS!
HEY GUYS, WE ARE THE MYSTERY CLUB: WE WILL SOLVE THIS MYSTERY BY OURSELVES!
I'VE GOT AN IDEA...
WHAT ARE YOU DOING?
I'M DOWNLOADING AN APP.
THIS IS NOT THE TIME FOR VIDEO GAMES!

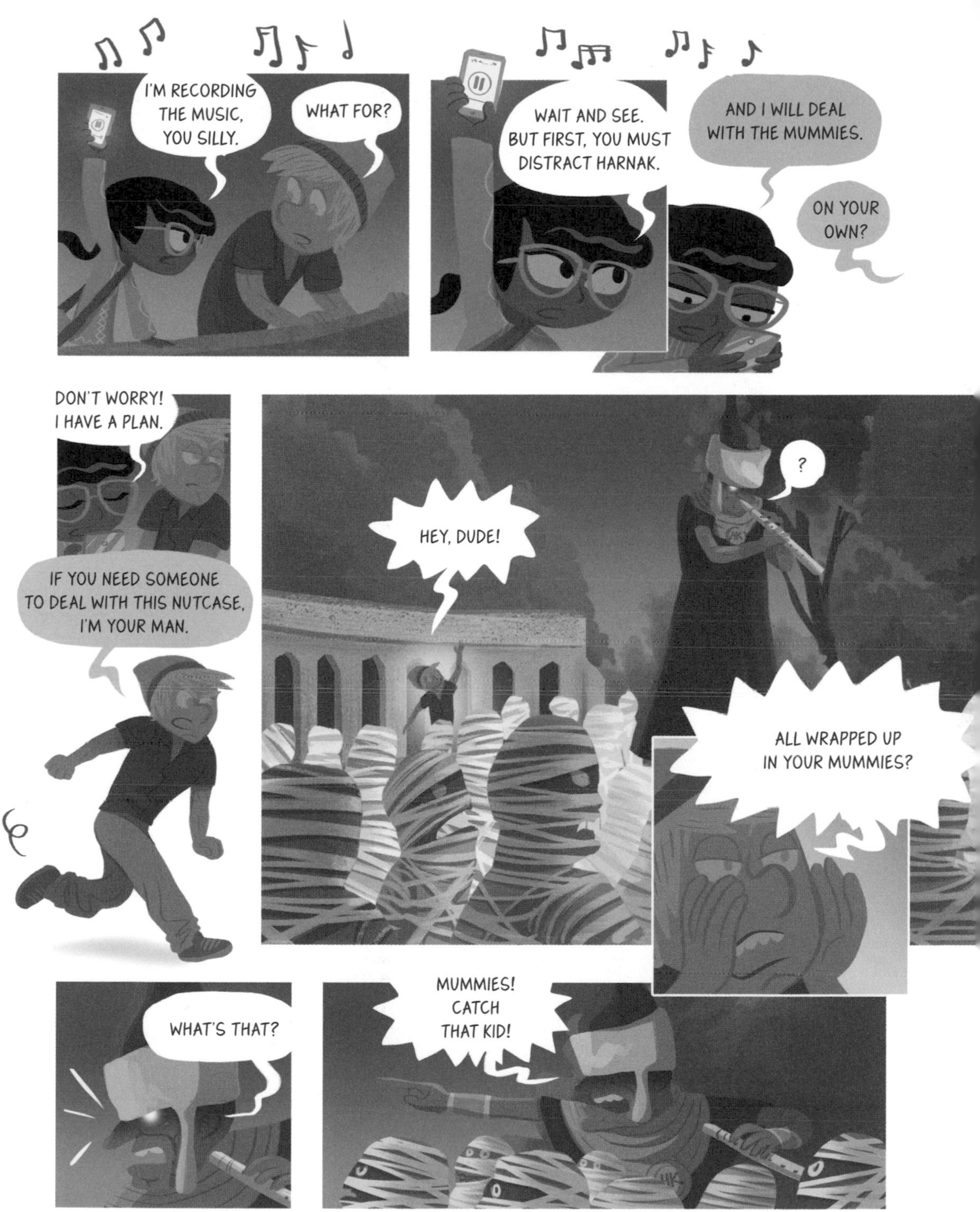
I'M RECORDING THE MUSIC, YOU SILLY.
WHAT FOR?
WAIT AND SEE. BUT FIRST, YOU MUST DISTRACT HARNAK.
AND I WILL DEAL WITH THE MUMMIES.
ON YOUR OWN?
DON'T WORRY! I HAVE A PLAN.
IF YOU NEED SOMEONE TO DEAL WITH THIS NUTCASE, I'M YOUR MAN.
HEY, DUDE!
?
ALL WRAPPED UP IN YOUR MUMMIES?
WHAT'S THAT?
MUMMIES! CATCH THAT KID!

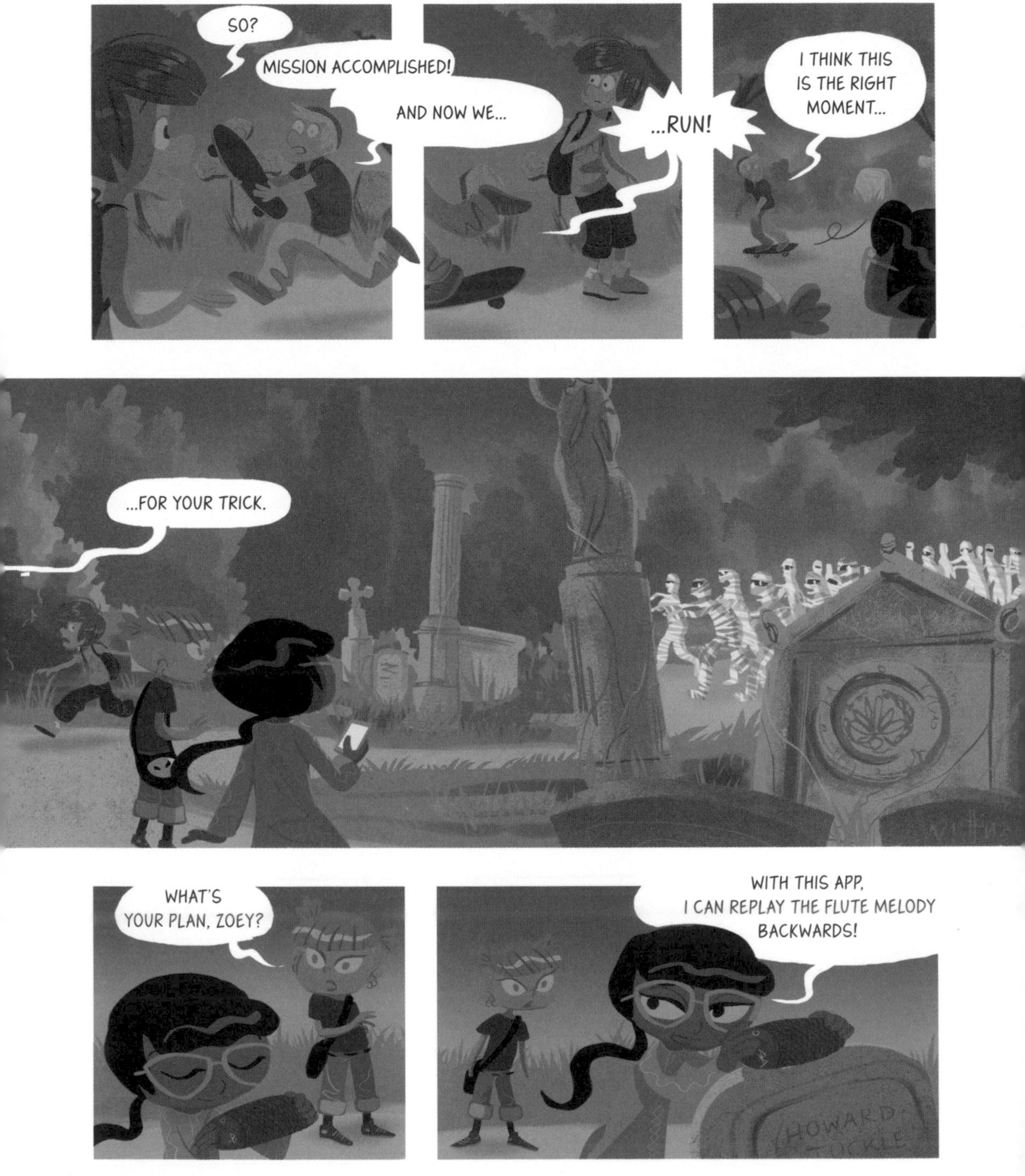

SO?
MISSION ACCOMPLISHED!
AND NOW WE...
...RUN!
I THINK THIS IS THE RIGHT MOMENT...
...FOR YOUR TRICK.
WHAT'S YOUR PLAN, ZOEY?
WITH THIS APP, I CAN REPLAY THE FLUTE MELODY BACKWARDS!
HOWARD TICKLE

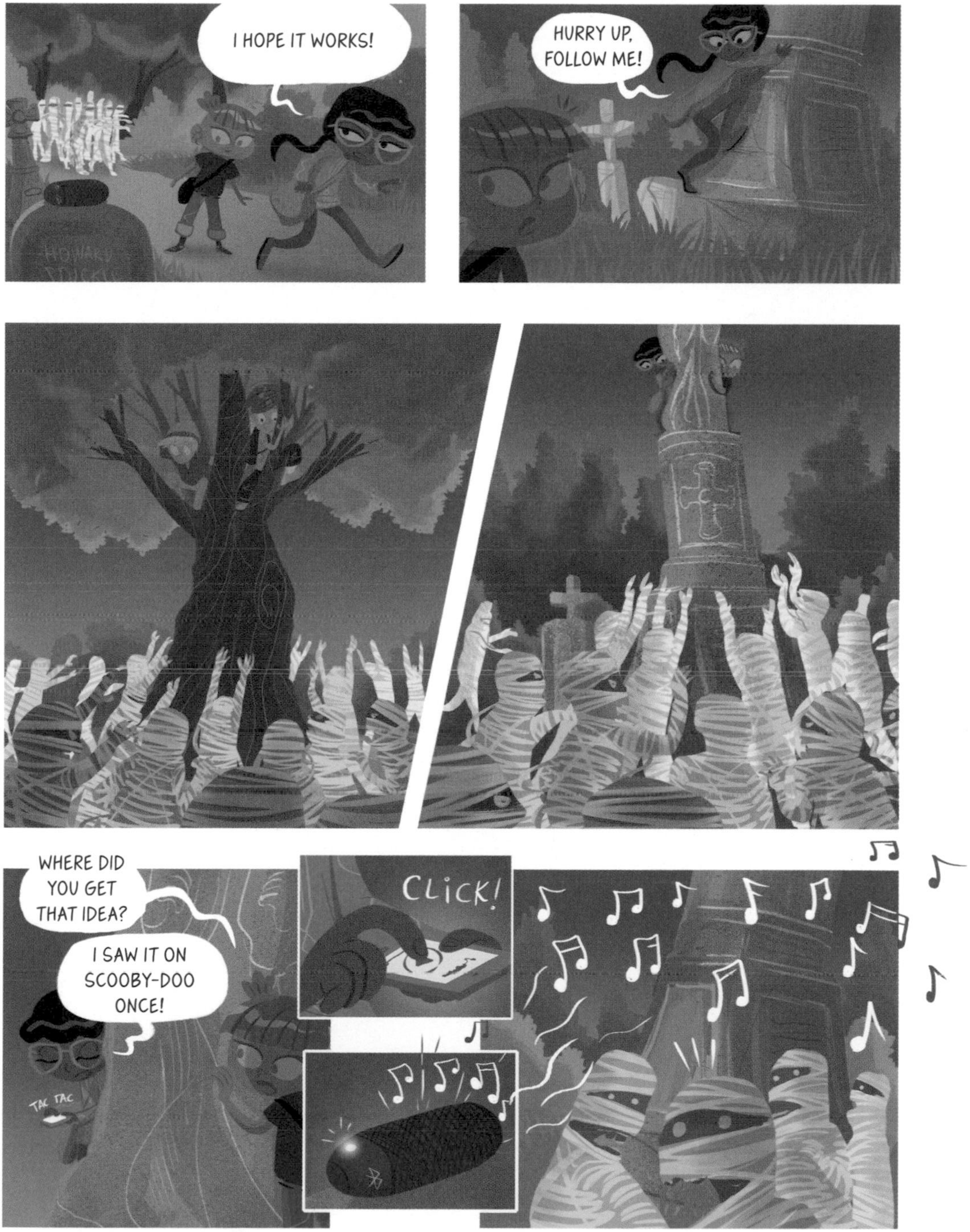
I HOPE IT WORKS!
HURRY UP, FOLLOW ME!
WHERE DID YOU GET THAT IDEA?
I SAW IT ON SCOOBY-DOO ONCE!
TAC TAC
CLICK!

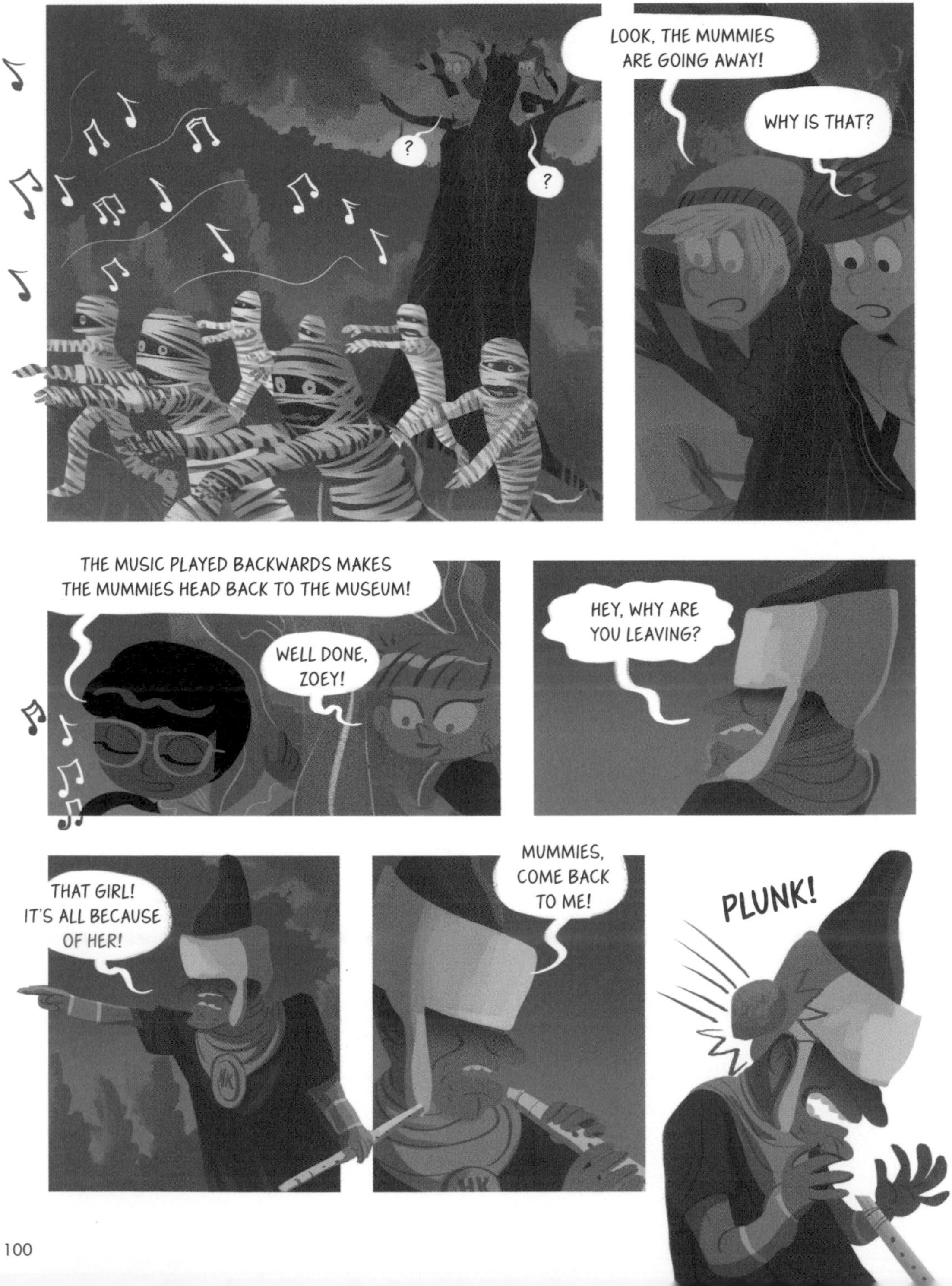
?
?
LOOK, THE MUMMIES ARE GOING AWAY!
WHY IS THAT?
THE MUSIC PLAYED BACKWARDS MAKES THE MUMMIES HEAD BACK TO THE MUSEUM!
WELL DONE, ZOEY!
HEY, WHY ARE YOU LEAVING?
THAT GIRL! IT'S ALL BECAUSE OF HER!
MUMMIES, COME BACK TO ME!
PLUNK!

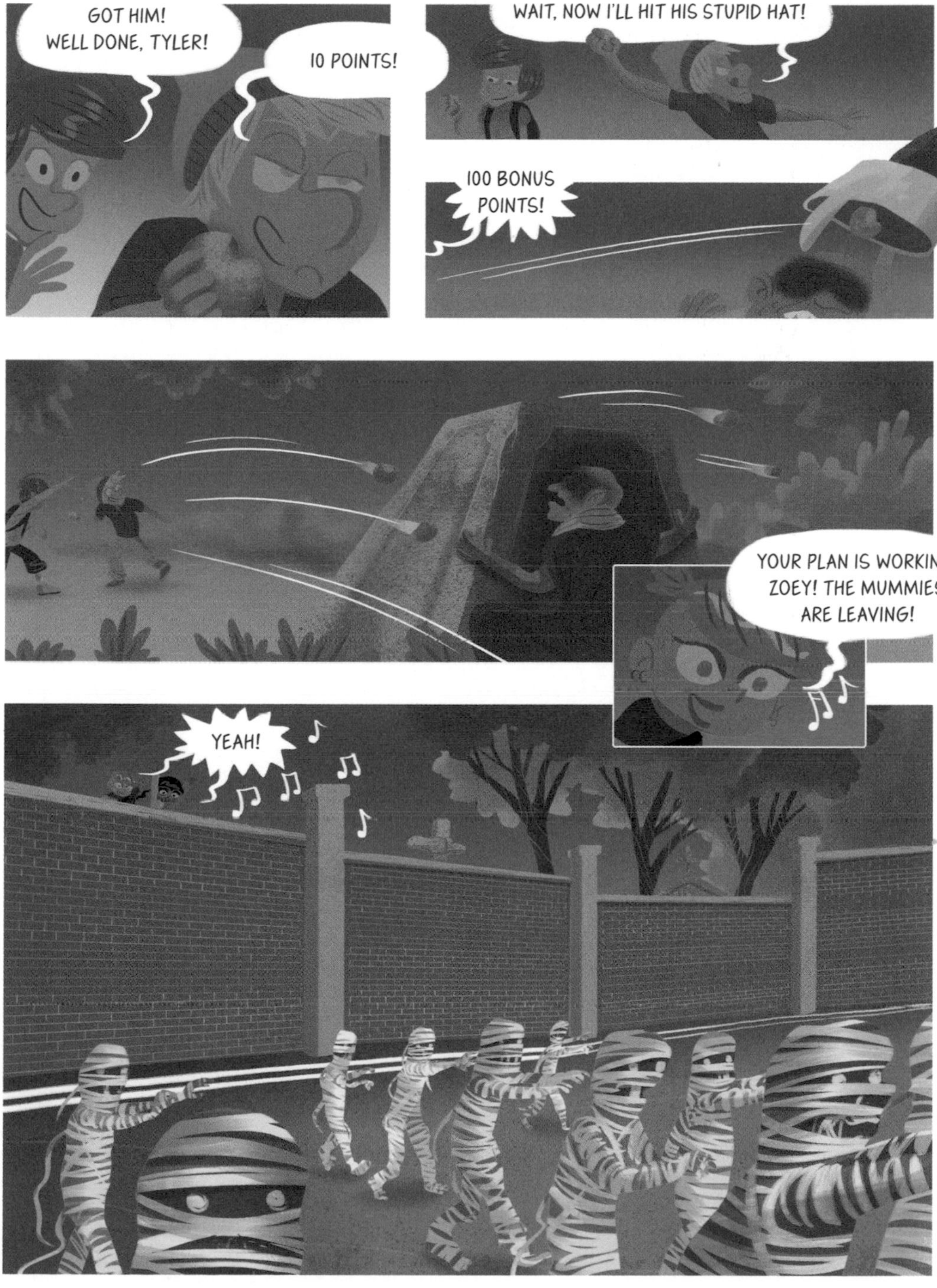
GOT HIM!
WELL DONE, TYLER!
10 POINTS!
WAIT, NOW I'LL HIT HIS STUPID HAT!
100 BONUS POINTS!
YOUR PLAN IS WORKING, ZOEY! THE MUMMIES ARE LEAVING!
YEAH!

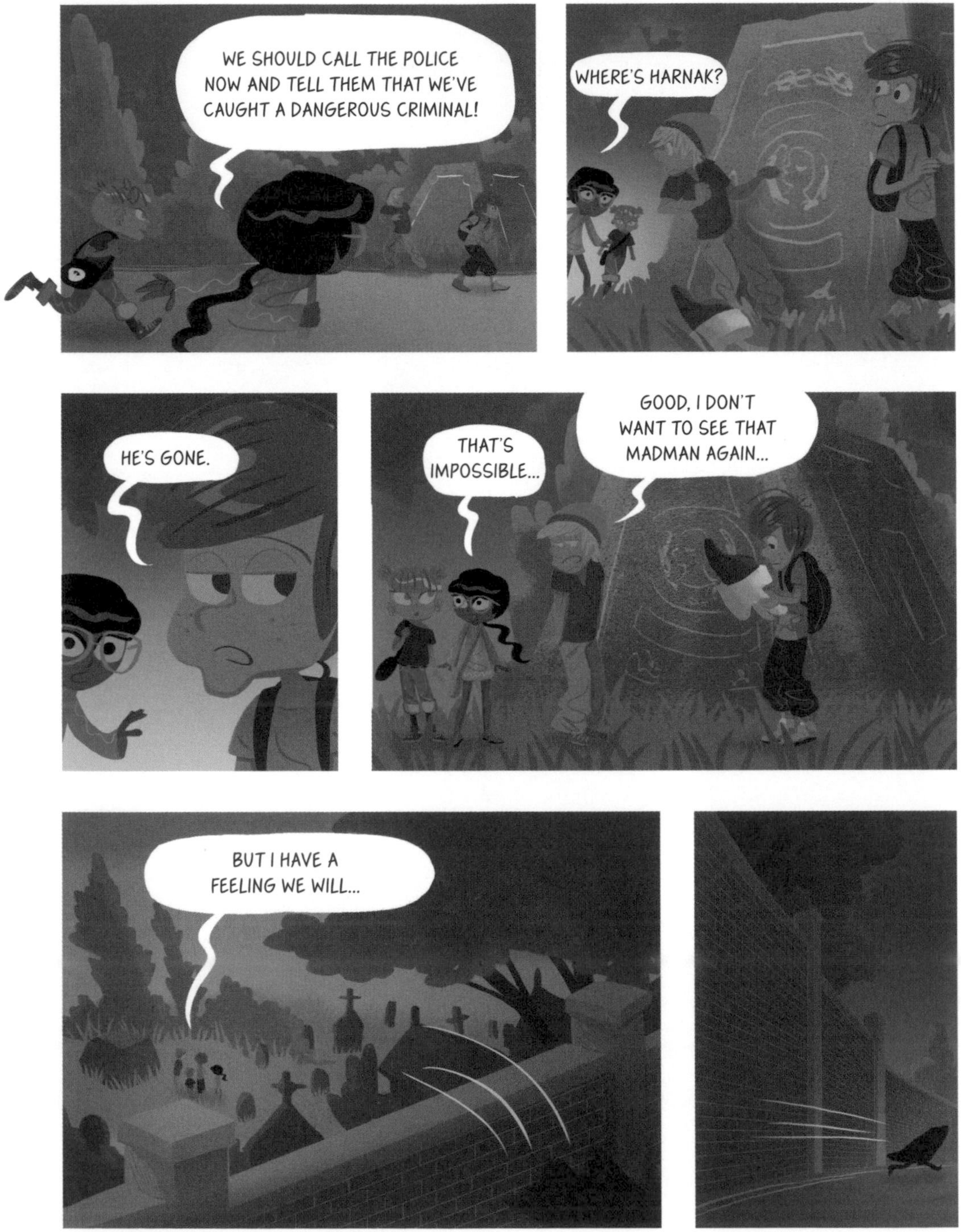
WE SHOULD CALL THE POLICE NOW AND TELL THEM THAT WE'VE CAUGHT A DANGEROUS CRIMINAL!
WHERE'S HARNAK?
HE'S GONE.
THAT'S IMPOSSIBLE...
GOOD, I DON'T WANT TO SEE THAT MADMAN AGAIN...
BUT I HAVE A FEELING WE WILL...

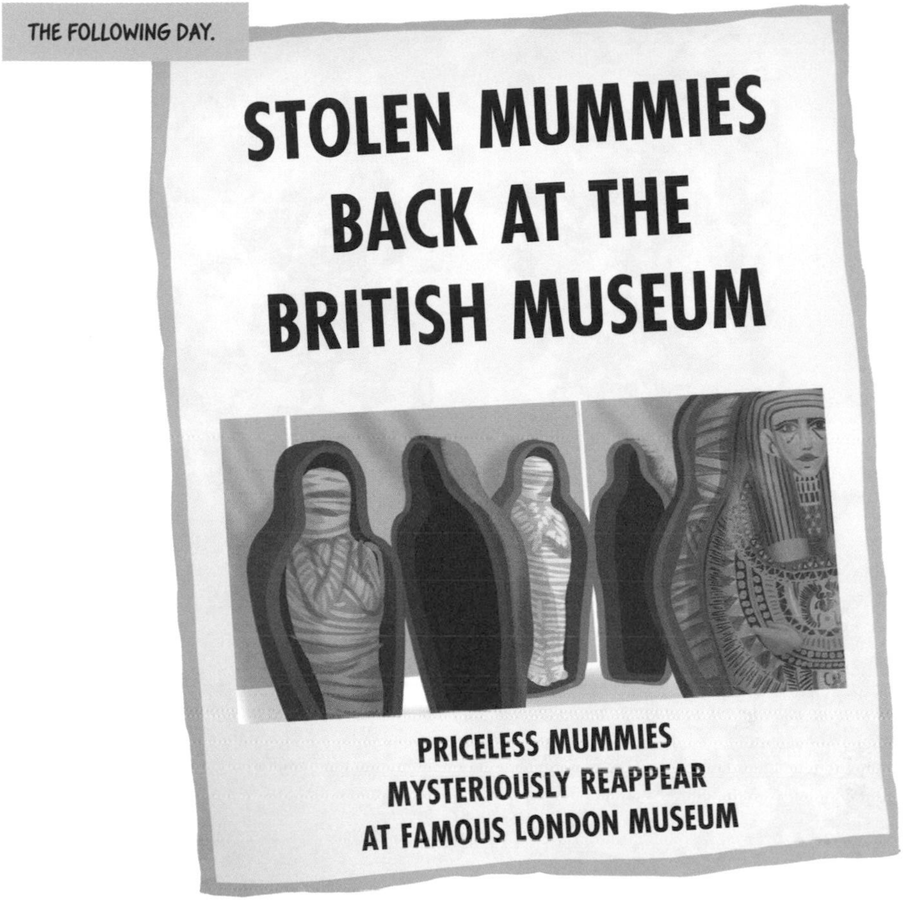
THE FOLLOWING DAY.
STOLEN MUMMIES BACK AT THE BRITISH MUSEUM
PRICELESS MUMMIES MYSTERIOUSLY REAPPEAR AT FAMOUS LONDON MUSEUM

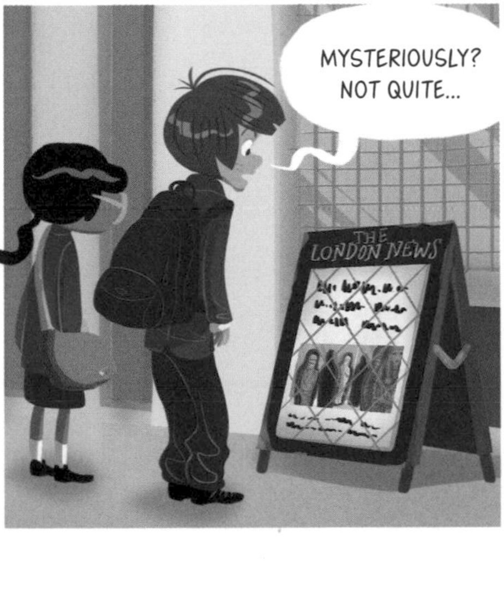
MYSTERIOUSLY? NOT QUITE...
THE LONDON NEWS

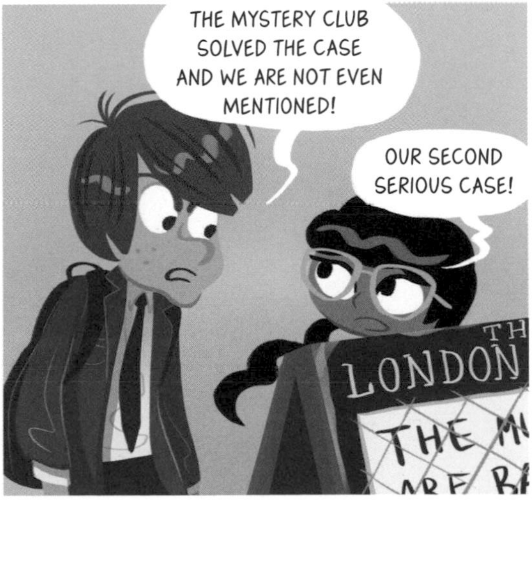
THE MYSTERY CLUB SOLVED THE CASE AND WE ARE NOT EVEN MENTIONED!
OUR SECOND SERIOUS CASE!
LONDON

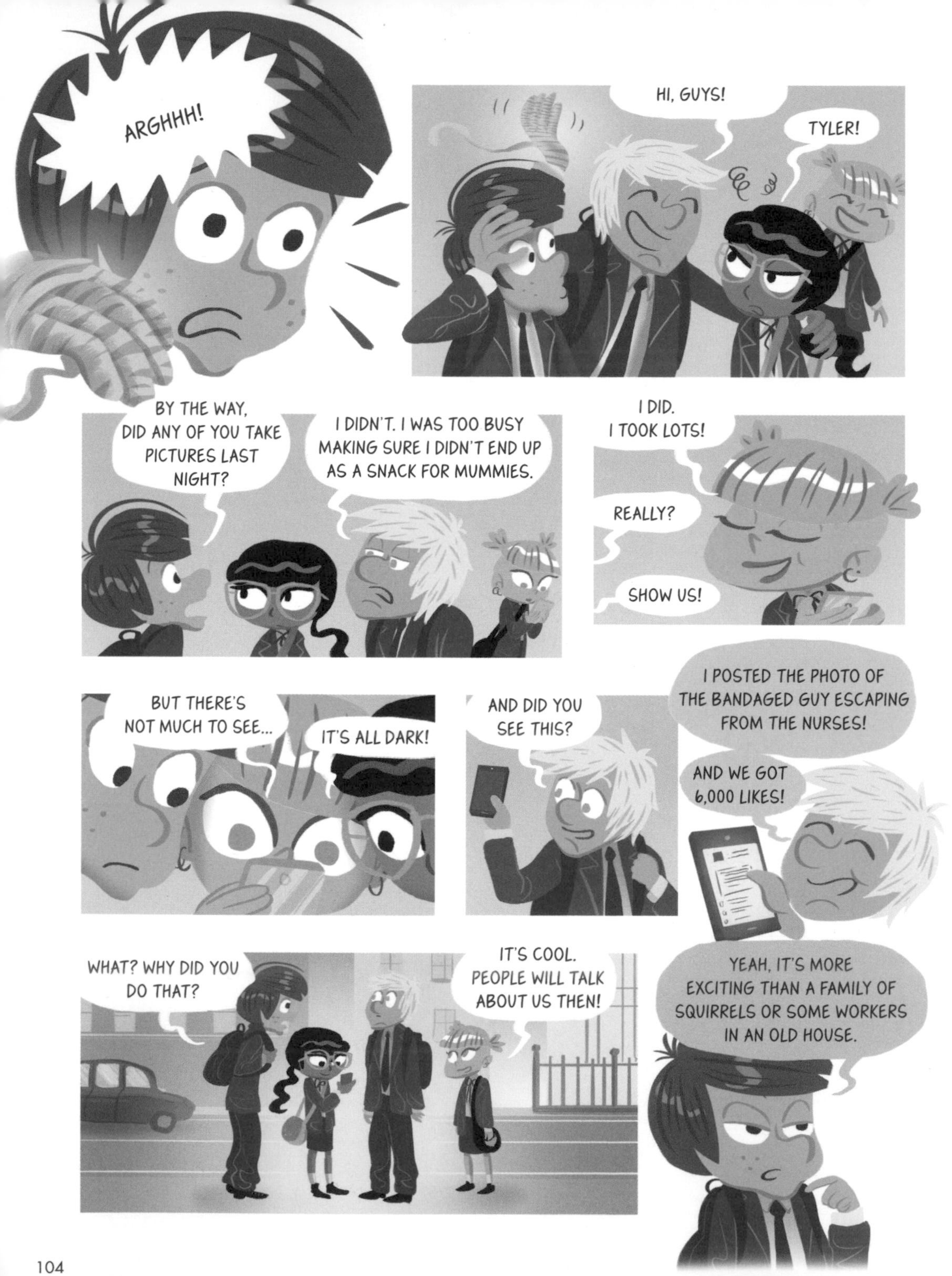
ARGHHH!
HI, GUYS!
TYLER!
BY THE WAY, DID ANY OF YOU TAKE PICTURES LAST NIGHT?
I DIDN'T. I WAS TOO BUSY MAKING SURE I DIDN'T END UP AS A SNACK FOR MUMMIES.
I DID. I TOOK LOTS!
REALLY?
SHOW US!
BUT THERE'S NOT MUCH TO SEE...
IT'S ALL DARK!
AND DID YOU SEE THIS?
I POSTED THE PHOTO OF THE BANDAGED GUY ESCAPING FROM THE NURSES!
AND WE GOT 6,000 LIKES!
WHAT? WHY DID YOU DO THAT?
IT'S COOL. PEOPLE WILL TALK ABOUT US THEN!
YEAH, IT'S MORE EXCITING THAN A FAMILY OF SQUIRRELS OR SOME WORKERS IN AN OLD HOUSE.

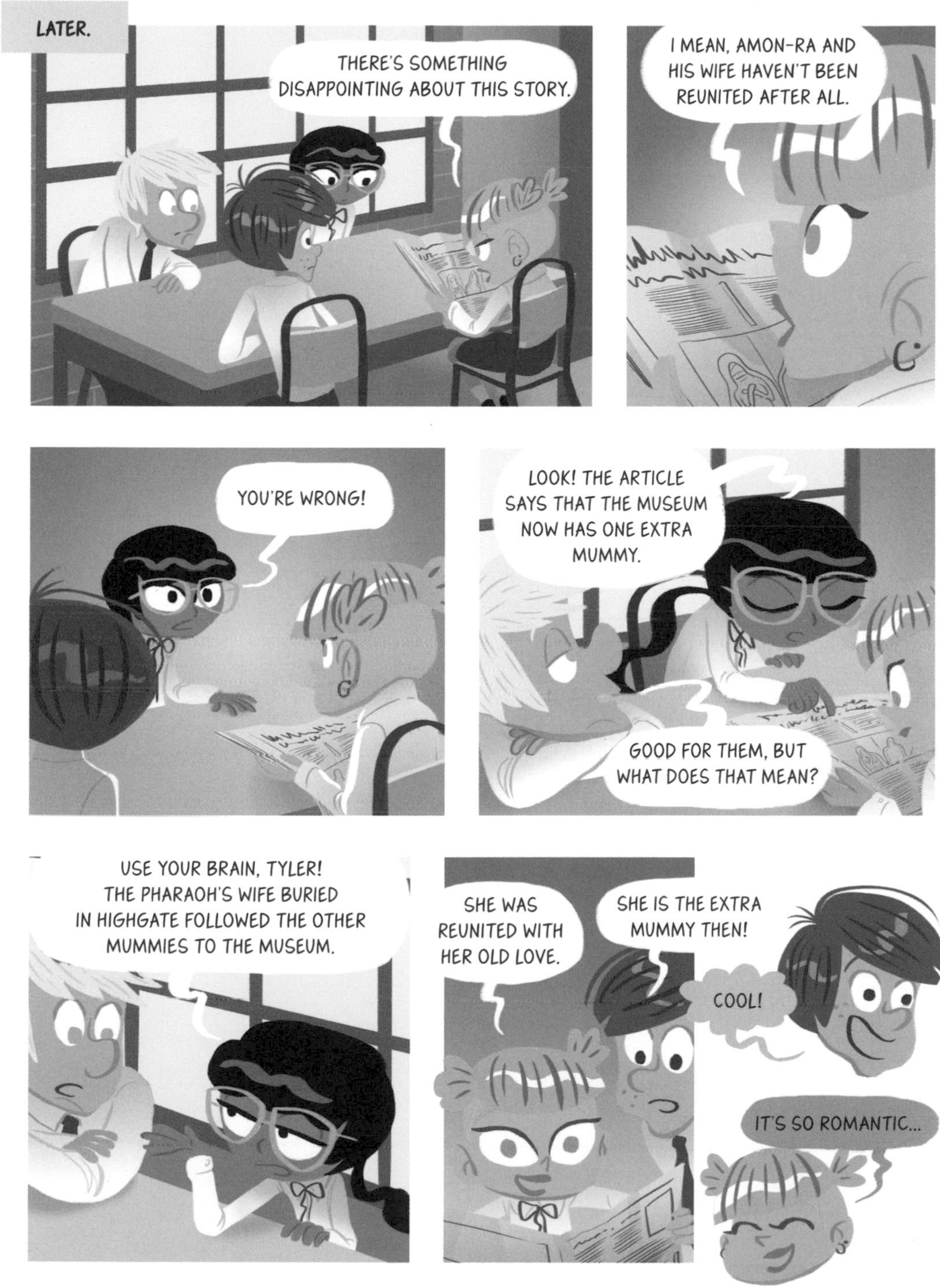
LATER.
THERE'S SOMETHING DISAPPOINTING ABOUT THIS STORY.
I MEAN, AMON-RA AND HIS WIFE HAVEN'T BEEN REUNITED AFTER ALL.
YOU'RE WRONG!
LOOK! THE ARTICLE SAYS THAT THE MUSEUM NOW HAS ONE EXTRA MUMMY.
GOOD FOR THEM, BUT WHAT DOES THAT MEAN?
USE YOUR BRAIN, TYLER! THE PHARAOH'S WIFE BURIED IN HIGHGATE FOLLOWED THE OTHER MUMMIES TO THE MUSEUM.
SHE WAS REUNITED WITH HER OLD LOVE.
SHE IS THE EXTRA MUMMY THEN!
COOL!
IT'S SO ROMANTIC...

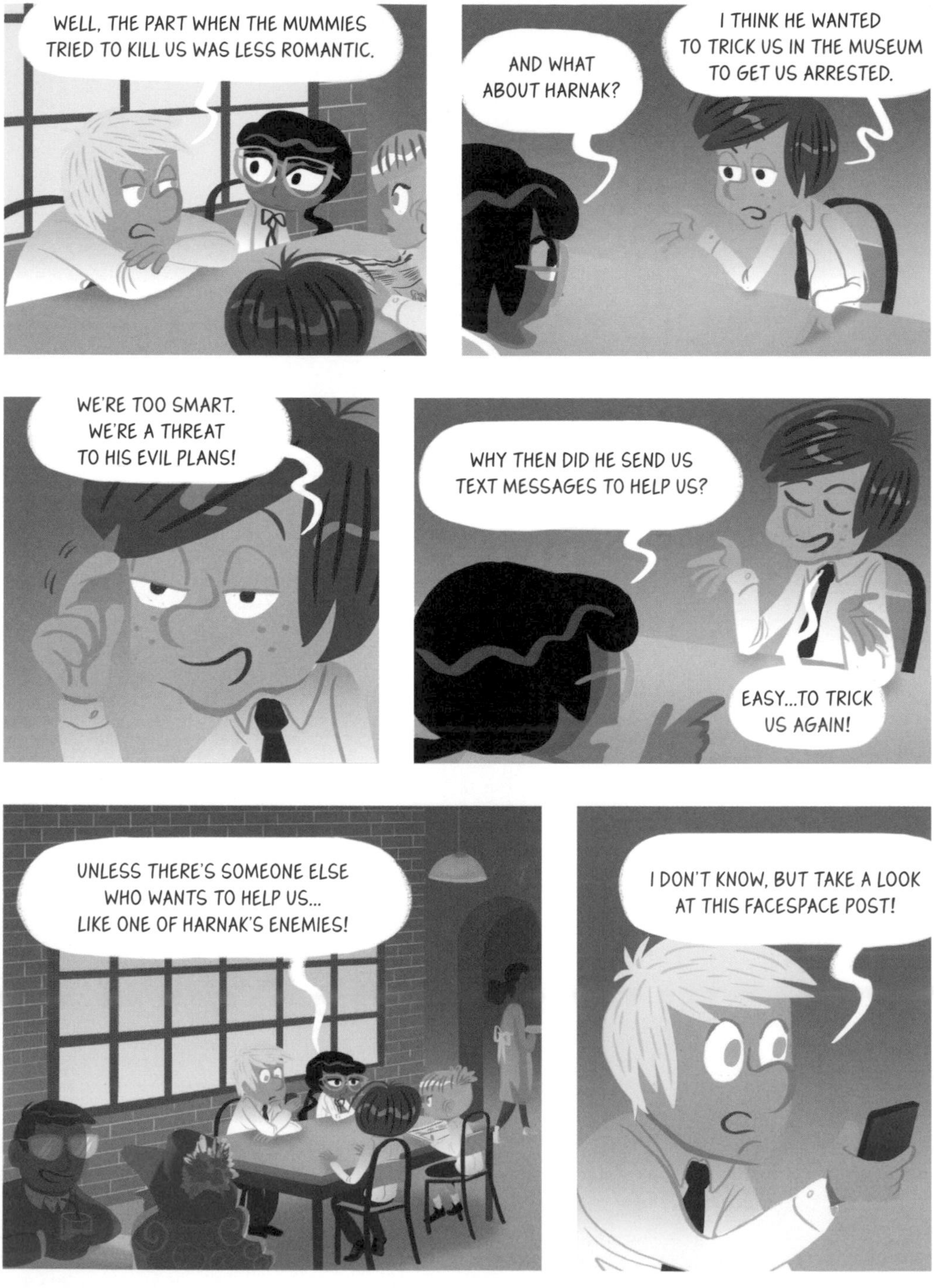
WELL, THE PART WHEN THE MUMMIES TRIED TO KILL US WAS LESS ROMANTIC.
AND WHAT ABOUT HARNAK?
I THINK HE WANTED TO TRICK US IN THE MUSEUM TO GET US ARRESTED.
WE'RE TOO SMART. WE'RE A THREAT TO HIS EVIL PLANS!
WHY THEN DID HE SEND US TEXT MESSAGES TO HELP US?
EASY...TO TRICK US AGAIN!
UNLESS THERE'S SOMEONE ELSE WHO WANTS TO HELP US... LIKE ONE OF HARNAK'S ENEMIES!
I DON'T KNOW, BUT TAKE A LOOK AT THIS FACESPACE POST!

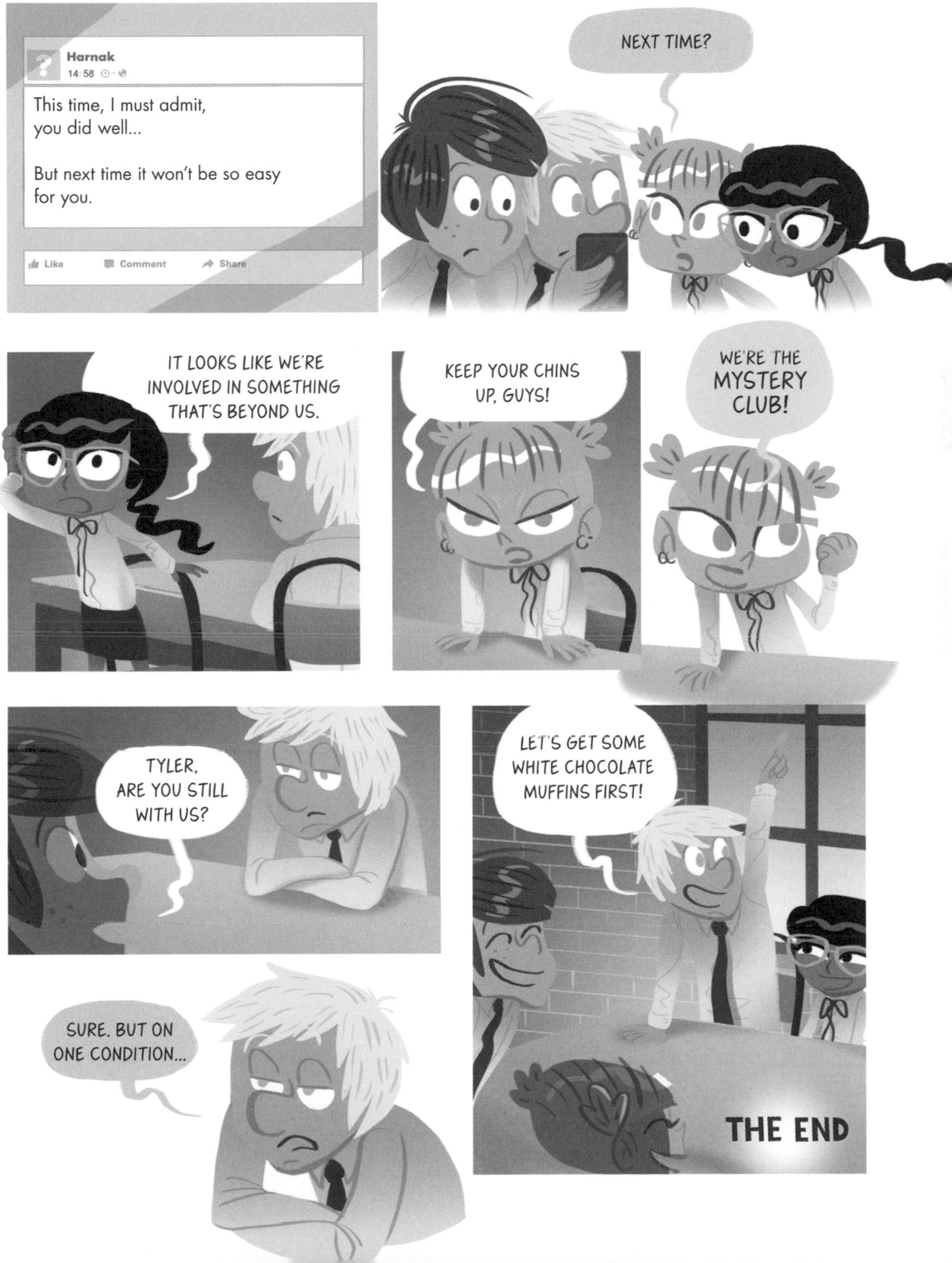
Harnak
14:58
This time, I must admit,
you did well...
But next time it won't be so easy
for you.
Like
Comment
Share
NEXT TIME?
IT LOOKS LIKE WE'RE INVOLVED IN SOMETHING THAT'S BEYOND US.
KEEP YOUR CHINS UP, GUYS!
WE'RE THE MYSTERY CLUB!
TYLER, ARE YOU STILL WITH US?
SURE. BUT ON ONE CONDITION...
LET'S GET SOME WHITE CHOCOLATE MUFFINS FIRST!
THE END

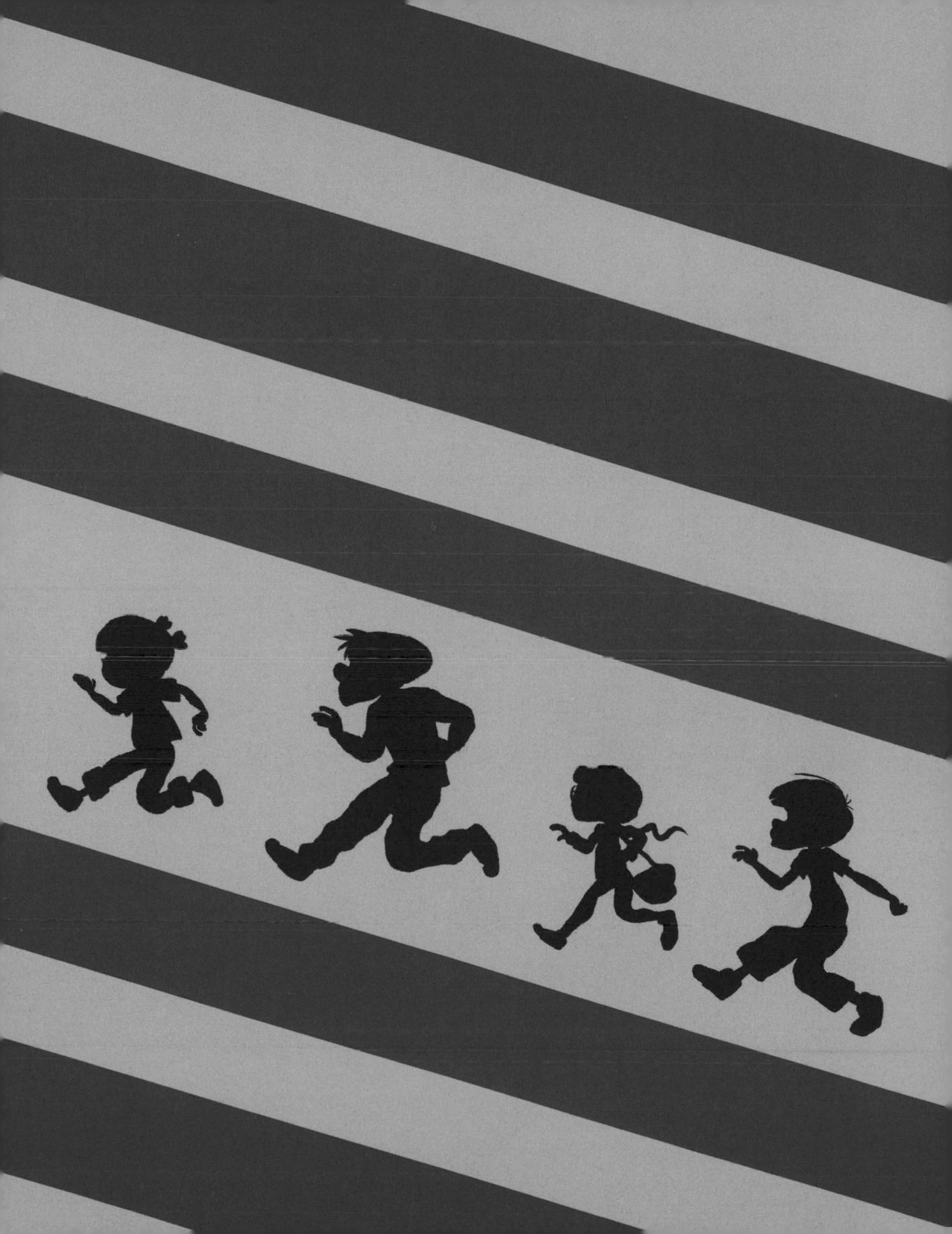

Davide Cali is a Swiss-born Italian author, working primarily in children's literature and graphic novels. He lives in Italy.

Yannick Robert is a French illustrator and author working in both France and the United Kingdom. Along with working in children's publishing, he also creates comics, animation, pop-up work, and more. He lives in Toulouse, France.